I0586471

MASTERS OF THE SUN

Dawn of Enlightenment #1

MICHAEL KINGSWOOD

ABOUT THIS BOOK

The world ended ten years ago, but life goes on. For Jack Simmons, that means a life spent hunting and trapping with his friend and mentor, and trying not to think about what he lost all those years ago.

Of course, even after the end of the world politics rolls along. And when the trade caravan brings word to Jack's town of a new force rising in the west, a force rumored to have magical powers, Jack finds himself thrust on a journey with a man he does not trust in a quest to discover the truth behind the rumors. What he finds there will change him forever, and usher in a new era for mankind. Assuming it does not kill or enslave them all first.

Enjoy the book! After you're done, please come to Michael's website and sign up for his mailing list. Guaranteed to be spam free, he uses it to announce new releases and special promotions for his fans.

❦ I ❦

TOP O' THE MORNING

Jack awoke with a start, sitting bolt upright. He could still hear screams ringing in his ears. He sat still for a moment, cradling his head in both hands, then with a quick inhalation, he wiped the beginning of tears from the corners of his eyes and stood up.

Pre-dawn light, visible through the cracked window glass, glimmered in the east, casting a pale illumination into the room. It was a small room, but serviceable. His narrow pallet, covered with rough blankets, a chamber pot barely visible underneath, stood against the wall opposite the window. A pump-action shotgun was propped against the wall near the head of the bed, several boxes of cartridges neatly stacked nearby. In the corner next to the foot of the bed was a table with a washbasin and pitcher beneath a cracked wall mirror. In the other corner, near the window, stood a small wood stove. A wooden rocking chair was nestled near the stove, along with another small table stacked with a pile of books. Along the wall next to the window was a series of hooks and pegs that held his clothing.

Jack moved mechanically to the washbasin and half-filled it with water from the pitcher. He swirled the water for a moment with his fingers, thoughts wandering. It had been ten years now. Ten years dreaming the same dream. Ten years waking up in a sweat early every morning, no matter how chilly or warm the weather, the grief and pain fresh in his mind.

Memory was hard to shed, the more so since it was literally burned into him. He looked up from the basin to the mirror, his gaze lingering on the scars that adorned his chest, neck, and the left side of his jaw. Three days of stubble adorned his chin, patchy where the scars prevented growth. The lines on his forehead and at the corner of each eye seemed deeper than he remembered. He looked like hell. Old, beat up, tired. Better than it could have been. Better than...

With a snort, he got about his business. That was enough belly aching, and there was work to do. He shaved quickly, gritting his teeth at the combination of cold water and a dulling blade. He really needed to put his razor to the whetstone one of these days.

First things first.

Moving with a purpose, he washed his teeth with a rag near the basin and ran his hands through his hair. Then he did his business in the chamber pot, donned a shirt, a patched leather jacket, a pair of jeans, and stomped on his boots. He grabbed his shotgun and overnight backpack and plopped a wide-brimmed hat onto his head. Then he left the room, a slight limp in his stride.

A narrow flight of stairs outside his door took him to the first floor. The house itself was small: just the one room upstairs, and downstairs a common room and two more bedrooms. And the bathroom and kitchen, for all they mattered.

The remnants of the last night's fire still smoldered in the fireplace in the common room. A fairly large stone model, the fireplace was old-fashioned, in keeping with the rest of the décor. The spit and cooking rack in the fireplace was obviously a change from its original design. Several pots and pans hung from hooks installed in the mantel, another recent change, and an ample supply of firewood and kindling was neatly stacked off to the side next to a standard set of fireplace tools. Aside from the fireplace, a simple wooden table with four chairs, an old sofa, its stuffing sagging in several places, and a full bookshelf completed the room's furnishing.

Jack set his shotgun, hat, and pack down on the table and knelt in front of the fireplace, wincing slightly as he bent his right leg.

Grabbing a poker, he stirred the smoldering embers, then blew into them slowly. Next, a handful of kindling went into the fireplace and, within moments, a small flame flickered to life. He set about building the fire with more stout pieces of wood. It only took a few minutes for the fuel to catch and he stood with a satisfied nod.

On one of the hooks over the mantel was a roughly made cast iron teapot. Jack filled it from a water barrel in the kitchen and sprinkled in some tea leaves from a small box on the counter, then hung it to heat from the spit in the fireplace.

The teapot began to whistle as he returned from the kitchen again, a loaf of bread and several strips of jerky in hand. Placing those new items on the table, he went back to the fireplace and removed the teapot. He had just returned to the table with the pot and two cups when the door to one of the bedrooms opened and a man stepped into the room.

Older than Jack by a large margin, well into his sixties probably, the man's hair was mostly silver, with a few strands of black remaining. It hung limply to his shoulders, framing a deeply wrinkled, but strong face. Blue eyes that were still sharp gazed at Jack beneath bushy eyebrows.

"Got the tea ready for me, I see. Did I ever mention I like that you get up early?"

"Every morning," Jack replied. He poured a cup and handed it to the older man. "Good thing for you I do or you'd miss half the day."

"Bah! I'm not so far gone as that. Not yet, anyway." Sitting down at the table, the older man sipped at his cup and pursed his lips slightly. "You don't have to come today, you know. No one will think less of you."

Jack sat opposite him, his own cup steaming in his hand, untouched for the moment. Drawing a deep breath, the younger man shrugged. "I owe you better than that. I'm coming."

"Hmmph. Whatever debt you think you owe was paid years ago. Ain't nothing holding you. I've often wondered why you remain here. You must have kin in the country somewhere. Some of them may have survived."

"You wouldn't last out here on your own and you know it. Remember the raids last spring?"

The older man made a dismissive gesture, snorting with derision. "A few lads barely off their mama's tit. Wasn't a one of them had anything but a stick or a couple rocks. One shot from Vera and they high-tailed it." His eyes flicked toward the wall near the door to his room, where a scoped, bolt-action rifle hung on a rack. Looking back at him, the older man pointed a finger meaningfully at Jack. "And you know I coulda taken any three of them together bare handed, if it come down to it."

"That's not how Billy and Steven tell it. They said there were a dozen of them, some with pistols. Good thing Billy had his machine gun with him." Jack shook his head. "I should have been here. If those two hadn't come by to deliver eggs..."

"Those two tell tall tales and you know it, boy. It wasn't anything I couldn't handle. Besides," the older man's eye twinkled in the firelight and he grinned mischievously, "you had prettier company to attend to."

Jack's face darkened, his lips turning down into a scowl. "I want none of her."

A loud snort was the older man's initial retort. "It's been long enough and you ain't getting any younger. Why..."

"No!" Jack slammed his cup down onto the table, splashing his tea. His scowl deepened, his gaze dropping to the floor. His jaw worked and for a moment he struggled to find the right words to explain himself, to no avail. Instead, he shook his head forcefully.

"Alright. Alright. Have it your way. But when you get my age, don't come crying to me if you find yourself wishing you'd done different."

Jack just grunted.

Both men sat in silence a time, eating breakfast and sipping their tea. Finally, the older man pushed his plate away and stood. "Well. We'd best get to it. Caravan's due in town around noon and we don't wanna be late. I'll get us some grub for the trip." With that, he strode into the kitchen. When he returned, Jack was still sitting at the table, nursing his tea and his thoughts. The older man laid a hand on his shoulder and gave it a gentle squeeze. "Come on, youngster."

Jack started, then stood as well, managing a half-grin. "After you, old man." He took the food and stuffed it into his backpack, then hefted his shotgun and, once more donning his hat, followed the older man out the door. As they got outside, they paused momentarily on the porch as the older man slung his rifle over his shoulder.

"Don't know why you keep wearing that hat. No one's gonna mistake you for anything but a city boy."

"I like the shade."

The older man chuckled and stepped from the porch. In front of the house was the rusted hulk of a pickup truck. Weeds grew up through the engine block and the tires had long-since decayed away, but amazingly the windshield was still intact. Jack eyed the remnant of days past as they turned left toward the pasture and the waiting cart.

"So much lost," he murmured to himself.

The older man heard though. "It can come again. Don't think it can't."

Jack shrugged but made no other reply. He turned toward the curing shed, leaving the older man to retrieve and hitch the horse. Swinging the door open, he beheld the fruits of the last six months of his labor. Meats from a number of game animals hung from hooks in the ceiling, carefully smoked to preserve them. Through a door at the back of the shed were the pelts. He and the older man spent many a day in the woods beyond the property, trapping and hunting. The older man was right, in some ways Jack was still a city boy. He'd always considered himself a fast learner, but it seemed like it took forever, once he was back on his feet, to learn how to do it right out in the woods. It had helped to have a task to focus on though, and eventually he'd gotten to the point that even some of the more adept locals in town remarked at his prowess.

It took an hour or so to load the cart and hitch the horse. The sun was fully visible above the tree tops as the older man clucked and shook the reins to get the horse moving. Jack checked that he had a cartridge chambered in his shotgun. Even though there hadn't been a raid in months, that didn't mean there couldn't be raiders lurking in the nearly seven miles between the house and town.

Once that was a quick drive, hardly worth considering. Now the road, once paved in asphalt and at least marginally maintained, had deteriorated through years of neglect. The pavement was pitted and cracked and weeds poked through in numerous places. In one or two places, a bush or sapling had managed to take root and grow up through a deep crack. Nevertheless, it was still faster than traveling cross-country. And certainly it was faster than three years ago, before the older man traded for the horse and cart. For a moment, Jack's shoulders and back seemed to ache from the memory of exertions required to get their wares to town using just a litter. This way was much better. If they were lucky, they'd make it with an hour or more to get set up before the caravan arrived.

The caravans were a recent occurrence, also. They first appeared five years ago, a meager band of two carts and one litter filled with various items the caravan masters had dug from some old Walmarts and Kmarts. Where they had found stores that hadn't already been plundered, Jack had no idea. But in the years since, the caravans had grown in size and frequency. Based out of Forest Hills, about one hundred miles west of town, they claimed to make a circuit of every pocket of civilization in a 200 mile radius. Even the raider camps saw visits from the caravans, or so the rumors said. These days, they came to town twice a year, bringing with them items and money.

Barter was the main way folks did business in town before, but now most dealt in Forest Hills Caravan Scripts. They were just little pieces of iron with "FH" stamped on one side and a number indicating the value of the script on the other, all but worthless in and of themselves. But back when there was a USA, what was a dollar but a piece of paper with some ink on it? Jack had some schooling in economics, back before the Troubles, and he understood that it was the idea behind the currency that was important, not its physical makeup. All the same, he found it fascinating how quickly people began to place value in those scripts. Some held out, decrying their neighbors for exchanging the products of their labor for something so seemingly useless. Others resented the influence of those living so far away from the little world of the town and its surroundings.

Still, there was no denying that life after the caravans was better than life before. Jack could almost begin to think that maybe the older man was right. Maybe it was possible to rebuild to the way it was. Except that every time the caravans came through, there were fewer old-tech products and more that were obviously handmade and of lower quality. Fewer products were made from metal; how many had the equipment or skills to run a forge? More and more products were wood or stone-based. The decline from high-tech to stone age was obvious, and as far as Jack could see, there was little to be done to stop it. No, it was better not to hope for what could not be. Better to accept things as they were and make do.

The journey passed quickly, with little conversation. The road to town from the older man's property had never been heavily travelled, even in the good days before the Troubles. At first, the road passed through woods and an occasional field, but after a couple of miles they began passing houses, long abandoned or burnt out, then an old shop or two. Finally they reached a sign, faded but legible, announcing the town limits. Still there was no sign of habitation, save the carcasses of years past, until the road turned a corner around a fair-sized hill.

It had been almost a month since Jack last came into town, but the older man had just returned from the town council meeting four days earlier. Jack was surprised to see a pair of towers as the central, inhabited area of town came into view. The towers were nothing spectacular; more scaffold than anything else. They stood about ten feet tall, with a rising gate blocking what remained of the road between them. The beginnings of a low palisade wall extended from the towers in both directions. Jack assumed it was meant to make a circuit of the main population area. An armed man was posted in each tower and a third at the gate.

"What is this?"

"Don't tell me you forgot the talk on defenses after the raids that convinced you I couldn't survive on my own."

"I remember nothing got done, whatever the council talked about."

"Too true. Well, at the last meeting, Beatrice got pissed and told the other council members they needed to put up or shut up. Everybody claimed they wanted a wall, but no one was willing to give the time and effort to make it. So she announced she was putting her hands on the project, on her own if need be. I tell you, that shook things up. Old Geoff Crenshaw wasn't having none of that. You know how he and Beatrice have it out for each other and he wasn't about to let her have all the credit for getting the wall built. Once he got onboard, the rest just fell in line and pledged to get started construction the next day." The older man wiped his nose on the back of his hand and gave Jack a wry grin. "Guess they really did it."

"Crenshaw's younger than you, last I checked."

"Well he don't act like it most days."

The cart neared the checkpoint and the guard at the gate raised a hand in greeting. Olive-skinned, with dark hair and eyes, he was short, but solidly built. He carried a bow and Jack could see a full quiver over his shoulder. No surprise there. With ammo becoming more and more scarce, bows were common now. In the years since the Troubles, folks from town had scouted out all the sporting goods stores, Walmarts, and any other place that might have ammo within a day in all directions. Those that hadn't already been looted during the Troubles had only limited supplies, so the town was basically left with what it had. Fortunately, Kevin West-field figured out early how to make bows and fletch arrows after reading some old wilderness survival books in the library.

Still, it would be nice to have more guns. Back at the house, Jack and the older man were also starting to run low on ammo and they hoped the caravan might have some. Shooting a bow was all well and good, and a man got more bragging rights for being able to hit accurately with one than with a gun, but Jack preferred to keep his shotgun for as long as possible, thank you very much.

"Hello, Tobias. Jack." The guard nodded to both men in turn. "Been a while. Things okay out there?"

"Nothing worth complaining about, Percy," replied the older man. "How's guard duty?"

"Boring, but it beats pulling weeds in Beatrice's field." Pushing down on the counterweight, he swung the gate's arm up out of the way. "You'll want to get a move-on to the market field. More outriders from the caravan arrived an hour ago. They're making better time than they thought and will be here in a half hour or so now." He glanced at Jack, his lips pursing slightly. "Don't want to have trouble, right?"

The two men in the cart exchanged glances. "We'd best get moving, then. Thanks Percy," said Tobias as he flicked the reins.

As the cart pulled through the checkpoint, Jack noticed Percy's eyes following him, an almost expectant expression on the other man's face. Shaking his head, Jack breathed a soft curse. "Looks like no one's forgotten."

"Hard to forget about *that*, youngster."

"Maybe Ortiz won't be with the caravan this time."

Tobias snorted. "Fat chance of that. He's the security foreman, after all. Don't worry. He's a professional. Doesn't hold grudges."

"We'll see."

❧ 2 ❧

RULES OF DISCIPLINE

The caravan market was set up on the old high
school football field. It was the logical choice: large
open area, room to graze the pack animals out of
people's way, large indoor facilities if the weather didn't coop-
erate, centrally located. The more nostalgic folks in town
objected at first, memories of good times and past glories
before the Troubles weighing hard on their minds. But eventually even the most stubborn had to admit that there would
be no more state championships.

The town population before the Troubles was about
twenty-five thousand. Now less than a twentieth of that
number remained. Whether because folks left seeking kin,
were killed outright in the Troubles or in the riots and
fighting that followed, or died in the aftermath from the star-
vation, disease, and despair people everywhere encountered
before they learned how to live off the land again, it made no
difference. The town and, by all appearances the whole country, maybe even the whole world, would never again be the
way it was.

The field was bustling when Jack and Tobias arrived.

Trade folk were rushing to finish preparing the displays for their wares: cereals and produce, whiskey and wine, wood-worked items, livestock, the list went on. Even a few ladies from Hempstead House were on hand, dressed suggestively to entice the presumably lonely caravan men. Tobias raised an eyebrow as the cart passed their spot.

"First time they've been allowed to set up shop here. Wonder how Liselle convinced folks to allow it."

"It wasn't discussed at the council meeting?"

"Nope. Guess they knew what my vote would be without having to take it."

"No big mystery there, what with you and..."

"Ain't got nothing to do with it, youngster. Don't matter that I'm close with Liselle. I got no cause to tell anyone they can't make a living as they see fit, long as they ain't setting out to hurt someone else."

Jack nodded a silent concurrence, sparing the ladies a quick glance. "Some object to the morality of it, though." Seeing the older man begin to retort, Jack held up a hand to forestall it. "But let's not go there."

Tobias sniffed, but said no more. He turned the cart and stopped at the home side of what once was the fifteen yard line. Setting up was simplicity in itself: Tobias unhitched the horse and led her over to the grazing area while Jack pulled a couple of stools and a folding table from the cart. Lowering the tailgate to reveal the pelts and meats, he set up the stools and table in front, arranging a few of the more high quality choices on the table.

By the time Tobias returned, all was in readiness, so the two men spent some time mingling with other townsfolk, renewing acquaintances and examining items for sale. The buying and selling wouldn't start in earnest until the caravan arrived and set up. This afternoon would mostly be marked by music, dancing, and a kick-off feast, with the official market opening in the morning. But it wasn't just the caravan masters who engaged in commerce at the market. Over the years, the caravan market had become the chief catalyst for economic activity in the area. People from a number of nearby settlements, too small to make it worth the caravan stopping, came to participate. A few travelled as long as three days to get there, so the market had become exactly what the name implied and there would likely be a chance to do business before the official start. Besides, the caravan masters typically made the rounds while their hands set up to get a feel for what they may want to buy in the morning. For those two reasons, everyone laid out their wares early. But it all hinged on the caravan.

After about fifteen minutes or so, the assembled crowd hushed as a group of riders arrived. Sixteen hard-looking men on sturdy horses took up station in the near end zone. More than before, though many faces were familiar from previous visits. But that had been true during most visits from the caravans. More wagons and carts meant more guards, of course. They had upgraded their equipment noticeably since Jack last saw them. All had pistols on their hips and most carried assault rifles: M-16s and M-4s from the look. Two men had machine guns and one in the rear looked to have a grenade launcher.

More striking was their difference in attire. Each wore camouflage fatigues and what Jack heard the Army used to call "Full Battle Rattle", helmets, elbow and knee pads, and armor plates on their chests, backs, and thighs. Where the hell had they gotten *that*? The only other person Jack had seen with that kit was Billy Gershwin, who left his Army post and returned to town during the Troubles.

"What, did they take over an old Army base?" Tobias muttered, echoing Jack's thoughts. "There'll be no dealing with their swelled heads now."

Jack was forced to agree. Caravan guards tended to be overbearing and arrogant. But then, he supposed that was part of their job, wasn't it? All the same it made dealing with them difficult, sometimes. Jack winced, the memory of the caravan's last visit heightened by the guards' arrival. He found himself knuckling the small of his back without realizing it for a moment. Once what he was doing registered, he forced his hands down to his side, but it was all he could do to not clench his fists. Maybe no one else noticed.

Tobias gave him a gentle nudge with his elbow, putting the lie to that hope. "Calmly, youngster. It's ancient history."

A grunt was all Jack could manage in reply before the arrival of the caravan main grabbed their attention. Fifteen standard wagons and carts, each pulled by a pair of horses, followed by a wagon that was boarded over and reinforced with iron. That would be the money wagon. Then came a larger wagon that was pulled by four horses and looked more a moving house than anything else. The caravan masters rode there. The rear guard, another sixteen men armed and armored as before, completed the column.

A contingent of people stepped forward from the towns-folk and gathered at the five yard line, awaiting the caravan's arrival in what looked like an official capacity. Seeing them move, Tobias sighed and stepped forward as well. "Time to kiss the ring." Tobias was one who, while he appreciated the caravan masters' economic impact and respected their profes-sionalism, didn't care for them much personally. Probably his least favorite duty as a member of the town council was dealing with them diplomatically. Jack didn't envy him that, either, for that matter.

It took a few moments for the caravan to arrange itself, but eventually the house-wagon came to a halt before the assembled welcoming committee. Eleven people represented the town: the ten council members in line and the mayor standing in front. Tobias stood behind the mayor and to her right, managing to look dignified despite his dislike of pomp and circumstance. Jack was amused to note that Geoff Crenshaw and Beatrice Collins stood on either end of the line, as far from each other as possible. The members of the council, and the mayor, were all the big money people in town, except Tobias. He was elected because nearly everyone in town respected him, most of the others because folks either owed their living to them or wanted to. They all had brains, but some of them couldn't find their backsides with both hands. Politics never changed, it seemed.

The house-wagon driver got down and moved back to the door. He fished under the cart for a moment, giving time for one of the guards to dismount, sling his rifle, and join him. The guard's fatigues and armor differed from the others; while they all had a red "FH" emblazoned on their helmets and breast, his was golden yellow. That would be Ortiz.

The driver finally retrieved a set of removable stairs, mounted them in place below the door, grasped the doorknob, and looked at the security man. Ortiz took a moment to carefully look over his men's positioning and the arrangement of the townsfolk. Apparently satisfied, he nodded. On cue, the driver opened the door and three men descended from the wagon.

The men varied physically as much as any three would: one tall and muscular, the second chubby and balding, and the last shrunken and frail. At the same time, there was a...sameness...about them. Each wore a freshly-pressed navy blue business suit with a blue tie, highly polished black leather shoes, and carried a briefcase. They walked with the same brisk pace and, once stopped before the welcoming committee, stood in line abreast in the exact same pose with heads high, looking straight ahead with expressionless faces.

Jack recognized the elder man immediately. Grymanski

(Jack had never heard his given name) had led every caravan since the first, and however frail he might appear, he had proven himself shrewd and hardy. The balding man was also familiar, but Jack had never seen the third before. Where was Graeber?

"Welcome to Glennville, gentlemen," said the mayor.

At the greeting, Grymanski's expressionless façade broke. Stepping forward with a smile, he took her hand in both of his. "My dear Ms. Lang, it is a pleasure to see you well." His voice was soft and slightly raspy, but kind, with a subtle British accent. He took in the on-looking crowd at a glance. "And to see that Glennville has been growing, just as we have."

"May I offer you some refreshment, Mr. Grymanski?" At about where the fifty yard line would be, a large tent had been erected. Several long tables, and one smaller table on a raised platform, were laid out there. A buffet table to the side was covered with food of various sorts and a platoon of cooks and helpers manned fire pits at the foot of the bleachers. No doubt they would be hard at work all afternoon.

Grymanski nodded and offered the mayor his arm. "Very kind. If you will accompany me?" The two began to walk, with Ortiz following closely behind. Grymanski's colleagues and the council also followed at a short distance. "We have a great many things to discuss," the old caravan master said. "Much has happened. There are changes you need to be aware of and decisions your town will have to make."

The mayor's eyebrow quirked upward in surprise. "Decisions?"

"A moment, my dear," said the old man. The pair was passing in front of Jack's cart and the caravan master stopped, turning to regard him for a moment. Ortiz did as well. Jack found the hard stare from the security man unsettling, but then who wouldn't? Ortiz was lean and muscular, and carried himself like a coiled spring, ready to move into action in a heartbeat. A puckered scar ran down his right temple, across his cheek, and to the corner of his mouth. He'd seen his share of scuffles, no doubt.

"Mr. Simmons, isn't it?" said Grymanski. "I trust there will be no...outbursts from you this time." The old man's tone was still kindly, but it had a harder edge as he addressed Jack. Down the line of council members, Jack noticed Tobias shaking his head, no doubt in warning.

"Graeber started that trouble, not I."

Ortiz's eyes narrowed and for a moment he looked as though he was about to move on Jack, but Grymanski's raised hand stopped him. The old man shook his head, making a soft tsking sound before answering. "Ah yes. I'm afraid Mr. Graeber's behavior during our last visit was...unacceptable. He has been terminated and is no longer a member of the Forest Hills Caravan Company."

Taken aback, Jack looked with confusion from Grymanski to Ortiz and back. "But...I thought..." Standing next to the old man, the mayor looked just as confused as Jack. "Why..."

"We discipline our own, Mr. Simmons. It would not do if we were to allow our executives to be set upon by anyone. It sets a bad precedent. Fortunately for you, Mr. Graeber's actions were egregious, else Mr. Ortiz would not have treated you so gently. I trust you'll remember that in the future, hmm?"

Grymanski turned the mayor away and resumed their walk. He said a few words to her, but though she nodded along, it was obvious from the stunned expression on her face that she wasn't really listening for several moments. For that matter, everyone else in earshot looked disbelieving as well. They thought forty lashes from a cat-of-nine-tails was *gentle*?

"I've hung men for less," growled Ortiz, giving Jack one last glare before moving to catch up with the caravan master.

The rest of the column followed, the new caravan executive giving Jack an appraising look as he passed. The council members avoided looking at him, except Tobias, of course. He stopped momentarily and gave Jack a wry grin.

"Guess that means you're famous."

"Great."

Tobias chuckled softly and clapped him on the shoulder, then moved to catch up with the group. Jack shook his head for what felt the eighth time in the last minute and sat down on his stool. He suddenly didn't have any appetite for the feast.

NEWS AND DECISIONS

Tobias worried over Jack sometimes. Hell, just about all the time. He had been through a lot. That day ten years ago, the day the Troubles began, was hard to forget. Tobias remembered sitting on the couch at home watching Good Morning America when all the power went out and his electronics fried themselves. Moments later, he heard the sputtering sound of a dying engine and rushed outside just in time to see a small plane crash into the tree line at the end of his yard. By the time he got there...

He'd seen and done a lot of things, but damned if he would ever forget that crash site. Several fires burning. Leaking fuel spreading inexorably toward the flames. Jack trying, in spite of his injuries, to pull his passenger out of the fuselage. Her desperate pleas for help turning into screams of unimaginable agony as the leaking fuel ignited and flames engulfed her. Jack fighting vigorously as Tobias pulled the younger man away and forced him to the ground to put out the flames on his clothes. If Tobias had brought his gun, he'd have put a bullet in the woman to end it, but without that option, she screamed and screamed for what seemed an eternity. There was nothing to be done except to drag Jack away and try to not listen.

He'd have driven Jack straight to the hospital, but his truck wouldn't start. The phone was dead, so he couldn't call for help and there was no way he could carry Jack all the way to a doctor by himself. So he tended Jack's burns and other injuries as best he could and hoped for the best. He would call for a doctor once the phones were repaired.

But days, then weeks, passed and they never were. The younger man was beside himself with pain and had to be tied down to keep him from thrashing out of the bed. Tobias put him on a steady diet of whiskey, which helped a little, but it was a hard several weeks for both of them. Only after Jack became coherent enough to speak did Tobias learn his physical wounds were the least of his torment. The woman in the plane was Jack's wife, Susan. Her loss had eaten at him ever since.

Small wonder he was reluctant to move on, but after the incident with Graeber, Tobias thought maybe Jack had decided to try making a new life. Serena certainly seemed willing, and Jack could do a lot worse. But then, he just shut off. Tobias had tried on a few occasions to encourage him, but just like this morning, he ended up hitting a wall.

Bah! Like he was one to talk. Tobias had never settled down, never married. He always preferred the bachelor lifestyle and who was he to think that Jack couldn't want that, as well? He had the benefit of having known the alternative, after all. But then, Tobias knew that wasn't the reason, however much he might like to tell himself it was. Jack had never let himself get over what happened. His pain or guilt or whatever prevented it. The only thing he was willing to do was work for Tobias to, as he put it, repay him for saving his life. Tobias' objections that Jack didn't owe him anything made no difference. So Tobias worked him, hard as he could. What else was he to do?

"I think Jack struck a nerve."

The words snapped Tobias back to the present. He had been only halfway paying attention to where they were going, just following the rest of the councilors as his mind wandered. He hadn't noticed Beatrice falling back to walk at his left. A bit older than Jack, in her early 40s, she was still more than handsome. Black hair to just below her shoulders, green eyes, a winning smile, and nicely rounded figure. If he'd been twenty years younger, she'd be just his type. And he was quite sure she knew it. Beatrice didn't miss much.

He looked sidelong at her. "You figure?"

Beatrice nodded slowly, favoring Tobias with a conspiratorial smile. "Oh yes. They couldn't do him like Ortiz wanted before, because of what Graeber did. It's been worrying them ever since, the thrashing he gave their man. You don't think it was by chance the old bastard walked past your cart, do you?" One eyebrow lifted to accentuate her words. "Do you really think that conversation was for Jack's benefit?" Her eyes made their way back to the caravan men at the front of the line.

Tobias followed her gaze as he mulled over her words. Jack had looked pretty shook up at the end of the brief talk. For that matter, so had everyone else...Ah-ha. Very clever. "No, I s'pose not."

Beatrice nodded. "They'll be a little extra watchful this trip. A little more cautious, I think. Could be useful." Useful for what, Tobias didn't even begin to guess. She always seemed to have some scheme or other in the works.

Beatrice left his side as the group reached the tent. The elevated table was set for fourteen and each had their assigned place. The three caravan men sat on one side, Grymanski in the middle, with Ortiz standing behind them watchfully. Mayor Lang sat opposite Grymanski. The other councilors were arranged by seniority on either side of her. Beatrice and Geoff flanked her, no doubt annoyed at being so near each other. Tobias had only been on the council longer than a few others, so he sat three people down from the Mayor on her left. The whole setup almost resembled one of those old arms reduction talks from the Cold War days.

They all sat and servers quickly made a circuit of the table, filling cups with water and some of Vincent Cho's wine. Grymanski stood, lifting his wine cup. "I propose a toast to our mutual health and a continued profitable friendship." There was general agreement around the table and all took a drink. Tobias was impressed. Vincent had been aging this batch since he first started, seven years ago, and it was his best yet. Even Grymanski seemed to like it, and from what Tobias had gathered, he was a hard one to please.

Mayor Lang cleared her throat as she set her cup down. "Mr. Grymanski, you mentioned some news and some changes?"

"Indeed. Late last year, our northern caravan discovered several people in one of the settlements creating fake payment scripts." He reached into the inner pocket of his coat, pulled out a number of iron pieces, and handed them to the mayor, who passed them down the line for the councilors to examine. The pieces looked very close to a Caravan Script, but they were not completely circular and the "FH" was slightly off center. They would probably pass a cursory comparison, but obviously not a more thorough one.

Grymanski continued. "Obviously, this was unacceptable and we made our displeasure with those who made and used the counterfeits known in no uncertain terms." He paused for a moment, his eyes growing hard as his gaze swept down the line of councilors. Tobias was sure the counterfeiters were decorating an oak tree somewhere, from the look in the old man's eyes. Several of his fellow councilors swallowed audibly. They got the message too. "In order to lower the odds of this sort of thing happening again, we have put new procedures in place. Mr. Peterson has taken Mr. Graeber's place as our finance manager. He will explain."

The new man, the young muscular fellow, nodded and leaned forward in his chair. "From now on, we will produce a new series of scripts each year. This year will be series one, next year will be two, and so on. Henceforth, caravans will only accept scripts in payment from the current or the previous series. The series number will be stamped on the scripts below our logo."

From his coat pocket, Peterson withdrew a small bag. It clinked as he handed it to the mayor. "Here are some samples. The caravans carry enough scripts to change out all those that have previously been issued. People may change their scripts free of charge. However, they can only change scripts that are currently valid, so I would advise your people to change all their scripts now, because they will not be accepted for change or purchase when we come through next."

The mayor pulled the drawstring on the bag and poured a few scripts into her hand. The councilors on either side of her gasped in surprise. Peterson nodded, continuing. "Also, as you can see, we have changed our minting methods. From now on, one script coins will still be iron, but ten will have some copper mixed into them, fifty some silver, and one hundred some gold."

"Where in tarnation did you get enough to do that?" asked Geoff, drawing an amused grin from the caravan man.

"There is a lot of gold and silver lying around since the Troubles, you know. Believe me, Mr. Crenshaw, we have a more than sufficient amount of ore."

Geoff blinked, his eyes narrowing. Tobias was wondering

the same thing Geoff probably was. They hadn't been introduced, so how did Peterson know him? Before Geoff could open his mouth to voice the question, Grymanski spoke again.

"We appreciate that this will come as an inconvenience to some of your citizens. For that reason, we will remain in Glennville longer than we have in the past, a full week, to give all a fair chance to change their scripts." He fixed Mayor Lang with a direct stare. "Unless you object, of course, Ms. Lang."

"No, not at all, Mr. Grymanski. You and your men are welcome here," she replied quickly. Many of the other councilors spoke up, voicing the same sentiment.

Grymanski gave the briefest of nods, barely acknowledging the council's agreement. No doubt he took it as a given. "In that case, there are other items to discuss. Mr. Harris?"

The balding man cleared his throat. "As you know, our caravans interact with many other settlements. Most, like you, are valued trading partners. However, we have recently expanded our routes and have made some interesting and troubling discoveries." As he spoke, he lifted his briefcase onto the table and opened it. Pulling out a small stack of papers, he paged through them for a moment before continuing. "Ah. Here it is. We found this in a small settlement a short distance south of Atlanta."

Harris handed his chosen paper to the mayor. Tobias was far enough down the table that he couldn't see any details except that the page was beginning to yellow with age and was torn around the edges, and that it had something handwritten in what looked like charcoal on one side and faded typed words on the other. The mayor looked at the handwritten side briefly, her eyebrows rising. "Is this true?"

"We cannot know without verifying the claim ourselves. We sent a small caravan further south to make contact, but they had not returned when we left Forest Hills to journey here. If they confirm what this paper says," Harris peaked his hands just below his chin, "Mayport could be the first place we've encountered that has managed to generate electricity since the Troubles."

An excited murmur began among the other councilors, but was quickly silenced as Harris raised his hands in a calming gesture. "Or, it could end up being nothing. Just wishful thinking. We'll know in a few months."

Looking back down at his stack of papers, Harris pursed his lips and hesitated for a moment before continuing. "The second piece of news is less encouraging. Our western caravan encountered a number of recently burned-out settlements..."

"How do you know it was recent?" inquired Beatrice.

Harris leveled a stern stare at her, receiving a quirked eyebrow in response. That lady has spunk, Tobias thought admiringly. After a long moment, Grymanski cleared his throat, and Harris, looking a trifle put down, continued. "We know, Ms. Collins, because each time, the townships were still smoldering. As with the others, this caravan had ventured further than before. But finding only burnings, it turned back for Farrah's Crossing, our western-most trading partner. The caravan had just visited two weeks before, but when it returned, Farrah's Crossing, too, was burning."

He picked up another sheet of paper and slid it across the table to the mayor. "It was different than the others: fires were still burning, so the raiders could not have left more than a few hours before the caravan arrived. The security detachment found one person, severely wounded, lying in a thicket on the outskirts of town. She was bleeding out from two belly wounds, but was able to tell what happened before she passed." He pointed at the paper. "This was drawn from her description of the standard the raiders carried."

The mayor frowned and held up the page for the other councilors to see. It, too, was drawn in charcoal and resembled the old "Don't Tread On Me" flags that had enjoyed resurgence in popularity during the years after 9-11. However, it was different in that the snake was coiled around an eagle and appeared to be biting it at the base of its skull. "That is mildly disturbing," murmured Chuck Lawson, to Tobias' left.

"Indeed, it is, to those who remember the original," intoned Harris. "But not as disturbing as the rest of her tale. The raiders were not the normal rabble the town had become accustomed to repelling. They were organized. Trained. And they were equipped with weapons she could not identify. She told of men hurling lightning and killing with a pointed finger." Shaking his head, Harris' expression almost appeared compassionate for a moment. "She was obviously delusional from the blood loss. But she was clear on two things. First, the raiders butchered the dead in the same manner one would an animal, even smoking the meat. Second, the survivors were stripped and tied into a long line of prisoners, no doubt from the other burned out towns. The leader of the raid said something about them being honored to serve the Masters before literally running them out of town ahead of his men."

Tobias was sickened. Butchering a person like that could only mean one thing. He could see the other councilors were coming to the same conclusion he was. Expressions ranging from disgust to horror, many a mixture of both, were plain on their faces. Harris slowly put the papers back into his briefcase and closed it, then leaned back in his chair, his hands clasped on the table. Grymanski again spoke, his eyes seeming especially sharp as he looked from one councilor to another.

"In light of this new discovery, we have determined that we should look to our defenses. You have come to a similar conclusion, as we noted on our arrival. However, if the woman's description of the raiders' skill and equipment is even close to true, your little wall will not save you. Indeed, I fear for all of the free settlements in the region should these raiders choose to visit." His raspy voice took on a paternalistic, almost gentle tone. Obviously a ploy, since that old bastard was anything but gentle. "For that reason, Forest Hills is extending an invitation to all our trading partners. We wish to form a consolidation of settlements. A mutual protection pact, if you will. We are hosting a conference in four months' time, after the New Year, at our headquarters, where we will negotiate the details. Glennville is welcome to send a delegation, if you wish."

If anyone had a pin to drop, Tobias was sure everyone within twenty yards would have heard it in the silence that followed.

❦ 4 ❦

AT THE MARKET

The rest of the afternoon and evening passed uncomfortably for Jack. At first, he kept his distance, but after a while, he crept closer to the banquet tent. Most of the people at the market were gathered in a loose ring around the tent. By tradition, they kept a discrete distance so the council and the caravan masters could speak in relative private, but Jack could almost taste the anticipation in the crowd.

The caravan always brought news from the other settlements, and lately the occasional letter or package as well. Most in Glennville had kin in other areas of the country, and despite the long odds, a fair number still held out hope of learning at least some were alive somewhere. In a few cases, that hope had been proven true. But even when news of kin was lacking, everyone wanted to know that life continued in the world beyond town and was eager to learn of it.

Jack moved toward the front of the ring and members of the crowd parted to let him pass. As they did, he noticed many giving him sidelong looks. Did they truly distrust and dislike him so? After all these years, he thought he'd earned a place here. He had come to enjoy going to town for the day: mixing with his neighbors, having a dinner that was cooked with skill for a change. But ever since the incident with Graeber, the townsfolk were standoffish and uncomfortable around him. Except for Serena and one or two others, it seemed the rest wished he were gone, or that he'd just let that bloated, sanctimonious, lecherous scumbag have his way with her. Some neighbors, letting their desire to stay in the caravan's good graces override respect for their own. Maybe Tobias was right. Maybe he should...

He stopped. There she was. About ten feet ahead, she hadn't seen him yet, thankfully. Wavy auburn hair hanging to just below her shoulder blades, toned arms and legs, and a nice hourglass figure: he didn't need to see her face to recognize her. She was engaged in conversation with Jeremy Higgins and Denice Fairshaw. Jack quickly altered course, moving away from the trio. Maybe he could get away before she noticed.

But no, Denice nodded in his direction and Serena turned just as he was about to make his escape. She smiled warmly at him and raised a hand in greeting. He hesitated, almost going to her, but instead turned and shoved his way through a couple of farmers from the other side of town. He caught, from the corner of his eye, the smile fading from her face, replaced by disappointment, then hurt, before she disappeared into the crowd behind him. He felt a pang of guilt, but quickly pushed it away. Better to not lead her on.

After a few minutes, he spied Logan Pierce. Younger than Jack by five or six years, with dark skin and close-cut black hair, Logan was one of the few who treated Jack the same as always. Tobias' closest neighbor before the Troubles, Logan had accompanied Tobias and Jack on many hunting expeditions. He had been, if possible, even more of an indoors guy than Jack at the beginning. His computer science skill set did not translate well in the new world and he and Jack had naturally become close in the months after Jack's recovery as Tobias taught them both how to survive in the wild. Lately, Logan lived inside the town proper and made a living helping Geoff Crenshaw with his herd.

Logan clasped hands with Jack as he walked up. "Good to see you, brother," he said.

"How's ranch life treating you?"

Logan shrugged noncommittally. "Pays the bills."

Jack snorted. Like there were that many bills these days. He opened his mouth to reply, but a general murmuring from the crowd drew his attention to the banquet tent. The caravan masters had stood from the table and were filing out, Ortiz obediently following. Normally, the mayor followed the caravaners out and announced the beginning of the feast, but today, she remained at the table, in conversation with the council members. From the gestures of all present, it appeared to be quite heated.

"What's the deal?" a townsman nearby wondered aloud, echoing Jack's thoughts. No answer was forthcoming though, as the council's deliberations continued for several minutes. Finally, the mayor brought it to a halt with a firm gesture and stepped out of the tent. Her raised voice carried to the crowd with ease. The reaction to the news of the changes to the caravan scripts was mixed among the people near Jack and Logan, but when the mayor announced the start of the feast, any grumbling stopped. It was hard to stay mad when faced with better food than was available for most of the year.

The tent held enough seats for about two hundred people, but Jack and Logan didn't linger. They instead filled plates from one of the buffet tables and trooped back to Tobias' cart. Theft was rare in town. Small wonder, considering justice was swift and harsh these days. Nevertheless, it was best not to take chances. Logan stayed just long enough to finish the meal. But duty called, so he hurried off to check on Crenshaw's livestock, leaving Jack with a promise to catch up later in the evening.

Jack did a bit of business that afternoon with some local farmers, trading game meat for vegetables and some baked goods. Grymanski and his chubby colleague made the rounds as well. No doubt the new guy was overseeing things with their wagons. There were no thinly veiled threats when they came by this time; it was strictly business. As usual, the pelts attracted their attention more than the meats. Meats could help see the caravan home, but the pelts could fetch a better price in trade later. Also as usual, they wasted no time on small talk, but instead looked the merchandise over quickly, took a few notes, and moved on.

Tobias returned to the cart not long after the caravaners left. The older man was more subdued than normal. He settled onto the stool next to Jack without a word, and for a long time, he stared into space.

"Looked like quite an argument there." Jack ventured, to break the silence.

"Eh? Oh. Wasn't nothing. Just the usual bickering."

"Yeah. Sure." Jack stood and pulled a sturdy wooden box from the cart. "Well, now that you're back, I'm going to go change our money."

Not waiting for the older man's reply, Jack moved away. There was already quite a crowd of people wanting to change their coins. Jack looked back after he'd queued up in line. Tobias was still sitting on his stool, frowning in thought.

The dancing began at dusk. Gena Massey and her band set up on the raised platform under the tent, where the council and caravan masters held their palaver. Their repertoire was a mix of classic rock and country western, with selections to appeal to most folks in town. The townsfolk gathered in a loose ring just inside the tent to listen, and those who were so inclined danced before the stage. It almost reminded Jack of a high school dance, the way most folks were slow to get on the dance floor. Jack didn't venture too far inside the tent, contenting himself instead to linger near the benches where Harlan Jeffries had his whiskey casks set up.

Logan returned shortly after the festivities began, but only said hello for a moment before he spied Lydia Stevenson in the crowd nearby. With a grin and a fist bump for good luck, he made his way over to her. She beamed a smile when Logan said hello, and before long, they were making turns on the dance floor. Jack chuckled and shook his head. He could remember a time when he enjoyed dancing. It didn't seem so long ago some days; others, it seemed an eternity.

"Looks like you could use a refill, Jack."

He turned toward the speaker and held out his cup. Harlan was a few years older than Jack. He was short, with a bulging belly beneath the apron he always seemed to wear. He wore his black hair short except for a mullet at the nape of his neck and had long sideburns that came all the way down to his chin. He would have fit in well in a biker gang, back when they still existed. Jack had never asked, but he had the impression Harlan had done some time. He made mean whiskey, though. Jack nodded in thanks and tossed him a script in payment as Harlan handed his cup back, then raised it to his lips and took a sip.

Wandering away a bit, his eyes lingered on the dancing figures beneath the tent. There was Tobias and Liselle. Jack had to hand it to him, Tobias sure could move. For that matter, so could she. They made a good couple. For all Tobias' talk about never settling down, Jack wouldn't be surprised if he popped the question one of these days.

Jack's wandering feet eventually took him around the tent completely and he found himself back near Tobias' cart. He paused, looking back at the festivities under the tent, then, with a tiny shrug, he walked over to his stool. Taking a moment to fish flint and steel and a short length of twine from a toolbox in the back of the cart, he proceeded to strike sparks onto the twine.

In a short time, it began to smolder. He blew softly onto it to kindle the flame. He had a cigar in his pocket, the last from the stash he purchased when the caravan last came to town. In the morning, he intended to stock up again. But for now, it was a beautiful night for a smoke. Biting off the nub, he puffed the cigar alight from the burning twine, then snuffed out the little flame.

Settling down onto his stool, he leaned back against the cart and looked up at the stars. He sat that way for a long while, not really thinking. Just looking, puffing, and sipping. He didn't notice a shadowy figure approaching until the person was standing in front of the table where he'd set up the pelt display.

"Hello, Jack."

He jerked forward, nearly tumbling off his stool in surprise. As he regained his equilibrium, he recognized the speaker. Serena covered her mouth with one hand to cover a little giggle at his expense.

"Sorry," she said, laughter in her voice. "I didn't mean to startle you."

"Well you did."

Even in the darkness, Jack could see the mirth fading from her face. Pushing a lock of hair back, she looked down at the ground for a moment before speaking again.

"Do you...want to come and dance?"

He was tempted. Much as he knew he couldn't give her

what she wanted, he still felt drawn to her. But it wouldn't be fair. He drew a deep breath and forced himself to look away.

"No. Thanks."

From the corner of his eye, he saw her nod slowly. She opened her mouth to speak, but, after a moment, shut it again. Slowly, she turned and walked back toward the tent. He saw her look back once. Maybe he was imagining it, but it looked as though she wiped her eyes. Jack felt a twinge of heartache, but shoved it down. He had no business feeling that for another woman, not after Susan. With a deep sigh, Jack took a long draw on his cigar, then a longer swallow from his cup.

"You're an idiot, Simmons."

Jack hadn't seen Ortiz standing there. The security man was leaning against a wagon across from Tobias' cart, his arms crossed over his chest. The two men shared a look briefly, then Ortiz shook his head and walked off toward his caravan's wagons. In spite of himself, Jack felt ashamed.

MIDNIGHT RIDER

T he two weeks after the caravan left passed without
fanfare. Jack and Tobias went back home and spent
the time as had become their autumn routine: three
or four days hunting each week to stock up on meat for the
winter, followed by a couple days of upkeep on the house and
grounds.

Then, unexpectedly, Tobias announced he was returning
to town for a council meeting. Normally, the council met
every month unless something emergent happened, but with
the caravan's extended stay, they had conducted far more
business than normal and Jack assumed they would have little
else to discuss. So much for his assumption.

Jack had no desire to return to town, so he was left alone
at the house for a couple days. Which was just as well, with
all the winter preparations to make. Without the older man's
distracting talk, Jack was able to accomplish a lot in that
time. It was hard work, but necessary. And it helped to keep
his mind focused on the tasks.

Except in the evenings. When dinner was done and there

was nothing to do but watch the fire and sip on a drink, he found his thoughts drifting back to that morning, so many years ago. He'd been so proud of himself, getting his pilot license. Just had to show Susan how much fun it was to fly themselves cross-country to see her folks. And then he botched a simple dead-stick landing because he didn't watch his airspeed. Bad enough he dreamt of it constantly, but those evenings alone in front of the fire... Why was it so hard to move on? Tobias was right, this was getting ridiculous. But tell himself that as he might, the memories remained, stronger than ever, and with them, the second-guessing and guilt.

He drank himself to sleep on the couch the first night. On the second, when Tobias returned, Jack was sitting at the table, sipping on his second cup of whiskey and puffing on a cigar, watching the fire. He didn't even notice Tobias come in until the older man hung Vera on her hook and tossed his hat onto the table.

"Getting a head start on me, I see. Anything interesting happening?"

Jack roused himself with a start. "Replaced some shingles on the roof today. Took a couple turkeys yesterday."

Tobias sniffed and grabbed a cup, then sat down at the table and poured himself some whiskey. "I said interesting, youngster." He took a sip and nodded appreciatively at the flavor. "Don't much matter, I s'pose. I got enough interesting to carry us both."

Jack raised an eyebrow in response. No doubt Liselle had made things interesting indeed for the old scamp after the council meeting adjourned the previous night. Tobias held his gaze for a moment, but, seeming to read Jack's mind, he coughed and looked away toward the fire, flushing slightly.

"Not that kind of interesting." He took a larger sip from

his cup. A long moment of silence followed, then the older man ran his tongue over his lips and said, "There's an expedition in the works to Forest Hills."

"Forest Hills? What for?"

"They've called for a palaver of sorts and invited Glennville to send representatives."

Jack frowned. "Is that what had the Council all spun up while the caravan was here?"

"Partly. Guess everyone figured there was more going on than just the money change out. Grymanski and his boys gave us some news, but we didn't want to let it out until we decided what to do."

Over the next several minutes, Tobias related the caravaners' story about the burnt out settlements and the strange raiders. Jack listened in silence, taking it all in. When Tobias finished, Jack stood and walked to the fireplace. Taking a long drag on his cigar, he leaned one elbow on the mantel and looked back at the older man.

"Bad way to go. Who is the Master? And what's it got to do with us going to Forest Hills?"

"No idea. But whoever they are, them raiders got the caravan company spooked. They want to set up a mutual protection pact."

"What, so if they get hit, we have to risk our butts to rescue them?"

"More preemptive than that, I think. They didn't go into details, wanted to leave that for the palaver to work out."

"Great. So what idiots are going to make that trip, with winter coming on?"

Tobias cleared his throat. "Well, there's Beatrice Collins, Geoff Crenshaw..."

"Naturally."

"...Dwight Goodwin, Serena Telmen. And you."

Jack choked on his drink, sending a wide spray across the room. "*What*?!!!"

Tobias gave Jack a direct look. "Council wants you to go along."

"You can't be serious! Hell no, I'm not going. Especially not with...." He stopped his sentence and took another drink. A long one. "What do they want me for anyway?"

"For one thing, you're about the best tracking and hunting man in town." Jack opened his mouth to protest, but Tobias held up a silencing hand. "Don't waste your breath. Most weeks, you get as much game as I, and a fair bit more than any other guy around here." Jack closed his mouth, a deep frown on his lips as the older man continued. "Someone needs to be on that trip who can keep an eye out for trouble between here and there, forage for supplies, things like that, and I'm getting a bit old for this sort of thing. But beyond that..." Tobias' eyes twinkled and he grinned mischievously. "Beatrice thinks you make Grymanski nervous. And so do I."

Jack snorted loudly. "Not that it would matter even if it were true. Grymanski's probably not the big decision-maker there. You realize that, right?"

"Yup. Still can't hurt to unsettle him though."

"Maybe. Why the others? I understand Geoff and Beatrice. But Dwight and...Serena?"

Tobias gave him a long-suffering look. "Dwight's retired Army, remember? Only one in these parts who really knows military strategy. And Serena's a lawyer. Professional negotiator. You got a better notion who to speak for the town in this?"

Shrugging, Jack replied, "Guess not. But I'm not going. Find someone else."

"Bah. It'll do you good to get out from under me. And besides, ain't it about time you gave that girl the time of day? You've got her more frustrated than..."

Jack pulled his cigar from his mouth and pointed force-fully with it toward the older man. "Don't start in on that again, Tobias. I...." He broke off suddenly. Did he just hear something outside?

"What's the matter...."

Jack silenced Tobias with a raised hand. There it was again. He stepped into the kitchen and looked out the window. Just then the horse began screaming in her pen and he saw several flashes of flame through the window. Jack's eyes widened. He could make out a half-dozen shadowy figures, three carrying burning torches. Two of them had entered the horse's pen and were attempting to rope her. The others were approaching the house. Fast.

Oh crap.

"Raiders!" he shouted and raced back into the common room.

The window where he had just been standing broke as a rock came flying into the room behind him.

Tobias had already pulled Vera off her hook and was switching off the safety. "Shotgun upstairs?"

Jack nodded and bolted for the staircase. When he was halfway up, he heard the front door break open and the report of Tobias opening fire. Vera's 30-06 rounds were loud enough outdoors. Inside, Tobias' first shot was almost deafen-ing, but Jack still heard a gurgling scream and a solid thud, followed by shouts of chagrin and the sound of booted feet running.

It only took Jack a second to grab his shotgun and ammo pouch, then get back downstairs.

By then, Tobias was on the front porch. One raider was down just outside the doorway, blood pouring from an entry wound in his solar plexus. His legs kicked and both hands clutched at the wound, but it was obvious he wasn't long for this world. Jack stepped on him as he rushed out to join the older man.

The torch the downed raider had been carrying was lying on the ground before the porch, illuminating the area in front of the house. By its light, Jack could see the other three who'd approached the house duck around the corner, heading out back.

Tobias rushed to follow. Not a good plan, to follow them blindly, but there was no time to discuss the matter. Jack hurried after Tobias and heard another shot right as he reached the edge of the house. He rounded the corner in time to see a second raider, this one holding a torch, fall...and the torch bounce into the curing shed.

Tobias stood about twenty feet ahead of Jack, sighting in on the two raiders who had roped the horse as they rode away on her back. Jack almost thought the other two had fled as well until he saw a shadow moving behind Tobias and to his left.

Shouting a warning, Jack raised his shotgun to his shoulder. Pain lanced through his left hand as something struck it hard and he reflexively dropped the shotgun. He just got a glimpse of Tobias starting to turn toward the approaching shadow, but then it was all Jack could do to defend himself.

The raider came on in a rush. A left jab caught Jack in the jaw and he reeled backwards. A heartbeat later, he saw a flash of something shiny and felt a burning across his chest. If he hadn't been pushed backwards by the punch, the knife probably would have taken him in the throat, but he was in no condition to feel lucky. The front of his shirt was quickly becoming soaked and the raider pressed the advantage.

Jack retreated, barely avoiding another slash. Then another nicked him in the shoulder before he could get away. The raider was quick!

Jack was in trouble and he knew it. Another slashing

attack, from left to right, got him on the thigh as he retreated again with his guard up. He couldn't take much more of this.

The raider attacked again, a long, arcing slash that cut Jack's guarding forearms, but went just a little too far out to the side at the end.

Jack made his move, stepping forward as the raider began to recover from the swing. His forearms struck the raider's knife-arm at the elbow, and in a quick move, Jack's right hand grabbed the raider's knife hand at the wrist while he drove the edge of his left into the inside of the raider's elbow joint, forcing the arm to bend double. A quick step forward with his right foot and a twisting of his hips, and the raider was on the ground on his side, Jack's right knee in his kidney and the knife, now under Jack's control, at his throat.

In the firelight, Jack saw the raider's eyes grow wide with fright. "NO!" he said, his high-pitched voice quavering from exertion and sudden terror.

Jack hesitated just long enough to say, "Yes" into the raider's ear.

Then, with a quick wrist movement, he moved the knife across the raider's throat. He felt a warm gush on his hands. As Jack stood up, the raider's hands went reflexively to his throat, trying in vain to stem the flow. He voiced a long, soft, gurgling groan and his entire body spasmed for a few moments, then went still.

Jack hardly noticed. Tobias was on the ground.

Jack, beginning to feel a bit faint, stumbled over to the older man. As he got closer, Jack could see the last raider lying beneath Tobias. His head was bashed in, probably from the butt of Tobias' rifle. Kneeling down next to the older man, Jack rolled him over and saw a knife buried hilt-deep into his side. He was unconscious, but still breathing. That was something at least.

He needed to dress Tobias' wounds and get him to town for help. But when Jack stood, his head began to spin.

No. Can't pass out.

Thinking that didn't stop the dark spots in his eyes from growing larger. Jack hardly felt the impact with the ground as he fell. His last thought before it all went black was to wonder if he was going to learn there really was a heaven, so he could see Susan again.

❧ 6 ❧

LIVESTOCK

For once, there were no dreams. Perhaps that was the reality of heaven. Just floating in unconsciousness. Not thinking. Not feeling. Not dreaming. Just peace. How long he floated in that state, Jack couldn't say. At some point though, faint, lingering pain intruded. The exact source of the pain was hard to determine, but it was there. Over some time, it slowly grew, becoming more pronounced and localized. His chest, shoulder, arms, thigh. His knee and hand. His wrists and ankles. All sent fiery signals of injury to his groggy brain. He fought against them, his unconscious somehow trying to maintain sleep to avoid the full awareness of his wounds.

Then he felt movement and his eyes cracked open. The brightness of many torches would only allow that much. Over several minutes, all he could see was glare. All he could feel was pain and a swaying sensation. People were talking nearby, but their voices were just a low murmur to his ears. Eventually, he awoke enough to understand and to see.

Directly ahead, he could see his arms and hands, bound around a wrist-thick branch. From the feeling of his ankles, he surmised they shared the same fate, and looking down, he saw that it was so. But wait, he wasn't looking down. It took a long moment for him to translate, and understand, the side-to-side swaying feeling. Down was behind him. His hands and feet were bound, but he was dangling from the branch. With slow, difficult effort, he moved his head and saw that the end of the branch closest to his head stopped at another person's shoulder. He was being carried. But by whom?

The voices spoke again and Jack strained to understand what they were saying. After several long moments, seemingly forever, he managed to decipher the words.

"..weighs a ton."

"Stop complaining. You saw what happened at the house. Fighters fetch a good price."

Something about those words made alarm bells sound in Jack's mind, but he couldn't understand why. His thoughts were sluggish. There was something he wanted to know, but he couldn't quite recall what it was.

"Fine, but do we need the old one? Might as well bleed him and be done. Probably done for anyway."

Tobias! He must have survived too. Where was he?

"We lost four men at that house. Jared'll skin us if we don't get more in return than a single horse. Keep him." That was a third voice, coming from somewhere to Jack's right.

Tobias was alive, at least. That was a comfort. A small one, but it was something. Jack stretched as best he could, turning his head to try to find the older man. But it was to no avail. He couldn't see a thing, and whenever he moved too far, the pain lanced through his body with new fury. He tried to call to Tobias, but all that came out was a long, guttural groan.

"This one's awake! Put him out!"

Jack heard a soft whistling, then felt an impact on his

temple. He saw a brief flash of light before he again dropped off into unconsciousness.

When Jack came to again, he was no longer dangling from the branch: a minor improvement that was cancelled out by the tremendous headache he had in addition to his other injuries. At first, he worried the blow to his temple had left him blind, for though he knew himself to be awake, he couldn't see a thing. But shortly, his eyes adjusted and he was able to make out some details.

He was in a rectangular box, near as he could tell. Wooden walls, with just a narrow slit near the ceiling at his head and feet to allow ventilation. It looked as though the wall at his feet was hinged so it could be opened. Faint light came in through the slits and around the hinged area of the wall, barely illuminating the interior. The box was just large enough to hold a cot, where he lay, and to allow him to sit up, slightly hunched, atop it. There was just enough open floor space to allow for a pitcher and a plate to fit between the cot and the wall. From the smell, there was food of some sort on the plate, but Jack made no move toward it. From somewhere outside the box, he could hear the sound of a person weeping. Someone else was shouting to be let out and Jack could hear banging, no doubt from that person's fists or feet. Clearly, he wasn't the only one in captivity here. Wherever here was.

He tried to sit up, but the movement brought on an intense wave of nausea. Dropping back down onto the cot with a groan, he pressed his palms to his forehead, breathing heavily. After a moment, the nausea passed, but he didn't try to move again, instead taking stock of the situation prone. It appeared his wounds had been treated. He felt tight wrappings around the knife cuts and there was a splint on the last two fingers of his left hand. So apparently whoever held him didn't intend to kill him. Yet.

The box lurched suddenly, drawing Jack's attention back to the general feeling of motion that had existed since he awoke. He had thought it was due to after effects of the head blow, but apparently the motion was real. The box must be loaded onto a wagon. Testing a theory, Jack kicked the ceiling and heard a muffled curse from above. Wonderful.

There was little to do but wait for whatever came. That whatever sure took long enough, though. Over the next several days, it became clear that his captors weren't very concerned about his comfort. The pitcher and plate were neither removed nor re-filled, and after drinking and eating everything that had been given him by the end of the second day, Jack became famished and parched. While there was a chamber pot beneath the cot, it wasn't changed out either. So, relatively quickly, the pot overfilled and things became very smelly. The box was stuffy and hot during the day, even though it was getting on in autumn. By the middle of the night, it became downright cold.

His neighbors didn't help matters. There was another man in the box above him and in the one to his right. A woman was below him. If anyone was to his left, they didn't respond to his queries or knocks. He tried engaging each of them, but the most he ever got from any of them was tears or despairing comments to the effect that they were all doomed. Not that Jack was inclined to necessarily disagree. Rumors had persisted for some time that many raiders traded in more than just valuables from the settlements they targeted, but he had never given them credence. He refused to believe that people had degenerated so far as that. Facts were facts, though. He had, apparently, become livestock.

Jack was cooped up for five days, best he could figure, before they let him out. He had been dozing, the closest he came to actual sleep in his accommodations. The sudden cessation of motion, by then such a normal part of his environment, roused him, but it was the loud commotion outside the box that made him perk up and pay attention. Scraping. The sound of metal on metal and wood striking wood. Loud voices speaking in commanding tones and receiving softer, submissive, replies.

After what seemed a long time, it sounded as though the woman below him was being pulled from her confines, and from her shrieks, it didn't sound as though she was enjoying it.

Jack needed to be ready.

Forcing himself to a sitting position, he flexed his muscles as best he could to work out the kinks. His wounds were healing, but it would be some time before his fingers especially were whole again. Both were black and blue and swollen. He was pretty sure he would lose the fingernails, from the bruising and discoloration behind them. Back in the day, he'd seen a friend slam his hand in a car door: Jack's fingers looked just like his did, except worse. At least they didn't hurt as much as they had at first.

The woman's yelling grew fainter. A moment later, Jack heard a rattling outside his box, like a piece of metal being shaken inside a pot. Then there was a loud scraping and the hinged wall opened upward. The sudden brightness after days with only the slits for illumination was blinding. Reflexively raising a hand to shield his eyes, he could barely discern a man-shape silhouetted outside the box.

"Out!" barked the man. He gestured vigorously with his hand. Wait... That wasn't his hand he was waving around. It was a handgun.

Jack tried to obey quickly, but his muscles, used to the

confines of the box, were slow to respond. He took a long few moments to shuffle out, earning him an "Out! Now!" from the man. Finally, Jack stepped out of the box. As he stood up, his back protested with a number of pops from several places. He stretched, feeling almost luxurious as he raised his arms over his head for the first time in what felt forever. That was short lived, however, as a flash of pain erupted from his injured shoulder. The man had smacked him with the butt of his gun.

"Down!" Jack began to wonder if the man had any words over a syllable in his repertoire.

Now out of his box, Jack could see why he never got any response to his left: his was the last box in the wagon, in the second row up. The doors were on the driver's side of the wagon and were stacked three high and four across. The wagon itself was parked next to a scaffold that was apparently designed to disembark prisoners: three platforms spaced to align with the box doors and a single set of stairs that descended through the three platforms to the ground. From the corner of his eye, Jack could see the barking man raise his gun again.

He hurried away. Or rather hobbled away, but it was the best he could muster.

The barking man wasn't the only guard, naturally. A burly fellow was stationed at each landing and one at the end of each level of the scaffold. Their armaments were varied: two had bows, two spears, and two rifles. All had long knives, more like machetes, on their hips.

The guard at the bottom of the scaffold shoved Jack toward a fenced path, almost like the sort of thing Jack had seen used to direct cattle. Not far ahead, Jack could see a woman, no doubt the one beneath him on the wagon, being dragged between two more guards. She was sobbing, letting out an occasional high-pitched whimper. More guards were stationed periodically along the path.

With no hope of escape, Jack did all he could: he followed the whimpering woman down the path toward a moderately sized tent. It felt like a long walk to his cramped legs, though it was only about a hundred yards. The woman had already entered when he reached the open tent flap. The door was flanked by two more guards. They were unarmed, as far as Jack could see, but from the way they stood with their arms folded across their chests, he got the impression they didn't need any weapons to inflict harm. The only way to go was inside, so he drew a deep breath and went in.

The tent was about thirty feet on a side and lit by a number of lanterns on poles spaced around the periphery. At the end of the wall opposite from the entrance Jack came in, there was another open doorway. Along that wall were five desks, in front of which stood men in long white lab coats. Each wore stethoscopes around their necks.

There were four other prisoners present: three men and the woman Jack followed in. The men were naked, and being subjected to what appeared to be a medical exam, under the supervision of a guard. The woman stood, still clothed and flanked by her two guards, at her station. From this distance, Jack could see that she was young, around twenty, and quite attractive, even with the grime covering her features.

The doctor, Jack assumed he was a doctor, said "Strip down" to her, but she made no move to comply. A brief look of annoyance flashed across the doctor's face. He looked at her guards and made a twirling gesture with his index finger, as though to say "Get a move on, boys".

With a grunt, one of the guards pulled out his knife. The woman shrieked and dropped to the floor. "No!" she screamed, but the guard paid no heed, methodically cutting her clothing off while his partner held her down.

Jack felt a surge of outrage and almost moved to inter-vene, consequences be damned. But a sudden hard shove from behind moved him toward the last exam station. A guard Jack hadn't noticed along the tent wall moved to super-vise him. "Don't even think about it," breathed the guard into Jack's ear. Feeling the point of a knife in the small of his back, Jack nodded and began removing his clothing without waiting to be prompted.

To his right, the men were being guided out of the tent. The woman's guards hauled her to her feet. She tried to wrap her arms around herself to cover up, but they forced them up over her head. The doctor began his examination, heedless of her weeping. He paid particular attention to her pelvic region, even pulling out a magnifying glass and a small comb to examine her in greater detail.

Jack had little desire, or time for that matter, to observe as his own doctor began examining him. Much like exams he had endured before the Troubles, it wasn't particularly rough, but it was thorough. The doctor spent a fair amount of time on his wounds, removing the dressings to examine the scabbed-over cuts and his broken fingers. From time to time, he made notes on a clipboard.

After a bit, the exam was done. "You appear fit, all things considered," the doctor said to Jack, as though he should be comforted by that, then began re-bandaging him with fresh dressings.

Next door, the doctor stood and nodded to the guards. "No STDs. She'll earn well once she's broken in."

The woman paled, her already distraught features drooping and her eyes widening in terror. "No," she breathed.

The doctor just shrugged and looked past her to the guards at the tent wall. "Next."

The woman began screaming again, but her throaty denials and then her pleas were to no avail. Her guards grabbed her by the arms and dragged her away out of the tent.

"Reason number eight hundred it's good to be a guy, eh?" quipped Jack's doctor, his lips twisting into a sadistic grin. The grin faded when Jack didn't respond. Did he really expect Jack to find that funny?

The doctor tied off the last of Jack's dressings with a particularly vigorous tug that earned him a grunt in response, then jerked his head toward the exit.

Jack's guard shoved him and he moved obediently to the end of the tent. New prisoners had already moved into place at the first two stations. One of them was Tobias. It looked like he could barely stand. He was hunched over, grasping his side with one hand, but the older man managed a nod and a wink for Jack as he walked past.

Outside, the cattle chute led to a pair of large fenced-in areas, another hundred feet or so away. A secondary path led off to the right, toward a group of smaller tents. The two men who had been guarding the woman were standing on either side of the closed entrance to the closest of those tents. From within, Jack could hear the woman crying out, alternating between sobs, screams, and pleas to stop. The voices of at least three or four men also emanated from the tent. They were whooping it up, urging each other on.

Jack felt heat rising in his cheeks as outrage filled him. His one good fist clenched and he took a step toward the tent. This would not stand!

Before he could go another step though, a hard blow to the back of his head knocked him to the ground. "Got to pay to play now, boy," he heard from above. Someone grabbed him by his arms and pulled him to his feet. A hard shove got him started down the chute.

Jack stumbled several paces and collapsed onto the rail on the side of the chute. Breathing heavily, his ears ringing, he fingered the back of his head gingerly. His hand came away red with more of his blood and he glanced back toward the examination tent. He could see the guard who hit him cleaning off a pair of brass knuckles. Lucky he hadn't broken his skull!

Wishing he could do something to help, but knowing it was less than useless to try, Jack forced himself to his feet and limped down the chute toward the fenced areas. The fence was high, about ten feet, and made from thigh-thick logs. Horizontal slats of two-by-fours were nailed in place on the outside of the fence every foot or so, starting just a few inches above the ground. It looked as though it would be difficult, if not impossible, to scale or squeeze through from inside. It would be a futile effort to try, though, as there were a pair of guards on each run of the fence, which looked to enclose a square area around the size of two tennis courts.

Just before he reached the pens, the chute widened and he came to a table set up near the entrance. A squirrelly little man sat behind the table, which was piled with rough-sewn off-white clothing, and a guard stood at either side. As Jack approached, the man tossed him a pair of pants and a shirt.

Almost grateful, Jack donned the gifts without a word. They fit poorly: the pants were too tight at the thigh and the shirt too tight around the shoulders. But they were better than nothing at all. Once he had dressed, one of the guards moved him toward the gate into the fenced area on the left and pushed him inside.

Within, there were around fifty people, all dressed as he was and all men. All were dirty and looked malnourished and ranged in age from late teens to Tobias' age. Many of the men were injured, some worse than Jack was, some not. For a moment, Jack wondered at the lack of women, then realized they must be segregated in the other pen.

"Welcome to Hell, buddy," murmured a man nearby as Jack entered.

Not replying, Jack walked to the opposite side of the fence from the entrance. There was another gate on that side, this one closed. But Jack could see buildings through the slats on that side and that roused his curiosity.

Sure enough, when he got to that gate, he could see an old road extending off to the left and right, not nearly as overgrown as those in Glennville, and lined on both sides for a good distance by a number of large houses. What looked like a driveway led up to the gate. Directly opposite the driveway was another one, extending about 200 yards before ending at a circular paved area in front of a large, well-built building. Thick columns along the front porch of the building framed the large double-doors of its entrance and there was what looked like a large parking lot off to one side. A wrought-iron fence, mostly rusted now, lined the street on the large building's side from the closest houses to both sides of the turnoff to the building. It looked like there used to be a gate blocking the entrance, but there was still a rusting iron trellis rising high over it, joining the two fences on either side of the drive. Jack could just make out letters built into the trellis: Forest Hills Country Club.

Jack's jaw dropped.

7

FOREST HILLS

The last several days were, mercifully, a blur in Tobias' mind. The last thing he recalled clearly was hearing Jack's shouted warning and turning just in time to take a knife-cut in the belly. The raider was already so close, all Tobias could do was hit him with the butt of his rifle. How it all ended, he didn't know for sure, but the multiple wounds, and especially the exquisite pain in his side, told him enough.

When the door to his box opened, he thought for a moment that he'd finally passed and he was looking at the long tunnel toward heaven's light. Wasn't that what the books said happens when you die? He sure hoped that reality didn't mirror this day's experience because that first guy would be a terrible greeter at Walmart, let alone at the Pearly Gates.

It was all Tobias could do to hobble down the stairs and down the chute to the medical tent. On several occasions, he thought for sure he was going to fall and pass out again. His wounds were bad enough, but the fact that his mouth was dry as a desert and his belly felt like it was a hole stretching to

China just made matters worse. However, there was no way Tobias was going to give the bastards the satisfaction of watching him drop. So he forced his way forward, each step a lesson in misery.

Somehow he made it to the tent. Within, he got some comfort, as he spied Jack leaving, his exam complete. Tobias worried the younger man had been killed, when he was coherent enough to think about it, and was surprised at how badly the thought of Jack's demise hurt. The way his heart lifted when he saw that young grump surprised Tobias even more. He was glad for it though, since it gave him the strength to endure a little bit more. Amazingly, he made it to the men's pen on his feet, though he was unable to dress himself. He didn't trust his balance to put on the pants. And the shirt...well, the wound in his side constantly seeped blood, even through the new bandage that doctor applied. Tobias doubted he could even manage to raise his arm high enough to don the shirt.

Once within the pen, however, Tobias found his strength fading. He'd only gone a short way inside when he lost his footing and fell to his knees. He managed to catch himself, but his new clothing dropped to the ground in a heap. Though there were other men all around, no one made a move to help. He called out for Jack, but all that came out was a feeble groan.

Somehow, that was enough. The younger man appeared at his side, helping him to his feet and leading him to a shady area next to the fence wall. Ah, blessed luxury, was that a water barrel there in the shade? It was too much to hope for. But for the second time in as many minutes, hope won out as he soon found himself gulping down water by the ladle-full. There was some stale bread also, which was the most delicious thing Tobias had ever tasted. Never let it be said that a meal can't work wonders. He almost began to feel human again. Certainly his spirits were, if not soaring, at least trying to take flight, which was a marked improvement.

It was time to start thinking about getting out of here. "Know where we are, youngster?" he asked, between bites of bread.

Jack nodded, his lips turned downward in a deep frown. "Forest Hills."

Tobias coughed, the piece of bread nearly going down the wrong way. Forest Hills??? "You sure about that?"

"The sign over there says it all."

"Show me."

It took a minute to get Tobias back on his feet, and into his pants and shirt for that matter, but before long, he was looking out at the Country Club entrance. "I'll be damned," he breathed. He'd always pictured the caravan headquarters as a warehouse or some such. A country club? It figured, though. Grymanski and his boys always did act like a bunch of spoiled rich yuppies.

Speak of the devil. Was that the old bastard there, coming out of the country club? He wasn't alone: three other men in suits were walking with him. They were chatting about something amongst themselves, quite vigorously too. The group reached the center of the road and turned right. Not one of them spared a glance at the two pens.

"Grymanski! Come here, you little prick!" shouted Tobias, as best he could. Apparently, it was good enough, as the quartet stopped and looked his way. Grymanski peered closely at the fenced pen, frowning slightly as his eyes swept over Tobias and Jack. Then he shrugged and gestured for his companions to continue walking. The conversation resumed and the group soon walked out of view. They did not look back.

The next morning, the gate swung open and a squad of caravan guards entered, rifles at the ready. Tobias was not surprised to see Ortiz leading the squad. The lean security man wasted no time in finding the two men from Glennville. Coming to a halt before them, he spoke in his usual short, direct manner.

"Miller. Simmons. Mr. Grymanski will speak with you. Now."

"Hmmph. Will he? Alright then. Lead on, boy."

Ortiz's eyes narrowed, but he nodded and stepped away, gesturing for the squad to follow behind them. Jack glanced at Tobias, his expression one of concern. "Tobias..."

"Don't worry, Jack. Let's see what he has to say."

And so they followed Ortiz into the old country club building, Tobias leaning on Jack's shoulder most of the way. The entryway wasn't quite as impressive up close as it was from afar. The columns were dirty, the facade beginning to crack in places. The furnishings and decor within were better kept up: leather couches and chairs, hardwood floors, fine rugs. This had always been a place of wealth and the Troubles hadn't changed that very much.

They found Grymanski in a small dining room, seated at the head of a polished mahogany table. He was dressed in a suit, of course. A teapot and three cups sat in front of him. Two other chairs were set up opposite each other, halfway down the table. When the two men entered, he offered them a hint of a smile, but did not stand.

"Ah. Mr. Miller. Mr. Simmons. So good of you to..."

Tobias didn't let him finish the thought. He practically dragged Jack along as he stalked toward the old man, bellowing out a reply.

"Slave trading! Treating people like cattle! Gang rapes!

What the *hell* kind of business are you running here, Grymanski?"

The old bastard tsk-ed softly. "A profitable one, Mr. Miller."

The matter-of-fact reply took the wind out of Tobias' sails. That's it? That's all he had to say?

Grymanski continued. "We supply what settlements in the region require. The demand for human labor in Glennville is limited, so we seldom bring many for sale in your town. But others require a great deal. There is a settlement in West Virginia, for example, that is attempting to re-open a coal mine, a very labor intensive enterprise."

The old man's implication was not lost on Tobias. "We don't do slaves in Glennville," he replied flatly.

Grymanski looked amused. "Really? Then where, pray tell, does your Hempstead House get their new employees when older ones depart, hmm? Or did you believe all those young ladies happened to wander into town to work there by chance?" From his tone, the old man doubted Tobias really did think that...but if he did, Grymanski pitied him for a fool.

Tobias shook his head vigorously. "The devil you say. Liselle wouldn't get involved in nothing like that." And it was true. Liselle was a good, kind woman. She treated her girls well, everyone knew that. When one decided to leave the business, she always left town with a large purse of money to settle somewhere she could start fresh. And there was always another girl looking to take her place. Although, come to think of it, Tobias wasn't sure he'd actually ever seen those girls leave. Had anyone else? Liselle always said they...

Tobias' eyes widened. He began to get a sinking feeling in the pit of his stomach. No. It couldn't be.

"Ah. I see you begin to realize the truth, hmm? Any business must turn over its inventory from time to time. She is most discrete about it, of course." Grymanski's eyes twinkled.

Oh yes, he definitely looked and sounded amused. "I am sorry to burst your bubble, Mr. Miller. It is always difficult, discovering the truth about those we love. Are you sure you wouldn't like some tea?"

White hot anger filled Tobias. That condescending, amoral prick! "*Fuck you*, Grymanski, you shriveled little..." He wanted to finish his sentence, but something went twinge in his upper abdomen, near the deep stab wound. He began heaving hard, dry heaves that subsided after several long moments. Lord, that *hurt*! He wiped his mouth with the back of his hand and was alarmed to see it covered in blood. "Oh shit," he breathed softly before his knees turned to jelly. He knew it only took a second to fall, but it felt like he was moving in slow motion. He heard Jack shout his name with concern, then he struck the floor and passed out.

Grymanski closed the door behind himself and crossed the room quickly. The old man settled into a stuffed leather chair, a pair to the one Jack sat in. They were in a small sitting room in the second level of the Country Club building. Besides their chairs, the room was furnished with a small coffee table and a medium sized bureau. Light streamed into the room through a large window, supplemented by two oil lamps mounted on the wall. Jack had been sitting here, waiting for news. It seemed to take forever, though it was only an hour or so.

Grymanski cleared his throat. "Mr. Miller is alive." Jack exhaled loudly and tension flowed out of his body as rapidly as his breath. Then Grymanski continued and Jack felt a fair amount of that tension return. "But he may not be for long. His wounds are deep, but they were well bandaged. However, it appears the deepest was recently torn anew and the new tear penetrated his stomach. A trifling injury, easily treated, not so very long ago. But now..." He spread his hands helplessly.

"Isn't there something we can do? What about those Docs over in the tent?"

"I assure you, Mr. Simmons, we have an extensive medical staff, and in their travels, our caravans recovered a wide variety of medical instruments and medications."

"So what's the problem?"

Grymanski did not answer immediately. Instead, he stood and strode over to the window. Peering out toward what used to be the first tee, the old man sighed deeply. "Shortly after my caravan departed Forest Hills on our last expedition to Glennville, my partners decided to send a detachment of security personnel to investigate matters in the west more deeply. Fifteen men, well trained and equipped. One returned, but he did not have anything substantive to add to what we already knew. The troop was ambushed not far past Farrah's Crossing by a force with superior weapons and numbers."

The old man wiped his brow with a handkerchief, then turned to look back at Jack. "I, of course, learned of these events only upon my return. Had I been here, I've no doubt I could have persuaded my partners to take less aggressive action. But now..." He shook his head. "Now, I fear we may have roused these Masters' anger, whoever they are. At the least, they must surely suspect our presence and will send further probes eastward."

"Yeah, great. Thanks for the news update, but I don't see what this..."

"...has to do with Mr. Miller's situation? Or yours?" Grymanski moved back to his chair, but did not sit. "My partners' idea had merit: we need to know more about these Masters, as they call themselves. Where they're based, how many they are, how well equipped. And what their intentions might be. However, the notion that a straightforward military excursion could accomplish that was foolish at best and doomed to failure from the start. No, we need a small group, who can blend with and live off the land, who can pass unnoticed, as our eyes and ears."

Jack held up his hands to forestall further discussion. "Whoa. Hold it right there. I see where this is going and..."

"Indeed. It is fortuitous for both of us that you are here at this moment, hmm?" Finally sitting again, the old man leaned forward, his elbows resting on his knees. He regarded Jack with a direct gaze, an eyebrow lifting.

"I'd hardly call it lucky."

"No? Consider. I need a tracker. Someone skilled in the wild and observant. Someone who is not instantly identifiable as being associated with the Forest Hills Caravan Company. By all accounts, you are just such a man. Your town council, and your mayor, were quite vocal about your value and skill when they pled your case to me during the Graeber affair." Jack blanched. Why did that always have to keep coming up? Grymanski continued. "You, on the other hand, need medical treatment for your friend."

"Oh, you son of a bitch."

"Quid pro quo, Mr. Simmons. Be thankful the offer is even on the table. Were it not for Mr. Miller's status within your community, he would not merit our assistance at all. All the same, you cannot expect us to expend exceedingly scarce, and valuable, medical supplies without receiving payment of some kind, hmm?"

Jack was beginning to feel even more boxed in than he had in the slave wagon. "So you want me to wander off west. To somewhere. To spy on someone. On my own."

"I doubt they'll be hard to locate once you pass far

enough beyond our frontier. But you'll hardly be alone. Mr. Ortiz has volunteered to lead the expedition."

And the hits just kept on coming. "You can't be serious. You want me to go out into the wild, alone, with him? Hell no. Might as well shoot me now. That guy's had it out for me for months."

Grymanski sniffed and waved one hand in a dismissive gesture. "Hardly. Mr. Ortiz is zealous in the execution of his duties, as well he should be. But I can assure you he thinks no less of you than he does any other person who ran afoul of Caravan Law in the past. You needn't fear for your safety with him on this venture."

"Easy for you to say. I think I'm going to pass." He stood and turned toward the door.

"Don't make a hasty decision, Mr. Simmons, without considering the consequences."

Jack looked back at him over his shoulder. "What are you talking about?"

"Lest you forget, both you and Mr. Miller are now property of the Forest Hills Caravan Company. Now, you can either do as I ask, and earn treatment for Mr. Miller and freedom for both of you. Or..." Grymanski's voice became cold, hard, his eyes razor sharp, "...you can both go back to the labor pens, where Mr. Miller will almost certainly die in agony. And you will likely live out the rest of your days working in the darkness of a coal mine in West Virginia."

Jack swallowed hard and turned back to face Grymanski fully. The old bastard wasn't screwing around, that much was certain. Jack was more than boxed in. He was stripped, hog tied, and ready for gutting. "It looks like I've got no choice."

Grymanski leaned back in his chair and crossed his right leg over his left. With a slight smile, he replied in a relaxed, almost philosophical tone. "There is always a choice, Mr.

Simmons. The question is whether you're willing to pay the price for making it."

However Jack tried to spin it, Grymanski held all the cards and both he and Jack knew it. Hang it all. Jack hadn't even wanted to come to Forest Hills, let alone go wandering off west to find a group of people who might just as well eat him as say howdy. If Tobias wasn't in such bad shape... Well, he was, and Jack couldn't just let him die. The old guy was going to owe him, for a change, after this.

Reluctantly, Jack nodded. "Fine. I'll do it." Moving back to the coffee table, he held out his hand. "But I don't move a muscle until Tobias is treated and fully on the mend."

The caravan master shook Jack's hand. His grip was clammy, but firm. "Agreed. Welcome aboard, Mr. Simmons." Jack wished that didn't sound so final.

It was a week before Jack and Ortiz departed Forest Hills. That was partly because of the time required to treat Tobias. The Company's doctors worked on him through the night after Jack made the deal. By morning, they had him stitched up as best they could, but he was touch and go for another couple days.

Jack checked in on him as often as he could, but he was busy getting ready for the journey. Once Tobias' initial treatment was done, it seemed his every waking hour was taken up with some thing or other. First on the list was obtaining new clothing and supplies. The caravan company was well stocked, of course, but he had no money for payment. He tried once, and only once, to point out that his and Tobias' money was stolen by the same people who kidnapped them and it was probably somewhere in the Company's coffers by now. He nearly got into a fistfight. An appeal to Grymanski, that since he was now working for the caravan, they should provide supplies, only got him an employee discount, and a paltry one at that. That infuriated him, but he was in no condition to make a scene over it.

So he took to performing odd jobs to pay off what he owed for the goods he needed. That ended up filling most of his day every day. But by week's end, he had "purchased" a sturdy pair of boots, clothing for all manner of weather they might encounter, a couple of warm blankets, fishing gear, two good knives and a whetstone, a compass, maps, cooking utensils, and a .22 caliber rifle with a few boxes of ammo. He got the rifle cheap as it required a lot of work on his part to get it back into serviceable condition.

Tobias woke on the fourth day. Jack could tell he was not pleased about Jack's taking the mission, but considering the alternative, he didn't complain. Much. He did provide no end of advice about what to do in the wild and when they met up with the Masters, and about how to handle Ortiz.

That last was the part that truly concerned Jack. Over the course of the week, he interacted with Ortiz on several occasions. They reviewed maps and read the reports of the Company's previous encounters with the Masters, but the security man was gruff, abrupt. He clearly didn't want to work with Jack any more than Jack wanted to work with him. Grymanski could say what he wanted, but Jack wasn't entirely sure Ortiz wasn't just going to put a bullet in his back as soon as they were gone from Forest Hills. Or, for that matter, that it wasn't Grymanski's intention from the get go for him to do that.

On the bright side, with the extra time to heal, his wounds were much improved by the time they left. The deepest cut, on his chest, was still fully scabbed over, but the others were more or less healed. The swelling in his fingers was gone and he was able to move them again. He didn't have full range of motion yet, but it was better than before.

Finally the day of departure arrived. Jack and Grymanski met in the circular driveway in front of the Country Club building. Tobias insisted on coming as well, but he was unable to walk so the Company supplied a wheelchair for the occasion. Ortiz joined them a few minutes later, a pretty blonde woman and a small boy walking with him. Jack was surprised: he never figured Ortiz for a married man.

Grymanski cleared his throat when Ortiz arrived. "Two days from today will be exactly three months until the conference with the settlement representatives. It would be ideal if you were to return with information before the start. Good luck, gentlemen."

As far as inspirational speeches went, it fell completely flat. But then, Jack didn't really care what Grymanski had to say. He nodded to the old man and turned to Tobias. They clasped hands briefly.

"Good luck, youngster. Be safe." He took in Jack's new rifle with a glance and sniffed with derision. Looking sidelong at Grymanski, he added, "If I still had Vera, I'd tell you to take her instead of that pea shooter." The caravan master didn't even have the grace to look embarrassed. Jack shook his head and managed a grin of amusement. Good old Tobias.

To Jack's surprise, a groom led a pair of horses, outfitted for riding, from behind the building. It seemed the Company had decided to fork over some support for the expedition after all. Accepting the reins from the groom, Jack mounted his horse, a dappled mare, and waited for Ortiz. The caravan guard took a moment to squat and give his son a hug, then he kissed his wife goodbye. She clung to him as he pulled away and Jack could see tears on her cheeks. To his greater surprise, it looked like Ortiz wiped his own eyes before turning to his horse and mounting up. If he had been crying, though, it didn't show as he gave Jack a steely stare.

"Let's go," Ortiz said, nearly growling. With a swift kick to his horse's flanks, he set off down the driveway. Jack gave Tobias a farewell salute and nudged his own horse into motion. As he turned away, he couldn't help but wonder if he was ever going to see the old coot again. Somehow, he doubted it.

8

ROAD TRIP

It took most of a week to reach Farrah's Crossing. At first, they were able to follow Interstate 40 and made very good time, despite having to dodge abandoned, rusted out cars at regular intervals.

Then at the end of the second day, as they reached the off-ramp for a town named Jackson, Ortiz led them off the interstate. Jackson was sparsely populated, but the townsfolk were friendly and there was a small inn near the interstate with a room they were able to rent for the night. The next morning, Ortiz led them up a state highway, a smaller, less maintained road that, in a few places, was little better than simply going cross-country for the rest of the journey.

Jack counted and they didn't say more than a dozen words to each other in the entire first day. Ortiz just rode along, his eyes constantly scanning the undergrowth on either side of the road and his rifle always at the ready. Jack wasn't sure who Ortiz thought was going to attack them just outside Forest Hills, but he decided not to ask. Better to not start the trip off on the wrong foot.

That night over the campfire, which Ortiz insisted they

light within a pit deep enough to conceal its light from spying eyes, Jack tried to engage Ortiz in small talk, but he just grunted. Then, as soon as dinner was done, Ortiz doused the fire and bedded down.

Ortiz insisted on a lot of things besides fire discipline. One of them was maintaining a watch during the night. They swapped every three hours, as measured by an hourglass Ortiz had in his pack.

Jack had the first watch that night. When he woke Ortiz to relieve him the night had gotten downright cold, and it took forever for him to get even close to warm in his blankets. Consequently, he got much less than his allotted three hours' sleep when Ortiz nudged him to take the watch again. On the bright side, he hadn't been asleep long enough to get to the usual dream.

The night in the inn got him caught up. The next day, the third of the journey, as they were passing down the main street of an abandoned town, Jack decided to try breaking the ice again.

Nudging his horse forward to move up alongside Ortiz, he once again noted how the security man looked at every dilapidated store front as though expecting an attack. This time, Jack couldn't say he blamed him.

There was something oppressive about the leftovers from before the Troubles. Rusted out cars lined the streets in old parking spaces. At each crossroads, junkers were lined up as they no doubt had been that morning, waiting on a red light that would never turn green. Weeds now grew tall in every yard and through wide cracks in every sidewalk and every street. Windows were broken, signs were hanging at an angle, if they hadn't already fallen completely. Many buildings were burned out. It wasn't that much different from Glennville, except there were people in the remains of Glennville who had repaired and maintained at least part of the town. Here, it was just abandoned. Jack had used the term 'ghost town' before in the past, but had never seen a place that warranted the description more than this. The bare tree branches and fallen leaves of autumn just made it worse.

Jack cleared his throat. "Your son's a good looking boy."

Ortiz gave him a sidelong look for a second, then he grunted and went back to his scan of the surroundings.

Jack tried again. "Must be hard, leaving your wife all the time."

"What's it to you?"

"Nothing. Just making an observation."

"Don't. Voices carry farther than you think."

Jack rode in silence for a long few minutes after that. By then, the pair passed out of the town limits and very quickly the buildings became fewer. Ortiz seemed to relax a bit as they left the downtown area, so Jack decided to try again.

"You got a first name, Ortiz?"

Ortiz looked at him again and scowled darkly. His down-turned lips made that big scar look all the more ominous. Jack rolled his eyes, starting to become annoyed. Was the guy *trying* to be a jackass or was it just his natural default setting?

"Look, we're going to be together for a while on this trip. Supposed to be a team venture, right?" He tried a friendly smile, but wasn't sure how well it came across.

Ortiz sighed and looked away to examine a nearby copse of trees as they rode past. Playing stone again. Jack was opening his mouth to say something else when the security man replied. "Juan. Juan Fernando, after my grandfather."

"We share a name."

Ortiz gave him an annoyed look. "Finally, my long lost brother. Shut up." With that, he heeled his horse to a more brisk pace, leaving Jack alone again. He shrugged his shoulders. It was a start anyway.

In the middle of the afternoon, Jack took a four point

buck, to Ortiz's great consternation. The security man objected to the noise from the rifle. But seriously, many folks these days made at least part of their living hunting. A rifle shot or two in the wild wasn't likely to draw any more attention than anything else, to Jack's way of thinking. Besides, they didn't have that much in the way of edible food. There was only so long a guy could go on jerky alone, after all.

It took a bit of time to dress out the deer. Longer than he was used to, actually. Jack had to hit it so many times to fell it with the .22 that he spent half the time digging bullets out of the carcass, ruining a good third of the meat. By the time the rest of the meat was ready, it was nearing sunset, so they ended up setting camp near the kill. Not too near, of course. A roaming bear could ruin their whole night.

After dinner, Jack built up the fire and set about smoking the remaining hunks of venison. Ortiz watched with a sour expression, but didn't raise any more objections. Even he could see the sense in preserving the meat.

"Next time, I'm using your rifle," Jack complained. Ortiz had left his army getup back at Forest Hills since it screamed he was a company man. However, he still came loaded for bear. He had at least two knives that Jack knew about, a big revolver on his hip, and a tricked-out M-14, complete with a scope. The 7.62mm round the M-14 fired was a whole heck of a lot more powerful than Jack's .22.

"Not a chance, Simmons."

"Have it your way, but we'll get a lot more usable meat if I can take the animal in one shot."

Ortiz merely shrugged. Jack couldn't get another word out of him until it was time to bed down and he volunteered to take the first watch. Exhausted, Jack had no intention of complaining. He settled into his blankets and within a few minutes was sound asleep.

Susan smiled at him as they leveled off at thirty-five hundred feet. The Cherokee's engine purring contentedly, he leaned the mixture to just rich of peak and returned the smile. It was incredible how lovely she looked. Her oval face, hazel eyes, dark brown hair. Her physique, athletic without losing its curviness. The little bump in her belly. He was a lucky man.

They had departed the airport about forty-five minutes ago on their final leg home after a visit with the in-laws. The sun was about halfway to its zenith, the clouds scattered at about ten thousand feet. It was perfect Visual Flight Rules weather and they had a nice tailwind. It was hard to complain about anything.

Somewhere in his mind, he knew it wasn't real. But he wanted it to be. Maybe this once, the engine would keep running and they'd make it home. But no, it was all happening the same as it always did, the same as it had ten years ago.

The sound of electricity arcing and the smell of ozone drew his gaze to the instrument panel in time to see the radio display flicker and then go dark. A glance at his other instruments showed a similar pattern all throughout the panel: GPS, transponder, everything electronic was dead, wisps of smoke rising from the edges of each instrument. To make matters worse, the engine chose that moment to sputter and then stop altogether. "Oh shit," Jack breathed.

"Jack!" Susan's tone was a mix of fear, wonder, and confusion. His eyes moved to her, then followed her extended finger, pointing off to the north. Barely visible in the day-lit sky, a willowy...something...waved across the horizon. White, then bluish-green, then red, it was like a flicker of light through a fogbank, or refracted by a wave. As he turned his gaze to trace it out, it became more ephemeral as it rose higher into the sky until it disappeared entirely in the sun's brilliance.

"What in the..." Jack didn't finish the thought. He felt the aircraft buffet, the beginning of a stall. Airspeed indicated fifty knots, right at the edge of control. He needed to be about twenty knots faster, at best glide speed, to minimize his descent rate. Lowering the nose, his knuckles white as he clutched the yoke, he glanced at the altimeter.

Two thousand five hundred feet. They'd lost a lot already. He needed to fly the airplane, find a place to land. Trimming for seventy-three knots, he scanned the terrain nearby. There was a good-sized town to the southeast, but his chart didn't show any airports for at least twenty-five miles and there was no way he could glide that far, not from this altitude. What was nearby? Not far to their left was a small farmhouse and a sizable field. It was the only likely candidate nearby.

He turned into a shallow bank to point the farmhouse. One thousand five hundred. He thought about flaps, but decided against it. Better to minimize drag. One thousand. The farmhouse passed beneath his left wing.

The field stretched off to the left. He'd skirt the trees then turn onto a short final. They should make it. Five hundred feet. They passed over the treeline and he banked left again. Damnit, he waited too long to start the turn. Altitude was going fast, and they needed to clear the trees. Two fifty.

Jack pulled back on the yoke to help accelerate the turn. They were going to make it. The last few trees were just ahead. They needed to turn about another fifteen degrees. He pulled back a bit harder and instantly knew he'd made a fatal error. The plane buffeted again. Another stall! But before he could do anything, the left wing dropped and the plane turned over onto its back. The trees filled the windscreen.

He felt a jarring impact and heard Susan scream. The

branches seemed to almost caress the canopy as the plane fell into them.

"Wake up!"

He felt another impact.

"Wake up, curse you!"

Another impact. His eyes fluttered open. Where was he? Jack blinked away fresh tears and his eyes focused after a second.

Ortiz was standing over him, his foot drawn back to kick him again. Three previous kicks had left Jack's side hurting. He raised a hand to forestall fourth.

"I'm awake. Christ, Ortiz!" He sat up and probed at his side with his finger, wincing as he felt the area Ortiz had kicked. "I'm not sure you didn't break a rib."

"Your watch," was all Ortiz said by way of reply. He waited for Jack to get on his feet, then bedded down in his blankets without another word. In less than a minute he was snoring. Unbelievable.

Jack didn't bother trying to draw Ortiz out the next day, but amazingly enough, he did it on his own. They crossed the Mississippi early in the morning and by noon they were riding down an even smaller road, passing through a wide meadow. A cold drizzle had been falling all day, and although Jack had a rain cloak, it wasn't nearly what he would call good quality. The seams leaked in several spots, and before they'd gone very far, his back was totally drenched. Ortiz didn't look like he was any better off, but he was his usual stoic self for most of the morning. He looked troubled by something, though.

"Do you have any idea how much noise you make while you're asleep?"

Jack blinked in surprise. "What?"

"You spent half the time groaning and one time called out a woman's name: Susan? Quite loudly. Can't have that when we get to places where we need to go unnoticed."

A shiver went down Jack's spine, followed by a surge of heartache and then resentment. "Yes, well, I'll try to sleep quieter then."

"You need to do more than try. Could be our asses."

Jack threw up his hands. How in the hell was he supposed to control that? Ortiz frowned slightly at Jack's reaction. He remained silent for a long time, long enough that Jack thought he was content to drop the subject. No such luck.

"Who is she?"

The heartache returned with a vengeance. For a moment, he could almost see Susan's face, smiling in spite of the rain. Unbidden, he felt tears begin to well up and he had to bite his lip to keep from crying out. Forcing the feelings down, he managed some modicum of control before he answered.

"She...was...my wife."

Ortiz nodded slowly. "The Troubles?"

Jack looked over at the security man and was surprised to see an expression of empathy on his face. "The first day. Plane crash."

They rode in silence for the rest of the afternoon. The rain stopped an hour or so before sunset, right as they were stopping to set up camp. They were unable to find any wood that wasn't wet, so they had to settle for bread and jerky for dinner. By full dark, the clouds had begun to part and the light from the waxing gibbous moon gave a fair amount of illumination to the camp site. Ortiz leaned back against a log and looked up at the stars. His expression grew distant for a moment.

"The Troubles were hard on everyone, Simmons. Everyone lost someone."

"You think I don't know that?"

Ortiz lowered his gaze from the sky and toward Jack. His tone grew harder. "You don't know how good you had it. Glennville was small time. New York..." Exhaling loudly, he vigorously shook his head.

"You're from New York? I heard..."

"I know what you heard, Simmons, and it's all crap."

Jack swallowed. "Well then...what was it like? Really?"

Ortiz didn't answer for a long moment. He pulled a pipe from his saddle bags and a tin of what Jack assumed was tobacco. Jack was surprised: he hadn't seen Ortiz ever smoke before. In a few moments, the security man had the pipe packed and he set to work with his flint and steel. It took some time, but eventually the tobacco caught. He took a long draw and leaned back against the log again. Then his eyes went distant again and he appeared to physically gather himself, as though getting ready for an exertion. When he spoke, it was softly, almost as though he were afraid to give voice to the memories lest they take on a life of their own.

"I was back home on leave from the Corps, visiting my Mother and sister."

"The Corps?"

Ortiz gave Jack a long-suffering look and rolled up his left sleeve. In the moonlight, Jack could barely make out a tattoo on his upper arm: the Eagle, Globe, and Anchor with the letters 'USMC' beneath. Ah. That explained quite a few things about him.

Ortiz continued. "When the power went out, we didn't worry at first. But when my sister and I went for a walk and saw the power loss extended for blocks... For a little while, we thought it was 9-11 all over again. Turned out it was worse. You remember the videos of that big blackout in the seventies, all the looting?"

Jack nodded.

"The first three nights were bad, like that. The fourth..."

Ortiz scowled. "I saw a report once that said New York City only had enough food in its groceries to last two days total. Without deliveries, by the fourth night it sounded like food was becoming scarce. We heard fights and brawls continuously. Fires started, people were shooting each other. We had plenty of food to last a while, so we decided to barricade ourselves into the apartment. But we didn't have much to drink, and by the sixth day, we were out completely. By then, there were fires burning everywhere. Bodies lined the streets. In the afternoon, we saw a group of cops and thought they were finally going to re-establish order, so we opened the door and rushed downstairs to greet them. When we got outside, they put us down on the ground and asked where we lived. We told them and three of them went upstairs. They came back down loaded up with our food."

Ortiz's scowl deepened and he clenched his fists so hard his arms trembled. "My mother immediately began protesting and, without a word, their leader shot her in the head. Then he turned his gun on my little sister and dared me to say a word. I'm no coward, Simmons, but Maria was only thirteen..." The security man's features twisted for a moment, some deep emotion threatening to break through. With a deep exhalation, he regained control.

"When they left, it was clear we had to get out of the city as soon as possible, before things fell apart completely. Maria was hysterical and nothing I said brought her around, so I did the only thing I could think of." He made a smacking motion with his hand. "The look she gave me..." He paused for a moment before continuing. "But she was more calm, so I was able to drag her away. My mother owned a gun. I took a minute to run upstairs and get it. Then we left. The closest way off the island was the George Washington Bridge, but it was many blocks away. By evening, we were almost there. I had to face down at least a dozen looters and other scum, and put down four more, to make it that far. But within sight of the on-ramp, a dozen men surrounded us. I tried to fight them off, but you can imagine how that ended. When I came to, it was fully dark. They were gone and so was Maria. I didn't know where to even begin looking for her, so after a day or so of searching, I was forced to give up."

Ortiz turned looked back at Jack sternly. "My mother was killed in front of me and my sister was taken from me by force. She may be alive, but I doubt it. It ate at me for a long time. But I don't dwell on it now, don't let it rule me. I've moved on."

"Well aren't you the big tough Marine," Jack quipped, his voice heavily laden with sarcasm. This was the last thing he needed, to be lectured by Ortiz. Bad enough he had to hear it from Tobias, but at least the old guy was a friend. Ortiz was... Trouble was, Ortiz was right. Hadn't Jack harangued himself about this same thing, no matter how he protested to Tobias that he was fine?

"I've got people depending on me to come back, Simmons. You do as well, but you're too stupid to see it." Unbidden, the image of Serena, hurt as he rejected her, came into Jack's mind. He forced it away with a grimace as Ortiz continued, wagging his finger. "Get your shit together. Because I'm not about to take a bullet just because you won't let ghosts stay dead."

With that, Ortiz tapped out his pipe and bedded down, leaving Jack to take the watch. Jack didn't bother to wake him at the three hour mark. He just sat, alone with his thoughts and his demons, until dawn's light appeared on the horizon.

❦ 9 ❦

THE FRONTIER

Two days later, they reached Farrah's Crossing, or what was left of it. As the reports said, most of the buildings were burned to the ground, though in the months since the raid, many of them had become overgrown with shrubs of various sorts. There were signs that people had been there in the recent past: a hoof print here, some litter there, a small latrine hole that had never been filled back in. But taken as a whole, there was little to set this place apart from the wooded hills surrounding it. One thing Jack noted quickly: there was no river, not even a creek. So what the hell had Farrah crossed to warrant the name?

Ortiz chuckled when Jack asked the question. "She crossed over to heaven, Simmons. Town was named after the wife of the guy who first settled here. The story is they got into a big fight, and she was screaming so loud she burst an artery in her head. Dropped dead mid-sentence." The security man looked sidelong at Jack and smirked. "They say the guy was so happy, he decided to settle right where she fell to commemorate."

That was bad, but all the same, Jack couldn't help but

85

laugh in amusement. After a moment, Ortiz did as well. Shaking his head, Jack supposed all married men sometimes fantasized about that. He could remember many a time when he was so pissed at Susan that...

Any amusement Jack felt faded and he stopped laughing mid-guffaw. Guilt welled up within him. Laughing over the thought of a man's wife dying and him being perverse enough to enjoy it! As though Jack wouldn't give anything to have Susan back! He bit down on his lip to prevent himself from sobbing as, all of a sudden, the guilt turned into the pain of heartache and loss. Again. Eventually the episode passed, but his good cheer was gone.

All this was not lost on Ortiz. The security man's expression of amusement faded, becoming first wariness. He turned on his horse, looking around for a threat. Seeing none, he looked back at Jack in time to see the worst of the episode and frowned deeply for a long several seconds. Then he snorted and turned his horse away, toward the remains of the road leading westward out of town.

Jack kicked his horse's flanks to catch up. For some reason, Ortiz's expression of disappointment stung.

On the second day out from Farrah's Crossing, they encountered the first living people they'd seen since leaving Jackson. And they weren't friendly.

Jack and Ortiz were nearing the crest of a treeless hill, so they dismounted and crawled to the top on their bellies to take a look before just riding up. Ortiz was a big believer in not allowing themselves to be silhouetted atop a hill: they could be spotted from a long ways off doing that, or so he said. Jack was a bit leery about it, but after what they saw from the peak, he was willing to concede that Ortiz had been correct.

On the next hill, a bit less than a quarter mile away, three horsemen were riding across Jack's field of view. They were clearly visible at the top of the hill with the naked eye. Ortiz had a pair of binoculars though, and studied them closely for a moment.

"They're not carrying any standards or wearing any sort of uniform. But they're all armed."

Ortiz passed the binoculars to Jack. Looking through them, he was forced to agree. At best, the riders appeared ragged, but two had rifles. The third had what looked like a lasso loop on the end of a long stick.

"Shouldn't be too hard to get around them," Jack said. Lowering the binoculars, he was about to hand them back when fresh movement halfway down the riders' hill caught his eye. "What's that?"

"What?" demanded Ortiz, but Jack didn't reply immediately. The binoculars revealed a smaller figure, probably a child, running down the hill away from the riders. From time to time, the figure looked over its shoulder. Jack looked back up at the top of the hill again. One of the riflemen was pointing down the hill, toward the kid. His comrades made excited gestures and turned their horses in the kid's direction, thumping their heels into the horses' flanks.

"Son of a bitch!" Jack said aloud. Dropping the binoculars, he stood and raced down the hill toward the kid and the riders, unlimbering his rifle as he ran.

"Simmons! What the hell are you doing? Get back here!" Ortiz said angrily, but Jack paid him no mind.

He could see about where the kid was, but lost sight of the kid himself. There were trees in the valley between the two hills, and even without their leaves, they obstructed his view.

The riders were clearly visible cantering down their own hillside. That probably meant Jack was visible too, but he wasn't putting up nearly the dust they were. Besides, he was banking on them looking for the kid, not anyone else.

In about a minute, he was at the bottom of the hill and nearing the trees. From somewhere ahead, he heard the sound of men shouting and a high-pitched, child's scream.

Slowing his pace, Jack entered the tree thicket and continued ahead, moving from tree to tree to maintain cover. Before long, he saw movement between the trees ahead and he thumbed off the safety on his rifle.

Jack sprinting to cover behind the next tree, then peeked around and beheld the horsemen.

They were even more ragged than he thought from looking through the binoculars. They had long, unkempt hair and unruly beards. Their clothing was mismatched and badly patched, their shoes little more than sandals, despite the autumn chill. Their weapons looked well cared for, though. You had to have your priorities, after all.

Jack didn't have much inclination to admire their rifles at the moment, though. Focusing in on the kid, Jack could tell now it was a little boy, maybe ten years old. Sobbing, he was down on his knees with his back to the riders. The lasso on a stick was looped around the kid's neck and pulled tight.

"We told you not to try to run, didn't we?" growled the rider holding the lasso-stick. "You're gonna regret that, kid." He gave a firm tug on the stick and the kid slowly rose to his feet, grasping in vain at the rope around his neck.

That was all Jack needed to see. Careful to remain behind cover as much as possible, he raised his rifle to his shoulder and sighted in on the lasso-holder. "Let the kid go," Jack bellowed.

The three riders' heads swiveled toward him in surprise. Catching sight of him after a very quick scan, the lasso-holder chuckled. "Just one of you, hero. Think you're fast enough to get us all?" His two compatriots sneered and the one on Jack's right raised his rifle to his shoulder in a blur of motion.

Jack's shot took lasso-holder in the belly, doubling him over in his saddle. His compatriot fired a heartbeat after Jack, a much heavier round than Jack's from the sound of it. The bullet impacted the tree a foot or so above Jack's head, sending a small burst of wood splinters flying. That was close!

Jack dropped to one knee and shifted his aim to the rifleman who just fired.

The poor fellow had a nice-looking bolt-action, but in the time it took him to eject the spent brass and chamber a second round, Jack's second shot struck him in the throat. Speed of fire was one good thing about the .22, Jack decided.

The struck rifleman tumbled backwards off his horse, both hands reaching up to clutch at the wound. His rifle hit the ground a heartbeat before his head and shoulders did. From the awkward angle of his body and the audible snap of breaking bone as he struck the ground, it appeared his neck was broken in the fall.

That left just one rider and he was no longer on his horse.

Jack looked around for him, but had to duck back completely behind the tree as a bullet exploded the bark right next to his face.

Sliding around to the other side of the tree, he managed to spy his foe lying prone on the ground on the far side of his horse before another bullet zipped by so close to Jack's ear that he could feel the bullet's wake in the air.

Again Jack pulled back under cover.

His back pressed against the tree, he thought for a moment. Another bullet zipped by, past the tree on his right side, and a plan occurred to him. Yes, that just might work.

He slid down the tree until he too was lying on the ground. Then, taking a deep breath, he rolled to his left. Two and a half complete rolls took him out from behind the cover of the tree and left him on his belly, looking down the sights of his rifle. He squeezed off two rounds in quick succession.

The final rider's horse, struck twice in the shoulder, screamed and reared. When the poor creature's fore-hooves struck the ground as it came back down, the leg under its injured shoulder buckled.

The horse fell to the ground and began thrashing around. Its former rider, shouting a curse, was forced to scamper out of the way as the horse threatened to crush him in its throws of agony.

He didn't get far. Just to his knees, in fact. Then Jack's bullet took him in the eye.

Jack rose to his knees, turning his rifle back to the first rider.

By now almost back to the rise of the hill, the man was hunched over his saddle, but kicking at his horse's flanks vigorously. The kid, lasso still tight around his neck, was dragging limply alongside.

If the rider had left the kid behind, Jack would have been content to let him go. As it was, though...

Carefully sighting in, Jack squeezed off two more rounds. He watched in satisfaction as the rider stiffened and fell sideways from the saddle.

Ignoring the still screaming and flailing horse behind him, Jack raced over to where the kid lay. He dropped to one knee and hastily loosened the lasso, but froze as he heard a loud gunshot behind him. Expecting the worst, he looked back over his shoulder and breathed a sigh of relief when he beheld Ortiz standing over the now still corpse of the last horse. Jack had almost forgotten about him.

Ortiz had a face like a thundercloud as he walked, more like stalked, over to Jack. But Jack paid him no mind, instead focusing on the kid.

Carefully removing the lasso, Jack winced at the deep bruising around the kid's throat. First things first, Jack checked the airway. The kid wasn't breathing, so Jack administered two rescue breaths and checked again.

"What the *hell*, Simmons?" boomed Ortiz's voice from over his shoulder.

"Not now," was all Jack said as he checked for breathing again.

Still nothing. No pulse, either.

Jack hastily found the spot where the kid's ribs came together and measured upward a couple of finger-widths, then placed the heel of his palm over the kid's breastbone and began compressions. His last CPR certification was over twelve years ago. Was it twelve compressions or fifteen? He couldn't remember, so he went with twelve, followed by two breaths.

After three rounds like this, Ortiz glowering over him with his fists on his hips the whole time, the kid began to cough weakly. With a sigh of relief, Jack sat back on his heels and wiped his brow with the back of his hand.

He looked up at Ortiz, who looked ready to chew rocks. "You have something to say, Juan?"

"We're not here to play hero, Simmons. Our mission is to get information and live to bring it back. That's it!"

Jack stood slowly, wincing slightly as his knee popped. "So you'd have just left this kids to his fate, then. They probably meant to sell him to... Ah, I see. Looking out for the old profit margin, huh?"

Jack didn't think it was possible for Ortiz to look more mad, but the security man's reaction proved him wrong. Ortiz's eyes widened and his jaw worked for a moment, then he looked away. "I don't approve of everything the company does."

"Yeah whatever. You're sure willing to take the money from it though, aren't you?"

Ortiz stiffened, then turned and walked back toward the other hill. As he left, he said over his shoulder, "I'll get the horses. The kid's your problem."

They camped in another copse of trees a half mile or so down the valley from the battle site, so as to avoid bears or other predators that might be drawn to the corpses and blood.

Getting the kid there was an exercise in worry for Jack. The old adage, "Don't move an injured person," rang in his mind the entire time. But there was no help for it, and the kid didn't seem to have any neck injuries beyond nearly having been choked to death.

Ortiz managed to retrieve one of the remaining horses belonging to the dead men, as well as their rifles and ammo. So Jack hoisted the kid onto one of the horses with care, laying him belly-down across the saddle. Then he led the kid's horse slowly to the campsite.

The kid was thin, almost emaciated. His hair was straw colored and tangled, nearly to the point of dreadlocks, his complexion pale. His clothing was patched and worn and didn't fit very well. He lay limp for a long time, even after Jack took him down from the horse and wrapped him in one of his blankets.

Standing and backing away to let the kid rest, Jack looked down at him for a long several minutes. Long buried regret and loss bubbled up. The kid was almost...

"Dinner's ready," Ortiz said from behind him.

Jack turned and saw that Ortiz had built up the fire while he was tending to the kid. The last of their venison from

Jack's kill was heating on a stick. Ortiz was already eating. The odor made Jack's mouth water. He hadn't realized how hungry he was. Rubbing his hands together eagerly, he moved around to his saddlebag and pulled out his plate and eating knife.

As he turned back to the fire and began to cut off a hunk of meat, Ortiz spoke again. "You want to explain? Don't give me that crap about saving him from slavers. We don't know who those guys were and your face says there's something else going on."

Jack paused in mid-slice. Biting his lip, he looked back at the kid again. He was very still, but his chest rose and fell in an even, steady rhythm. With a grunt, Jack finished cutting the meat and backed away from the fire pit. He settled down Indian style and took a bite. Even though the venison was almost a week old, it still had decent flavor, if not much in the way of moisture.

He wasn't sure how he felt about talking about this with Ortiz. He'd never told anyone, not even Tobias. But they were stuck together for a while, and maybe it was time to get it off his chest.

Swallowing, Jack spoke. "My wife. Susan. She was..." He took another bite and chewed slowly. Between chews, he tried again. "If she hadn't..." He had to stop as the pain rose up again. Damnit, why was it so hard to say? Swallowing again, he forced the words out. "Our son would have been about his age." He nodded toward the kid.

Ortiz nodded. "I see."

"I see? That's all..."

The kid groaned and Jack moved to his side, his retort forgotten. Crouching next to the kid, Jack could see he was awake and reached out a hand, meaning to offer comfort. The kid recoiled, squirming to get away.

"Easy, kid. We're not going to hurt you."

The kid looked from Jack to Ortiz and back, then around the rest of the campsite in a quick, fearful scan.

"Those men are gone."

"You mean dead." The kid's voice was high-pitched, quavering. Jack didn't blame him for being scared.

Nodding, Jack offered his hand to the kid. "I'm Jack and that's Juan. What's your name, kid?"

The kid hesitated, looking at Jack's hand as he might a coiled rattlesnake. But eventually he took it in a tentative shake. "Simeon."

Simeon didn't say much more than that the rest of the night, despite Jack's attempts at conversation. He couldn't say he blamed the kid. He'd been through a lot. Still, he felt a bit put out about it.

🙋 10 🙋

TARNISHED DREAMS

Jack awoke with a start. For once his sudden awakening wasn't brought on by remembered pain and loss, but rather by surprise.

While he slept, Jack dreamt the same dream he always did. But it was different. When he looked at Susan's belly, beside him in the copilot's seat, it was flat. In a panic, he looked around and saw a little boy in the back seat. Who was that? Jack turned in his seat and looked at the boy more closely. He was younger, but the facial features were the same.

Simeon.

Back in the waking world again, Jack rubbed at his temples in confusion. Why the hell would he dream about the kid? And like that, of all things? These were his memories. His pain. Where did that kid get off intruding in them?

In spite of himself, Jack felt a deep anger, nearly rage, well up within him. He turned his head to regard the kid, asleep again in his blanket, and it was all Jack could do to not rush over and throttle him within an inch of his life.

Only his promise to the kid when he first awoke stopped Jack in that moment of ire. All the same, he found himself

95

out of his blankets and crouching, ready to spring on the boy, before he realized it. Christ, what was he doing? Jack's anger turned quickly to shame, then fear as he considered what he'd almost done.

"What are you doing?"

Ortiz's voice cut through Jack's thoughts like a dagger. He stiffened, unsure how to respond for a heartbeat. Then he managed, "Ready to relieve you."

Ortiz snorted. "It's barely been an hour. Hit the rack."

The security man's voice held an edge of command and a subtle overtone of menace. Did he suspect? Surely not. Regardless, it was with trepidation that Jack lay back down. Sleep was a while in coming, but eventually he drifted off again.

Like before, Susan's belly was flat but this time he managed not too look in the back seat before the plane crashed again.

The next morning dawned cold and cloudy. Frost covered the ground, stiffening their blankets and making the morning ritual quite uncomfortable until Jack managed to get the fire re-lit. Breakfast consisted of jerky and the last nubs of stale bread in their packs, with hot tea, brewed weak to stretch their remaining seasoning, to wash it down. However unsatisfying Jack found the meal, Simeon wolfed it down with vigor. Toward the end of breakfast, Jack queried him.

"How did you come to be out here, Simeon?"

The boy swallowed a hunk of bread before answering. "My Ma wanted us to live with the wizards."

Jack and Ortiz shared a quizzical look. "How's that again?" Jack inquired.

Simeon looked at them with an expression of confusion.

"You know, the Sun Wizards. They live in a castle down in Texas and practice their magic."

Ortiz snorted with derision. "No such thing as magic, kid."

"Where's your mother now, Simeon?" Jack interjected quickly, seeing the boy shrivel in reaction to Ortiz's comment.

Jack instantly realized he'd made a mistake. If anything, Simeon retreated further. He lowered his head, allowing his hair to cover his face. His chest heaved and Jack could hear him sniffling. Jack shared another look with Ortiz, who rolled his eyes. Jack would have thought he had a better understanding of and tolerance for kids. Guess not.

Jack stood, intending to comfort the kid, but Ortiz grabbed him by the arm, stopping him. The security man motioned with his head toward the horses and raised one eyebrow. Expecting to be taken to task, again, for something, Jack followed him.

Ortiz bent over to check his horses' shoes and spoke quietly. "I think we should help the kid find his wizards."

Jack blinked in surprise. Hadn't Ortiz just shot down the kid's fantasy?

Seeing Jack's expression, Ortiz rolled his eyes again. "Think, Simmons. He doesn't know technology from a hole in the ground. What do you suppose someone who grew up like he did would think of an iPhone? Magic, maybe? Whoever burned out Farrah's Crossing and took down our scouting party had high tech weapons. Wizards, Simmons?"

Jack looked back toward the boy. What Ortiz said made sense, but it felt like they'd be using him. "I'm not sure."

"It's where he wants to go anyway. Look at it this way: worst case, you've done your good deed for the year."

Ortiz lowered the horse's hoof and walked back to the fire. Jack followed slowly. He wasn't sure he liked the plan, but Simeon perked right up when Ortiz made the offer. The kid agreed quickly, wiping his nose with the back of his hand and smiling.

Simeon didn't have much in the way of directions to the lair of his purported wizards. All he'd heard is they had an installation, a castle he kept saying, somewhere northeast of Dallas. There wasn't all that much Texas between there and the borders with Oklahoma and Arkansas. Just hundreds of square miles. What could go wrong? Nonetheless, when they broke camp, they turned southwest.

The next two days were nondescript. They awoke, ate, rode, stopped, ate, slept. Save for the doe Jack took the afternoon of the first day, little broke the routine or altered in the scenery. By now, Jack had gotten used to abandoned vehicles, burned out or abandoned buildings, and the like. He'd long since stopped feeling as though unseen eyes were following them as they passed through a ghost town. Ortiz, though, remained as watchful as ever.

It was obvious that Simeon was becoming more comfortable around Jack and Ortiz. As the days drew on, he began chatting more, and in fits and starts shared the story of how he came to be on a quest for these supposed wizards.

The heartbreaking part was Simeon didn't know what happened to his mother, though he suspected she was dead. The two of them had lived in a moderate-sized settlement up near St. Louis until one too many raids convinced her and several others to look for a more secure place to live. Word filtered up that these wizards, or whoever they really were, had established a safe area. It didn't take long to decide the group was going to head down to Texas to live with them.

All went well for ten days, then the evening before Jack

and Ortiz met him, a group of armed thugs ambushed the small caravan. Most of the men were killed. The raiders had other uses for the women. Simeon saw his mother briefly during the initial assault and remembered her screaming at him to run. He managed to escape during the confusion in the aftermath of the battle, but he never saw her again.

Jack could tell the kid felt guilty for leaving without his mother. But he didn't blame Simeon one bit. His prospects had he remained with those raiders were bad. At best.

The morning of the third day, they reached Interstate 40 again. A road sign showed them only twenty-five miles east of a city called Fort Smith.

"Might as well have not gotten off 40 to begin with," Jack quipped, earning him a look of reproach from Ortiz.

"Believe me, Simmons, you did *not* want to go by way of Memphis."

"How come?"

Ortiz wouldn't answer.

After a brief deliberation, they decided to head into Fort Smith. If there were people about, they might have better information on where these Wizards could be found. If word had spread all the way to St. Louis, surely it had spread here too. For that matter, Jack was surprised they hadn't heard about these folks in Forest Hills before now.

When they reached Fort Smith, they found it was indeed still populated, though, just like everywhere else, its population was a fraction of what it was before the Troubles. Most of the town's activity centered around what used to be the University campus. It seemed a nice enough place and folks seemed friendly enough.

Until they asked about the Sun Wizards. People looked at them oddly and stopped talking. One woman they asked crossed herself and walked away as quickly as her legs could carry her. Even the bartender in a local saloon wouldn't say much of anything when asked about them. By the end of the day, they knew little more than they had at the start.

They paid for a night in an inn with the remainder of the venison from the doe. It felt good to sleep in an actual bed for a change. Simeon in particular remarked on how comfortable it was.

The next morning, when the Inn's grooms retrieved their horses, Jack found a folded paper tucked beneath his saddle blanket. Curious, he pulled the paper out.

"What's this?" he asked the groom, only to find the young man already gone. That was odd. He didn't wait to get a tip.

"What's what?" Simeon said.

Jack showed him the paper. The boy's eyes lit up. No doubt he enjoyed the notion of a mystery.

"Open it up!"

Jack complied. There was a message, written in a messy hand, as though whoever wrote it was either in a hurry or not very practiced with letters. Jack's eyebrows climbed high on his brow as he read it. The message contained detailed directions from Fort Smith to a town called Idabel, and from there to the Red River, where the message writer said they would find what they were looking for.

"That doesn't at all sound like a trap," Ortiz muttered, sarcasm dripping from his voice. "No one wants to say a word about these people and now someone leaves this?"

"Maybe they don't like wizards here," Simeon offered. "Maybe the person's scared to talk to us."

That was as good an explanation as any. In the end, they decided to follow the directions. There wasn't much else to do and the message pointed them in the direction they were generally heading anyway.

Five days travel, following the directions on the note, brought them to the town of Idabel. Or what was left of it. It was never all that large a town from what Jack could tell of its layout as they rode in. But it had been picked clean in the years since the Troubles. Now it was a ghost town just like so many they had passed through before.

They camped in the gymnasium of the old high school to get in out of a cold drizzle that started not long after they rode into town. Being indoors precluded a fire, but at least it was dry. As was his norm, Simeon fell asleep not long after dinner. Jack and Ortiz stayed up for a while after that, discussing their next move.

If they followed the directions exactly, they would take the road west out of town, then follow the road when it bent south. They'd hit the river after about fifteen miles, total. It seemed straightforward enough to Jack, but Ortiz smelled a rat. He proposed taking the road south. When they hit the river, they could decide what to do next. That seemed like a bit too much work to Jack, but Ortiz wouldn't budge. Eventually, Jack acquiesced to the security man's plan, if only to avoid arguing about it any further.

With the plan settled, they settled in for the night.

11

CITADEL OF THE SUN

They left Idabel at first light, heading due south per Ortiz's plan. The road travelled south for several miles, then bent east. Around noon, it bent back to the south again. Jack was just about to point out that they would have reached the river by now had they just followed the directions when he saw the glint of sunlight reflecting off water through the trees to the right.

They eagerly turned off the road and, after rounding a small hillock, they reached the bank of a moderately wide, slow-flowing river. It was hard to tell whether the river was deep or shallow, but Jack was not eager to find out. Maybe if it was summer time, it might be feasible, but it was the middle of November. No way.

"This must be the Red River," Ortiz said.

"If you say so. I hope there's a bridge around here somewhere."

Oritz didn't reply, but turned his horse to the right. Jack and Simeon followed without complaint. It made sense to go upstream. Worst case, it would become shallow enough to cross somewhere. Jack didn't want to think how far that would be.

It didn't come to that, of course. They camped by the riverbank that night, but very soon after they broke camp the next morning, they sighted a bridge crossing the river a short distance ahead. It was small: just two lanes, and those partially blocked by rusting car hulks. That wasn't so unusual, though.

The unusual part was what they found on the other side.

Two cars blocked their way, placed bumper to bumper across the road. A flagpole was erected off to the side, a white pendant fluttering in the breeze. Two men, carrying rifles, waited behind the cars. Dressed in red blouses with a white and yellow emblem of some sort on the left breast, they were clearly not random thugs.

The riflemen had apparently seen Jack's party for some time as they approached the bridge because they displayed no surprise at all when the party approached. They did, however, level their weapons at the three travelers.

"Halt!" said the one on the left. His voice, deep and gravelly, carried across the intervening distance easily.

The party obediently reined their mounts to a halt.

The rifleman spoke again, this time to his companion. "Get the Enlightened." The second rifleman nodded and ran to a modest-sized building a few yards down from the roadblock.

The building had the look of a bunkhouse, and from its rough construction, Jack surmised it was recently built. A fenced corral behind the building held a dozen or so horses. Yes, this was definitely more than just a couple of punks looking for toll.

Ortiz cleared his throat. Jack looked over at him and the security man nodded toward the flagpole. The breeze had picked up and the pendant was standing straight out. The breath caught in Jack's throat.

On the pendant was emblazoned the image of a coiled snake biting the neck of an eagle, with a blazing sun overhead.

The second rifleman returned to the roadblock, in company with another man. The newcomer was dressed in cowled black robes that were cinched around his waist by a red cloth belt. A trio of small flasks hung from his belt on his left hip and a rod of some sort was tucked behind his belt on his right hip. The man walked with his hands clasped in front of his belly such that they were both covered by his wide sleeves. He looked somewhat like a monk.

The first rifleman lowered his weapon as the monk reached the roadblock. The monk regarded the trio on the bridge for a short moment. Then he pushed back his cowl, revealing a youthful face, pitted with acne, and flowing brown hair that hung to just above his shoulders.

"You approach the territory of the Order of the Sun. State your business, travelers."

Ortiz and Jack exchanged a glance. Jack shrugged. What to say here? Simeon beat them to it.

"We want to become wizards!"

The monk's eyebrow quirked upward at the boy's words.

"Truly."

Simeon nodded excitedly and the riflemen to the monk's right, the first who spoke to them, chuckled with amusement.

"Don't know what he's asking for, do he?"

The monk looked disparagingly at the rifleman, and the fellow stopped laughing quickly. He cleared his throat and backed away a step, making a shallow little bow. Sniffing, the monk looked back at Simeon, then the two men.

"Do you seek to learn as well?"

Ortiz nodded and Jack followed suit.

This seemed to satisfy the monk, as he nodded and spoke again, his tone more welcoming.

"The Master decreed that all who wish to learn the higher truths be allowed to. We will see you safely to the Citadel."

The monk nodded to the two riflemen and they backed away. Then he pulled the rod out from behind his belt and pointed it at the cars. His faced scrunched in concentration for a heartbeat, and then, with the loud scraping of metal dragging across asphalt, the cars moved apart, opening a path for the trio to pass through.

Jack's jaw dropped. From the corner of his eye, he could see that Ortiz's had done the same. What the hell just happened?

The monk smiled faintly.

"Have no fear. I am Lucius, Enlightened of the Order. You are under my protection. No harm will come to you, so long as you cause no trouble."

Lucius did not travel with them. Instead, he dispatched four more riflemen and an older man, dressed similarly to himself, except his robes were white with a red belt, to be their escorts. The white-robed man introduced himself as Acolyte Ulysses, but said little else.

The escort led them down the road for the rest of the morning, past a few clusters deserted of buildings. Then, an hour or so after noon, they came to the top of a good sized ridge.

Looking down from the crest, Jack could see a small town nestled between a trio of hills. The town sat astride a fair sized stream that flowed from the hills and off to the north, toward the river most likely. It looked only large enough to support a few hundred people, but a sea of tents had been erected around it. Thousands of tents, ranging from tiny bits of canvas barely large enough to cover a single man to pavilions larger than the banquet tent used in Glennville for the Caravan Market feast. On the near side, new buildings were in the process of being constructed: large buildings that looked like dormitories or apartments.

That all was impressive enough, but the building atop the hill opposite the riders was what truly drew the eye. Massive, constructed of red stone of some sort, it was several hundred feet from one end to the other and at least fifty or sixty feet tall. The roof was capped with a dome in its center, the top of which reflected the sunlight like a properly-angled mirror will do. A single spire, rising another hundred feet or so above the dome, completed the structure itself. Jack could see the entire complex was surrounded by a crenellated wall, about thirty feet tall, with towers at each corner and a single gate. Flags waved from the top of each tower, as did a large one from the top of the building's main spire. The entire thing looked like a cross between a medieval castle and a mosque.

"Behold the Citadel of the Sun," said Ulysses, his tone reverent.

Ulysses led them down past the new construction and into town. Up close, the new buildings were quite large. Each could probably house a hundred families once completed. The construction crew consisted of several soldiers, dressed in their red blouses, overseeing dozens of workers. Even in the late autumn chill, the workers wore little more than rags. They were thin, poorly fed. Their eyes were downcast and their postures were slumped, defeated.

"Who are they?" Jack asked Ulysses, nodding toward the workers.

The Acolyte sniffed. "Traitors. Criminals. Prisoners of War. Waste of good flesh, but the Master frowns on execution except for the worst cases. So they work off their debt to the Order."

"For how long?"

"As long as it takes."

Jack had no response to that.

"Just who is this Master?" Ortiz asked.

Ulysses gave him a level look. "You will see."

They continued on into the town proper. Back before the Troubles, it clearly had been a one-horse town. The downtown area consisted mostly of a single main street, with a bar, a general store, a couple of restaurants, and a few other shops. A few residential streets were accessible from the main street, but that was all there was to it. Now, thanks to the tent city, it was bursting at the seams with people. Everywhere were soldiers going about their duties, men and women engaging in all manner of chores and commerce, children playing, and occasionally more prisoners performing menial tasks. Jack estimated there must have been ten thousand people encamped in the valley.

As they left the downtown area, the tent city closed in around them. The road to the Citadel cut a straight path through the tents, which stopped at the base of the hill. But as they made their way, it seemed the press of people actually increased. Individuals and families stood in groups looking up at the Citadel as though expecting something.

Ulysses noticed Jack looking quizzically at them and spoke again.

"Many come to ask boons of the Master. Here they wait until summoned to his presence."

That seemed a trifle pompous, though it made sense. A man only had so many hours in the day, after all.

A quartet of soldiers stood guard in the gatehouse. One of them, wearing the same blouse as the others except for the gold bars on his collar, stepped forward to meet them as they dismounted. He inclined his head to Ulysses and spoke in a respectful tone.

"Good day, Acolyte. What have we here?"

"Potential students, Lieutenant, here to see Reginald."

The Lieutenant looked them over, but said nothing. Instead, Ulysses addressed them.

"Here we part ways. Reginald has charge of student induction and early training. The Lieutenant will see you to his offices. Be well."

With that, Ulysses turned and re-mounted his horse, then rode back down the hill. His soldiers followed without a word.

The Lieutenant spoke as soon as Ulysses left.

"No one is permitted weapons within the Citadel except members of the Order or soldiers of the Legion. If you will hand over your arms, my men will take custody of them. You may retrieve them when you depart."

His tone strongly implied he would not take no for an answer. Even had it not, Jack saw no point in challenging the rules as their first act in town. Ortiz seemed to agree, as he unholstered his weapons and handed them over without complaint. Jack did the same, and after a few minutes, received a written receipt of his equipment from the soldiers. Very efficient.

Once that was taken care of, the Lieutenant waved over some grooms, who took their horses. Then, with a brisk "Follow me," he led them through the large courtyard to a set of double doors in the Citadel wall directly opposite the gatehouse. Solidly made of dark wood, the doors were around fifteen feet tall and probably ten feet across. A blazing sun, the same as the emblem on the soldiers' blouses, was inlaid into the doors, with what looked like gold and silver.

Despite their size, the doors were apparently very well balanced as they opened easily at the Lieutenant's touch. Jack and the others followed the Lieutenant inside and the doors swung shut behind them.

Reginald was young, in his late teens at most. He had curly blond hair, green eyes, and a slight build. Like Ulysses, he wore the white robes and red belt of an Acolyte.

His office was a short way inside the Citadel. It was relatively small and sparsely furnished, with just a simple desk, a pair of chairs facing the desk, and a couple of filing cabinets along the wall. Like the corridors they'd walked down to get here, the office was lit by natural light from a single window and by a soft, off-white glow from crystals resting on mounts in the walls. Or at least they looked like crystals. Each glowed equivalent to what Jack remembered from a 60 Watt lightbulb, though they gave off no heat that Jack could detect.

Reginald rose when the Lieutenant led them into the office. When told they intended to become students of the Order, he thanked the Lieutenant and dismissed him. Reginald looked the three of them over, spending more time on Simeon than the two men.

"I'm sorry, but no one may enter the training who is younger than thirteen."

Simeon opened his mouth to protest, but Reginald cut him off with a raised hand.

"No exceptions. You may assist the librarians, if you wish. There are several lads doing so while they await their coming of age."

Simeon shut his mouth and bit his lip, his head lowering in disappointment. Either not noticing or not caring, Reginald turned his attention fully on Jack and Ortiz.

"We admit new students every eight weeks. The next indoctrination begins in three days. I will see you have rooms assigned. Tomorrow, you will have your pre-admission interviews."

Ortiz asked, "What kind of interviews?"

"Nothing too strenuous. But we want to know who it is we're teaching. I encourage you to be as open and honest as possible. That won't be a problem, will it?"

Jack shook his head quickly and Ortiz followed suit. Reginald inclined his head slightly, almost as though returning a supplication. "Once your interviews are complete, I must ask that you remain in the Visitor Dormitory until you are summoned. The rest of the Citadel is for the Order alone, and those who serve the Order."

"What about the boy?" Jack asked.

"He will be housed with the servants." Reginald looked back at Simeon. "Assuming you wish to do so, lad."

Simeon nodded. He still looked dejected, but it looked like his mood was improving.

"Very well. Welcome to the Citadel, gentlemen."

❧ 12 ❧

QUESTIONS AND ANSWERS

Reginald led them out of his office and down the main corridor in the Citadel until he reached a large set of double doors that were propped open by wooden door stops. Through the doors, long rows of stacks filled with books were visible behind a large wooden counter. Off to the side, numerous tables were set up, a reading area for the library, no doubt. A man, wearing the black robes of an Enlightened, and a woman who was dressed in an Acolyte's white were seated behind the counter.

Reginald led them into the library and bowed slightly to the Enlightened man. He waited a moment to be acknowledged.

"Acolyte Reginald," the Enlightened said finally, his eyes flickered toward Jack and Ortiz, then Simeon, his lips turning downward into a half-sneer.

"Enlightened Horace, this boy..." Reginald glanced at Simeon questioningly.

Quick on the uptake, the lad replied, "Simeon."

Reginald cleared his throat softly before continuing. "Simeon seeks to learn the Higher Truths, but has not yet reached his majority. He would like to live and learn with the other children in waiting."

If anything, Horace's half-sneer deepened at Reginald's words. He was silent for a long moment as he looked Simeon up and down. Finally, he nodded. "Very well. We have room for another now. Acolyte Constance," he said in a tone of command, causing the woman in white to perk up and scurry over to his side.

"Yes, Enlightened," Constance said, bowing in the same way that Reginald had.

"Take charge of this boy and show him to the children's quarters. See that he meets the others and gets settled."

Constance frowned slightly, but bowed again and came around the desk to Reginald's side. Simeon, swallowing with what Jack assumed to be nerves in spite of his stated enthusiasm for the arrangement, gave her a small smile.

Instead of returning the gesture, she sniffed and said, "Come along then." With that, she turned and walked away toward a smaller door off in the corner of the room. Jack kicked himself inwardly; he completely missed seeing the door when they entered.

Simeon looked at Ortiz, then Jack, and smiled. "Thanks a lot, Mr. Oritz. Mr. Simmons. Guess I'll see you around."

"Count on it," Jack replied. Ortiz just nodded.

Simeon and Constance disappeared through the door. The sound of the door closing behind the lad was depressingly final to Jack's ears. He was surprised to discover he already missed the kid.

There was no time to grouse, though, as Reginald gestured for Jack and Ortiz to follow him. "I'll show you to your quarters now."

The Visitor Dormitory was a small building located caddy-corner from the main gate into the Citadel complex, not far from the stables. Jack and Ortiz were assigned a small room on the second floor, barely larger than a walk-in closet. Two cots rested against opposite walls with footlockers at their feet. Aside from that, the room was empty. There wasn't even a window. Instead, one of those glowing crystals, resting in a small sconce, provided light.

"Don't keep visitors for long, do you?" Jack quipped as he surveyed the arrangements.

Amusement flashed across Reginald's face quickly and he shrugged. "These quarters are only for short stays. People with business that requires a longer wait generally stay down in the town."

Jack thought back to the throngs of hopefuls in the valley below who were awaiting summons to see the Master. "How long do most people wait?"

Reginald looked at him askance. "As I said, we admit new students every eight weeks, so..."

"No, I mean people who aren't trying to be students."

"Ah, the petitioners. It depends on the nature of the person's request. And on the Master's schedule, of course. But they seldom wait longer than six months."

Six months! Jack couldn't imagine waiting around that long for anything. His disbelief must have shown on his face because Reginald raised an eyebrow and spoke again.

"Many who come to the Master are desperate. On their last legs. In those circumstances, a brief delay is not unacceptable when it comes with food and shelter for the duration."

Jack had to concede that point.

"Now then," Reginald said with a clearing of his throat, "the glow crystal is simple to use." He took the crystal out of its sconce and held it up for them to see. "Pressing with your thumb and finger in one of these combinations will select the desired light level: off, low, medium, or high." He pointed to five different points on the edge of the crystal. Each point was slightly discolored, making it easily visible. From the points' arrangement, four on one side of the crystal and one on the other, they were laid out to be actuated with the right hand. "The charge can last as long as a day, depending on the light level selected. There is an Acolyte assigned to recharge the crystals twice daily, so do not be surprised if you hear a knock."

Looking between Jack and Ortiz, Reginald waited for a moment, no doubt in anticipation of questions. With none forthcoming, he replaced the glow crystal in its sconce and went on. "Down the hall is the privy. At the end of the hall on the first level is the common area. Several books from the Library are available for reading and food is provided twice daily. You can expect to hear from the interviewing officers tomorrow afternoon or, at the very latest, the morning after. Good luck."

With that, Reginald departed. The door closed behind him with a solid thud and the click of the latch falling into place.

Jack began unloading his belongings into the footlocker. Thoughtfully enough, there was a padlock, complete with key, on the locker. That was something at least. He was surprised when he glanced over and saw that Ortiz was not doing the same. Instead, the security man was standing and staring at the door, a troubled expression on his face.

"What's wrong, Juan?"

A soft grunt preceded Ortiz's reply. "They say the Master allows all comers to study, but I wonder how true that is."

"How's that?"

"If he never learned about certain applicants, he didn't turn them away, did he?"

"Word would get around, though."

"Would it?" Ortiz looked at him with a grim expression and raised an eyebrow.

Jack swallowed, the implication behind Ortiz's words sinking in.

"We're in a dangerous spot, Simmons. Tell them the wrong thing, something that makes them think we're a threat of some sort, and..." Ortiz shook his head. "We need to make sure we have our story straight."

The evening meal was nothing special: boiled venison mixed with potatoes and a few pieces of various greens in weak broth to make a stew, along with almost stale bread. But it was free, so Jack didn't complain as he ate his fill.

The common area could seat fifty or so, but it was less than halfway filled with the other potential students. Or at least Jack assumed that's who they were. Jack counted sixteen of them. It almost felt like high school all over again, as the various people kept to themselves or their own little groups and seldom exchanged a word with anyone else.

That was just as well as Jack and Ortiz hashed out the final details of their story over dinner.

The night's sleep wasn't the most comfortable Jack could recall. Ortiz's snoring was amplified by the close walls and woke Jack up on more than one occasion. But at least it was indoors and somewhat warm. All the same, he felt more than a little groggy as he followed Ortiz down to the common area for breakfast.

Jack found a copy of Canterbury Tales on the shelf in the common area the next morning after a quick breakfast of bread and an apple. Bemused, he recalled reading it way back in Junior High, well before the Troubles. He lost himself in

Chaucer's stories for the rest of the morning and managed to not think about where he was or the potential danger he was in.

But shortly before noon, it all came home again when two men dressed in the red blouses of the Legion strode into the common area. Quickly spotting Jack and Ortiz, who was seated not far away and also reading a book, the pair walked over with a crisp, formal stride.

Clearing his throat, the older of the two, a man not much younger than Jack, issued a perfunctory, "Come with us," before turning and walking toward the door. Setting the book down, Jack shrugged and, with a glance at Ortiz, stood and followed the legionnaire out. Time to face the piper. The second legionnaire fell in behind them.

Their destination was another outbuilding in the Citadel complex's courtyard, smaller than the visitor dormitory but more solidly built. It almost looked like a fort in and of itself. Stepping within, Jack understood why. Legionnaires were everywhere, engaging in labor of one sort or another and causing Jack to surmise that the building was, if not the Legion's headquarters, then at least the command center for the Citadel's garrison.

Their escort wasted no time in showing Jack and Ortiz around, however, instead leading them through the entryway, down what appeared to be the building's main corridor, then to the right down a more narrow hallway that ended at a pair of stout wooden doors that faced each other on either sides of the hall.

Turning to face them, the leader of the escort pointed first at Jack. "That room," he said to Jack, gesturing toward the door on the left. Ortiz got the door on the right.

Jack grasped the doorknob and paused for a moment. This was it. With a deep breath, he turned the knob and stepped inside.

The door swung shut behind the escort as Jack sunk down onto his cot and leaned back against the wall with a sigh. Tension seemed to leave his body in a rush. For a moment, he just sat there breathing, trying to relax.

The interview hadn't been nearly as taxing as he thought it would be. But all the same, he felt wrung out, drained. Not that the questioning had been particularly difficult or harsh. But it was taxing, stressful, and Jack needed a moment to recompose himself. Looking across the room, he took some solace in the fact that Ortiz appeared to have a similar reaction, though the security man was more reserved about it.

"How'd it go with you, Juan?"

Ortiz shrugged. "Once I told them about my time in the Corps, they tried to convince me to just join up with the Legion and give over this bit."

Jack felt his brows rising on his forehead. "Oh? That would be right up your alley, wouldn't it?"

Ortiz nodded. "Probably. But it would look suspicious to just back away so quickly. It might be a good backup plan, though."

"Hopefully it won't come down to that. They didn't seem very concerned with the story, to me."

"They wouldn't show it in front of you. They're comparing notes on our discussions right now, though. We'll know if there are issues soon enough."

As usual, Ortiz was a ray of sunshine. He was right in one respect, though. It was out of their hands now. There was nothing to do but wait. And hope.

❧ 13 ❧

THE MASTER

T he next day passed without incident and Jack began to feel more certain that their stories had worked.

Then, true to his word, on the third morning after their arrival at the Citadel, Reginald summoned Jack and Ortiz, along with the sixteen other hopefuls. Jack surveyed the crowd. Young, old, thin, fat, male, female, the applicants apparently came from all walks of life from their dress and demeanor. But all had hopeful expressions on their faces as they assembled in the courtyard outside the visitor's dormitory.

Reginald addressed them briefly before leading them into the Citadel.

"You will be meeting with the Master this morning. If you are wise, you will show him the utmost respect. Failure to do so may have consequences beyond not being allowed to study here."

Reginald paused for a moment to let the words sink in. Jack felt a surge of relief, followed by excitement. It had worked! They were in!

Reginald wasted no time with further discussion. He

turned and led the group into the Citadel itself. They passed down a wide corridor and then up a wide, carpet-draped set of stairs to the second level. The stairs reminded Jack of those in the ending scenes of Gone With the Wind.

At the upstairs landing, they turned right and followed a narrower corridor lined every twenty feet or so with a pair of doors. At the tenth such pair, the corridor ended and Reginald chose the door on the right. Beyond was another, narrower, set of stairs. This staircase was not straight like the last one, but rather turned in a long clockwise spiral that eventually ended at a set of double doors.

Reginald stopped and, turning to face the group, smiled faintly. "Through these doors begins enlightenment," he said. Ortiz and Jack glanced at each other, exchanging raised eyebrows. It was sometimes scary how often they were thinking the same thing at the same time. Jack supposed they were rubbing off on each other.

The acolyte led them through the doors and into a plush, well-lit room. Tall, well-crafted shelves, all filled with a multitude of tomes, lined the walls on either side of the entrance. Thick carpets covered the floors. The ceiling was vaulted, rising into a dome at the center of the room. The top of the dome was glass or crystal and illuminated the room with natural sunlight from outside. Beneath the dome, a grouping of about thirty chairs was positioned facing a dais on the far side of the room from the entrance, upon which stood a simple lectern. A mural was painted on the wall behind the lectern, depicting a man touching a shining globe - the sun? - with his outstretched index finger. It looked very much like that old painting atop the Sistine Chapel of man trying to touch God. Indeed, the entire room felt much like a church, now that Jack thought about it.

"Please be seated. The Master will be with you in a moment," Reginald intoned. They obeyed, taking seats among those available. Just like in church, no one sat in the first few rows, Jack noted with amusement. After all had sat down, Reginald retreated to the doorway and, bowing, exited, pulling the doors shut as he went.

Long minutes passed and Jack began to wonder if Reginald had been playing a prank on them. Then, between one heartbeat and the next, a man appeared behind the lectern. A collective gasp went up from the gathered group, and not just because of his sudden arrival. The man himself was enough to startle.

He was tall, but slender, with greying brown hair pulled back into a ponytail at the nape of his neck. He had a close-trimmed beard and a hooked nose, and wore wire-rimmed spectacles. He was dressed in cowled, flowing red robes, trimmed in dark blue and cinched around his waist by a dark blue cloth belt.

He stood for a long moment with his eyes closed, his arms crossed over his chest, pressing a large tome to his body, his head lowered. Then he raised his head and opened his eyes. The crowd gasped again. His irises were a deep red.

Setting his book down atop the lectern, he smiled at the crowd. "Welcome to you, friends," he said, his baritone voice carrying easily. "I am Doctor Lewis Horbach. You have come seeking deep truths. Seeking power. Both are available to you here, if you have the courage, the commitment, and the wisdom to find them."

Jack was impressed. A glance at his fellow supplicants revealed that Horbach had, with just those few words, put most of them under his spell. They looked at him with something akin to awe, and no wonder. He spoke clearly and with confidence. But beyond that, he exuded knowledge of something that no one else had. It was compelling.

Horbach continued. "I first came to know the truths taught in these walls many years ago. At first, I was laughed at." A soft chuckle rippled through the small crowd, several members no doubt disbelieving such a statement. Horbach made a calming gesture, sparing the group a small smile. "I was a physicist, you see, and those who take that path are supposed to follow only hard facts, not truth. But I saw further than the others. They theorized about higher dimensions and parallel universes, but contented themselves that these were unreachable, and thus merely interesting, if unprovable, theories. I knew better. Looking at the writings of the ancients, I came to understand that man's long-forgotten ancestors had once tapped the knowledge and power contained in those realms for their own betterment. It was only the blinders of modern science that prevented modern man from doing the same."

He sighed sadly, his voice taking on a regretful tone as he continued. "But when I tried to express this to my colleagues, they mocked me, belittled what I was trying to reveal. Several advised me to leave the path of truth and return to the fold of conventional physics, with veiled threats of losing tenure if I did not. I could see the road ahead: like the church with Galileo, I was to be made an example of. A warning to others who would prize truth over dogma. So I left. I departed the university and made my way here. I was joined by a number of young visionaries who subscribed to my theory. Together we conducted experiments over the course of a number of years. For a long time, all our results were negative. Many of my assistants lost faith and left, but we who remained carried on."

"Finally," he continued, "even I began to doubt. In all of my experiments, there were tantalizing glimpses of a way to breach the barrier to the higher dimensions, but none bore fruit. I almost gave up." Bowing his head as he said this, he looked the epitome of sadness and despair. Glancing around again, Jack saw several members of the audience leaning forward in their chairs, concern etched in their faces. This guy was good.

"Then a little more than ten years ago, the answer came to me in a dream." Horbach looked back to the audience and smiled triumphantly, his eyes seeming to glow in the sunlight streaming from the top of the dome. "I was trying the different methods individually, but the answer was to do them together." He rested his hands on the top of the book on the lectern and leaned forward, fixing each member of the audience in turn with a piercing gaze. "In the morning, I told my assistants my revelation and they rejoiced. The experiments were designed to focus the necessary energy to a single point in a booth large enough to hold one person. Because we did not know what would happen to the person inside the booth, I entered myself. I believed in the rightness of my calculations, but even so I felt fear when my assistants energized the system. Foolishness."

Horbach drew a deep breath and closed his eyes. He shivered visibly as though from a remembered rapture. "Mere words cannot begin to describe what I saw and felt when the energy streams coalesced and I was lifted to the higher realms. There was a power and a presence I'd never imagined. In a glance, I perceived creation's breadth and majesty in its entirety. It was too much. I felt my mind straining beyond capacity and knew I was about to go mad. But then I felt as though I was being pulled and the boundaries of my perception shrunk to merely the contents of our galaxy. I marveled at the sight of stars being born and dying, of the black hole at the galactic center devouring entire star systems, of alien civilizations traveling the void between stars. Then my perception shrank once more, to encompass just our solar system. I beheld the strange creatures swimming in the cold seas of Europa and Titan, touched the nuclear reactions within our star, and was touched in turn by the fragile beauty of our little world."

He shrugged his shoulders, as though throwing off a weighty cloak, and opened his eyes. "Then I was back in my lab. It seemed a lifetime had passed, but my assistants quoted an elapsed time of only a few seconds. When I stepped from the booth, I was changed." He gestured to his red eyes and rolled up one of his sleeves, revealing red lines running down his forearm, stopping at a red ring around his wrist. It almost looked like a spreading infection, to Jack's eyes. "But the change was more than merely physical. I became aware of the natural energy around me, and over time I discovered that I could manipulate that energy, bend it to my will."

Raising his hand, he looked at his fingers for a moment and flames appeared from just above the tip of each, as though he was carrying five candles. The flames slowly grew in size until they were the size of small torches. Clenching his fist slowly, the five separate flames collapsed together into a single fireball floating in space. A collective gasp went up from the crowd as Horbach then rapidly spread his fingers again and the fireball turned into a fan of flame that extended from his hand over the heads of the audience to the wall opposite the lectern. Then the flame went out completely. Jack was surprised to see the wall was not even scorched, though he had felt the heat from the flames distinctly.

Horbach smiled again. "When I described my experience to my assistants, and especially after they saw what I could do with my burgeoning abilities, they rushed to enter the booth themselves. But for reasons I still do not fully understand, they could not access the higher realms as I had. Finally, I entered again and also failed to make the journey. I cannot explain why, except to surmise that the exact confluence of time, place, energy, and faith necessary to make the jump is exceedingly rare, almost impossible. What is it Jesus said to

Thomas? 'Blessed is he who believes, but has not seen.' My assistants knew the experiment was true. I did not, but I believed and risked the unknown to discover truth. Perhaps that extra element of faith is what allowed me to make the jump while my assistants could not."

"Of course, without being able to duplicate my experience, I knew my colleagues in Physics would never believe my account. So, despite having proved my theory true, my initial joy soon turned to sorrow. However, not long after that came the difficulties we know now as the Troubles. In the struggle to survive in a changed world, I discovered that a few of my assistants were able to learn to control the universe's energy as well. None could perceive the energy as I could: they required the use of certain substances to achieve even small effects that were becoming completely natural to me. But their relatively feeble abilities gave me hope and I realized the purpose of my life. Through my pupils and me, humanity would be saved from itself and lifted to a new level of civilization and enlightenment. I decreed that all who wished to learn be allowed to, provided they in return pledge themselves in service to humanity."

Horbach raised his hands out to his sides, palms out toward the crowd. "And so you have come. Most of you will be unable to learn. Of the few who are, only a minority will have the discipline and faith to learn the highest elements of the Art." His eyes flickered toward the tome atop the lectern for a heartbeat, then returned to the faces of his listeners. "But all will have the satisfaction of doing their part, however small, in the journey toward a better future."

An awed silence was the only response the small crowd could muster.

As soon as Jack closed the door to their room, Ortiz burst out, "That guy is a nutcase!" There was never any mystery where Ortiz stood, Jack had to give him that.

"Maybe, but what about all those things he was able to do? And what Lucius did with those cars?"

Ortiz snorted loudly, giving Jack a look that screamed 'You're an idiot' before replying. "Come on, Simmons. Didn't you ever go to a magic show back in the day? It's all sleight-of-hand and clever mirror tricks."

"...and fans of flame streaking across the room."

Ortiz threw up his hands in exasperation. "Don't tell me you *bought* his crap?"

Jack shook his head and sank onto his pallet. "He sure seems to believe it. So do his flunkies around here. And he looks the part." Sighing, he leaned back against the wall. "I don't know. You gotta admit he was pretty convincing."

"So is every con man."

Jack shrugged, conceding the point. "Well, we're going to have to play along for a while, at least, if we're going to find out anything useful. Did you notice how he never let that book out of his reach?"

Ortiz nodded. "Pretty obvious show. Made me wish I could play him in poker." He plopped down onto his pallet and leaned toward Jack, elbows on his knees. "He took it with him when he left. I'd bet good money he's got something important written down there. Probably designs to those weapons their troops have. The trouble is getting a look at it."

"One thing's for certain: we're not going to get anywhere close if we come off as thinking he's full of crap. No offense, Juan, but you should have seen your expressions in there. Obvious skepticism from the start."

"I'm no good at acting."

"Tell me about it."

Ortiz frowned hard at Jack for a moment, then grudgingly nodded in agreement. "Alright. I'll try."

"We'll need to check in on Simeon from time to time."

Ortiz's brow furrowed and his lips turned down in a scowl. What did he have against the kid? He opened his mouth to ask that very thing, but Ortiz beat him to the punch.

"I told you before, Simmons. Taking care of that boy is not our mission. We're here to obtain information and get back. Period."

"But..."

Suddenly rising to his feet, Ortiz pointed a forceful finger toward Jack. His hand shook and his eyes were alight with anger. "He's not your son, Simmons! Get that through your skull and keep your eyes on the mission or so help me..."

Clenching his fist, Ortiz pulled his hand back, as though preparing to throw a punch. For a second, Jack thought he was going to take a swing, but then, his face still dark with anger, Ortiz turned and stalked out of the room, slamming the door behind him.

❧ 14 ❦

TESTING AND ACCEPTANCE

That afternoon, Reginald mustered them again. This time, he led them back within the Citadel to a moderate-sized room on the main floor.

As Jack entered the room, he was reminded of chemistry lab back in high school. Three rows of long tables were set up in the room, each with seating for ten. Each table was set with five large basins and an equal number of pitchers, with a single cup in front of each chair. Two acolytes waited at either end of each table, holding large flasks. A lectern stood in the middle of the far wall between two chalkboards.

Reginald directed them to take seats and waited patiently while they complied. Once they were all settled, he walked up to a door in the corner. He knocked three times, then stepped to the side and stood against the wall, waiting.

Almost a full minute passed, then the door opened and a woman walked into the room. Dressed in the black robes of an Enlightened, she was still young, in her thirties somewhere, but her black hair was heavily streaked with grey. She wore a stern expression as she stepped up to the lectern and addressed them.

"I am Margaret, Enlightened of the Order. I am the Dean of Students. Those of you who go on to learn from the Order will be under my authority for the duration of your time as Acolytes."

She gestured toward the Acolytes at the tables and they began walking down the aisles between the tables. As they reached each hopeful's place, the Acolytes poured a greenish-grey fluid from their flasks into the waiting cups.

Jack peered into his cup after the Acolyte moved on and grimaced. The fluid was about the thickness of whole milk, but it gave off a harshly metallic odor, with just a hint of sour, like a lime. Bubbles rose to the top in a steady stream, similar to a newly poured glass of Coke. What Jack wouldn't give for one of those. It had been years since last he saw anything but empty Coke cans and bottles. He missed it. Particularly when compared with this concoction, whatever it was. Glancing around at his fellow hopefuls, Jack saw similar expressions of dismay on most all of their faces.

Their distaste wasn't lost on Margaret. The faintest hint of a smile appeared on her lips.

"Before you is the Dimensional Elixir. Some call it a magic potion, but that is not strictly accurate. The elixir does not cause any effects in and of itself. Its function is to allow the imbiber access to the energies of the Higher Realms."

"It smells like crap," said a young man in the row ahead of Jack.

Margaret turned her gaze onto him and raised an eyebrow. "As with most things in life, some difficulty must be endured to reach a higher goal." She moved her gaze to each hopeful in turn, then added, "This is the first test. Those who are able to withstand the elixir may have the ability to learn the art. Drink up. All of it."

This was not going to be fun. Gingerly, Jack took hold of his cup and raised it. The odor just got worse as the elixir neared his nostrils, though he was able to detect subtle undertones in the smell. Was that a hint of peach? Maybe walnut? Ortiz, sitting beside him, took a long draw from his cup, reminding Jack that he was stalling.

With a deep breath, Jack followed suit.

It, surprisingly, wasn't as horrible as he expected. It wasn't good by any stretch of the imagination, but he managed to force it down. It took effort though, and Jack was dismayed to see he still had about half of his cup to go.

With a grimace, he took another drink, trying to recall the techniques for chugging bad beer that he learned in college. Again, it took a large effort to swallow, but he managed to empty the cup.

Three fellows in the row ahead of him began retching into the basins on their table. A young girl behind him did the same. Jack was pretty nauseous himself, for that matter. He felt his stomach gurgling, as though the bubbling in the elixir had increased from his swallowing it, and felt sure he was going to be sick.

Then Ortiz *was* sick and it was all Jack could do to keep the elixir down.

The gurgling because more pronounced, and he began to feel a stabbing pain, like a really bad stitch in his side. He clutched at his belly and heard a groan issuing from his lips. This was bad.

A guy in the row behind him fell off his chair, thrashing and moaning in pain. Jack could relate.

The pain got worse, but as it did so, Jack's nausea began to fade. He'd rather have kept the nausea. The pain began to radiate out from his stomach, coming to encompass his entire abdomen, then his torso, then his arms and legs, until every inch of his body was racked in throbbing ache.

Then his head joined in, and it was as if his skull was going to crack open from within. He heard himself groaning loudly and felt himself pressing his palms to his temples. His vision went red.

And then, just like that, it ended.

Jack opened his eyes. Had he even closed them? He couldn't remember, but all of a sudden he felt great. His skin tingled, and he felt as though every hair on his body was standing on end, but a quick look showed that wasn't the case.

He looked around the room. The guy who'd fallen off his chair was sitting up on the floor, an expression of wonder on his face. One lady in the front row also appeared enraptured. Everyone else was either still being sick or slumped over the table, exhausted.

But he hardly noticed their state of sickness. He was too amazed at his *vision* to really notice what he was seeing.

It was almost as though he'd always been seeing in two dimensions, but suddenly he began to see in 3-D. Everything had more depth to it. The smallest details were easy to see, from the ant walking up the far wall to the tiny freckles on Margaret's nose. But more than that, there was a shimmering of sorts around each person in the room. It was almost like heat waves emanating from a stretch of highway in the middle of summer, except the shimmering spread in all directions from their bodies and only extended a few inches before fading.

Jack rubbed his eyes, expecting the strange effect to fade. When it didn't, he shook his head in amazement. What had that potion done to him?

A minute or two passed and Margaret nodded to Reginald. He took a step forward and cleared his throat, drawing all able eyes to himself.

"If you will follow me." His tone made it not seem a question, but a command. He gestured toward the doorway Margaret entered from. Jack was not entirely surprised to see the door swing open, apparently of its own accord. Reginald turned and walked through the door.

Jack got off his stool and followed the lady from the front row through the door.

———————

The doorway led into another classroom, this one smaller. Half a dozen individual desks, the kind found in many public high schools before the Troubles, sat in the center of the room, facing another lectern and chalkboard. Reginald stood beside the lectern, waiting. He gestured toward the desks.

"Take a seat."

The door closed behind them. Jack looked back to see that Margaret had followed behind them. She swept past them as they settled into chairs and positioned herself behind the lectern. The half-smile she offered them was more genuine this time.

"That you are here means you have potential. You should feel fortunate: barely ten percent of those who petition to learn can withstand the elixir."

The lady Jack had followed raised her hand. She reminded Jack of the quiet girl in class who was afraid to answer questions. Or to speak in general. Margaret raised an eyebrow.

"What is your name, Applicant?"

"Caroline, ma'am."

"What would you ask, Caroline?"

She swallowed audibly.

"What will happen to the others?"

"They will be ill for most of the remainder of the day and probably sleep the whole of tomorrow. But most will not be permanently harmed."

Relief showed plainly on Caroline's face, earning her a frown from Margaret.

"For which of your fellows are you worried? The young man seated next to you?"

Caroline nodded. "My boyfriend, ma'am."

"I see." Margaret leaned forward, her eyes growing hard. "Now is your first lesson. To join the Order is to leave outside relationships behind. It is forbidden for an Acolyte of the Order to fraternize with those who cannot know our Truths. So you must all decide, here and now, where your heart lies, for once you begin to learn, you will not be allowed to retreat from the Path." She looked each of them in the eye, lingering finally on Caroline. "You may leave now, if you wish, but this is your last chance to do so. What will it be?"

Caroline's eyes widened. As Margaret leveled the final question, she looked stricken. Caroline bit her lip, tears welling up. For that matter, the other man in the room, sitting to Jack's right, looked uncertain as well, though he was clearly not nearly as pained as Caroline. She struggled visibly with the decision, looking back at the door to the first class-room with an expression of hopeless longing.

Jack knew her answer before she voiced it, because as she sniffed loudly and wiped away her tears, something seemed to die in her eyes.

When Caroline looked back at Margaret, her gaze was firm, though her voice quavered a bit as she said, "I will stay and learn."

"Very well. And you?" She turned her gaze to the other man.

He cleared his throat before answering.

"Kevin, ma'am. I'll stay too."

Margaret looked, finally, at Jack. He shrugged.

"Jack. I'm in."

"So be it."

She looked at Reginald, who nodded and stepped forward. Reaching inside his robe, he withdrew three black rods, about seven inches in length. Each was topped by a crystal of some sort. They looked similar to what Lucius used back at the bridge. Reginald handed a rod to each of them, then stepped to the side. Jack turned his rod over in his hand. Despite its grainy feel, it was not made of wood. Nor was it metal or plastic. Jack couldn't quite put his finger on what the feel of the rod reminded him of. Margaret's voice pulled him away from his musings.

"You each hold a focusing rod. Though the elixir opens the door to the Higher Realms, only the Master can use the energies there without a buffer. The rod fulfills that role and aids in concentration."

She pulled out a rod of her own and held it up for them to see. Her eyes narrowed slightly and the space around her rod seemed to warp. It was as though darkness itself swirled around the crystal at the end of the rod. Then, that darkness was replaced by light and the crystal began to glow. Dimly at first, but with gradually increasing brilliance until it became painful to look at. Then, all at once, the glow stopped, leaving just a purplish afterglow in Jack's retinas.

Margaret spoke again. "Of course, it will take several attempts before you are able achieve even this small feat. If history is any indicator, only one of you will persevere to acquire the skill to truly master the Art and become Enlightened. But even those who do not can still serve the Order. Welcome, students."

With that, she stepped away from the lectern and swept out of the room. As the door closed behind her, Reginald stepped forward.

"I'll show you to your new quarters now. You will have one hour to retrieve any belongings you left in the Visitor's Dormitory and change into appropriate clothing. Then your instruction will begin."

❧ 15 ❧

NEW BEGINNINGS

The next four weeks were among the strangest, and most interesting, Jack had ever experienced.

By the time he finished moving his belongings into his new room, a small, spartan cell on the east side of the Citadel that was only a small step up from the Visitor Dormitory, the tingling in his skin had faded and his vision had returned to normal. He was relieved, because that strange perception was disconcerting. But he was surprised to also feel a bit of disappointment.

In his cell were two sets of white robes like the other Acolytes, except his had a white belt. A note directed him to change into the robe and leave his civilian clothing in the chest at the foot of his cot. He complied, though he felt a bit silly in the outfit.

Mustering back with his new classmates, themselves also wearing new white robes, they all compared notes. Jack was surprised to learn that their experiences had differed from his. To Kevin, the shimmering was grey-purple in color, while Caroline hadn't seen the shimmering at all. Kevin's vision had also returned to normal while moving in, but Caroline retained the enhanced perception. When Reginald joined them, they wasted no time in asking the reason for the differences. He looked un-surprised by the question.

"The elixir affects different people in varying ways. Some perceive the energies differently, some experience the effects for longer than others. The differences do not seem to correlate with a person's ability in the Art. They're just...differences."

The rest of that day was filled with lectures and concentration drills. When Jack got back to his cell in the evening, he was exhausted. As soon as he stepped into the room, his exhaustion turned to annoyance: the chest where he'd deposited his clothing was gone. The next day, he made a furious inquiry of Reginald, who had charge of them still, about his things. The Acolyte looked almost surprised at the question.

"Didn't the Dean make herself clear? You are required to leave *everything* behind to study here." He smiled kindly, then continued. "Don't worry. In a few weeks, you won't even miss them."

The next several days were also blurs of lectures, demonstrations, drills, and examinations. They were not given access to focusing rods again, or given any more of the elixir, for quite some time. Reginald explained they first had to understand how the Art functioned. And they had to know the Order's safety procedures by heart.

The thing Jack was most curious about was the elixir. If it truly was the only way to work the Art, he would need to learn how it was made. That would prove difficult, however.

"The formula for the elixir is known only by the Master and the Highest of the Enlightened," Reginald explained in response to Jack's question. "But I can tell you that it is deadly if not imbued with energies during the distilling process."

Jack frowned. "So how do you have enough?"

"How do *we*, you mean?" He sounded a bit amused as he made the distinction, but regained his serious, instructive tone as he continued. "The Highest take turns, working in pairs for two months at a time, to mix the elixir. Then selected members of the Order assist them in directing the energies to make it safe. They make more than enough."

Whether because he didn't know or because they were too new to be entrusted with any more information, Reginald would say nothing else about the elixir, except to reassure them that as their tolerance for the concoction increased, the initial sickness would become easier to suppress until, eventually, they wouldn't feel it at all.

At the end of the week, when they assembled in their classroom for the morning session, they found flasks and cups on their desks, along with focusing rods. At long last, it appeared it was time to actually learn some magic. Of course, that meant enduring the elixir again. From the trepidation on Caroline and Kevin's faces, it appeared they were looking forward to that part almost as much as Jack was.

It was just as bad as he remembered: it seemed to take forever to get past the nausea and pain. This second time around, Jack saw no evidence that he was developing any tolerance to the foul fluid. Oh well, at least it didn't leave a hangover when it wore off. The training session was good, though. Reginald walked them through the focusing exercises they'd practiced earlier in the week and Jack found he was able to make his crystal glow for a short while. His glow was feeble compared to what Margaret had accomplished that first day, but it was better than what Kevin managed. Caroline was a natural: her crystal emitted a bright, steady glow that outshone both of the guys. Even Reginald was impressed.

They didn't accomplish much beyond that for several

days. Each time, Jack was able to maintain the glow for a bit longer, until by the end of the second week, he could not only sustain the energies, and the glow, for the duration of the elixir's affect, but he could vary its brightness from the dimmest of glimmers to an eye-piercing beacon. He felt a certain sense of accomplishment at that, but Reginald made it clear that they'd barely begun to scratch the surface of the Art.

His time wasn't entirely spent studying, of course. Jack had evenings and the last day of the week free. During those times, he explored the Citadel complex thoroughly. He had the thought to check out the town and surrounding environs as well, so on his first free day, he headed out to the gate.

The guardsman on duty stepped in front of him, his hand raised in a halting gesture.

"Where do you think you're going?" asked the guard.

Jack blinked in surprise.

"Just taking a walk. Getting to know the lay of the land; you understand."

"You got a pass?"

"What is this, third grade? Get out of my way."

The guard frowned and made a gesture toward the guard-house. A moment later, another man, wearing a Lieutenant's gold bars on his collar, walked out. He took in the situation at a glance and, shaking his head with a soft chuckle, stepped over to Jack's side.

"Sorry, buddy. New students aren't allowed outside the Citadel walls without the Dean's permission."

"You're kidding me."

The Lieutenant shook his head, a pitying smile on his face. Jack ground his teeth in annoyance, but thought better of making a scene. Instead, he turned around and sought out the library.

Whatever else the Order might be, Jack had to admit it

was admirable in its efforts to preserve knowledge. Like the monasteries of old, Horbach had ordered his people to find and preserve as many books of learning and art as they could. On one wall in the library, near the entrance to the reading area, was a map that displayed the original home of each book in the Order's care. Virtually every large city in the Gulf Coast and lower midwest states was represented, particularly those cities that housed Universities. From the map alone, Jack estimated the Library housed several tens of thousands of books.

Jack enjoyed reading, but he didn't just go to the Library for books. He also wanted to check in on Simeon. Ortiz's objections not withstanding, Jack felt some responsibility for the lad, considering they took charge of Simeon and brought him here. Ortiz could claim he was projecting or whatever all he wanted, but that didn't change the facts, in Jack's eyes. He was gratified to see the boy settle in well with the library staff and spent as much time as he could, outside of his own studies, with him.

During those visits, it became clear that, before coming there, Simeon had never learned to read. Often Jack came in and found Simeon under the tutelage of one of the library staff or their young assistants, haltingly sounding out words. When he could, Jack helped with the lessons and was impressed at the progress the boy made. In retrospect, it made sense: growing up in the harsh reality of the old world's ruins, reading would be a luxury, and a difficult one to obtain. For that reason alone, Jack would have been glad they'd brought Simeon to the Citadel. But seeing him mesh with other kids his age, watching him laugh and play and slowly lower the shields he'd so obviously put up before, Jack became more and more convinced they'd done the right thing. And that the Order was, in this sense at least, a force for good.

Jack saw Ortiz once or twice in the first week, but not at all in the second. He was not at all surprised to see the security man wearing a Legionnaire's red blouse and marching in formation with a platoon of recruits. As they'd discussed before, it made sense. If Ortiz couldn't gain intel from the Order itself, why not from the Legion? Jack was surprised, however, to learn that new recruit quarters were within the Citadel complex; he would have figured they'd be out with the tents. But Reginald, overhearing him discussing the matter with his classmates before the start of class, explained it was the same concept as with the new students. Just as the Order wanted to control his comings and goings for a time, so did the Legion. All the easier to do that within a walled complex, Jack supposed.

Things changed abruptly at the beginning of the third week.

Reginald walked into the classroom at the usual starting time, but on this occasion he didn't go to the lectern like he normally did, but rather held the door open. A moment later, Margaret swept into the room. Jack was surprised: she hadn't graced them with her presence since the first day.

As she stepped behind the lectern, she gave them each, in turn, a challenging gaze.

"Reginald tells me you have learned a great deal of theory over the last two weeks and proved yourselves able to focus. Prove it to my satisfaction and you may proceed to applications."

For the next three hours, she grilled them mercilessly on the information Reginald had imparted. Her questions delved into the tiniest minutia of every topic, probing the limits of their recall and beyond.

Jack was surprised at how much he actually remembered.

Hyper-dimensional physics was not a topic he ever had any interest in studying, never mind thermodynamics, the precession of the equinoxes, and all the arcane topics that just a few weeks before he would have called the worst of pseudoscience.

That said, he was amazed at Caroline. She remembered every detail, answered each question without hesitation. When the quizzing was complete, even Margaret looked at her with something close to awe.

There was no praise forthcoming, though. They downed a dose of the elixir, then she spent the next hour and a half, until the very last of its effects wore off, pressing them on every concentration and focusing exercise they'd learned. When they finally stopped, Jack found himself covered in sweat and breathing heavily, as though he'd just run five miles. He had no idea simply concentrating could be so strenuous!

Margaret regarded them gravely for a time as they recovered from their exertions. Then, with a small smile, she looked at Reginald and nodded.

"Very impressive, Acolyte Reginald. Well done. You have leave to proceed."

With that, she left the lectern and strode from the room. Reginald watched her depart, then turned back to the class, wearing a smile of accomplishment.

"We'll break for lunch now. This afternoon, we will begin to learn some simple applications of the Art. You should be pleased. This is an important step on your path to enlightenment."

❧ 16 ❧

APPLIED ART

Jack surprised himself with how eager he was to get back for the afternoon's class. He didn't register exactly what lunch was that day, he ate so quickly. Kevin did as well, but Caroline ate at her normal stately pace, seemingly no more eager than normal for the afternoon's activities. She beat them back to the classroom, however, so Jack supposed maybe that was just an act.

Reginald returned a few minutes after they did. Seeing them all seated and ready, he took his place behind the lectern and spoke without preamble. "The simplest manifestation of the higher energies for a person of enlightenment is usually Force."

Producing his focusing rod, he pointed at a small cup on the lectern in front of himself. His brow scrunched for a heartbeat and the crystal on the end of his rod lit up. Three small marbles lifted from the cup and floated across the room to them, one landing on each of their desks.

Jack had seen the Art used a time or two; Lucius' display at the river sprang to mind. All the same, Jack found his jaw dropping as the marbles moved through the air. He knew without looking that his classmates were similarly impressed.

Reginald looked at them and spoke again. "Your task will not be as complex as what I just did. All you have to do is direct the energies into Force and move the marble across your desk."

That didn't sound so hard. Simple, even.

After downing another dose of the elixir, and enduring the requisite nausea and pain, Jack hefted his focusing rod. But he quickly learned that applying Force was far from simple. He tried, and failed miserably, to make anything happen. He tried again. And again. Still nothing except sweat, which began beading on his brow. Irritated, Jack looked over at Caroline and Kevin and saw they were having similar difficulties.

Seeing their lack of progress after what felt to Jack like an hour, though in fact it was only a few minutes, Reginald offered more guidance. "You have to focus on the marble. Direct your will to the spot you wish to push on," he said. "Just like hitting a pool ball with the cue."

That was easier to understand. But it was still easier said than done. Jack found, after a half hour or so, that he could make the marble wobble. But then, just like that, the crystal on his focusing rod would stop glowing and he would no longer feel the energy flow. Baffled, he tried again and the same thing happened. Looking to his fellow students, Jack could see they had the same problem, except their marbles trembled more than his had.

Seeing the confusion on their faces, Reginald chuckled softly and spoke up.

"Don't lose focus. You have to maintain focus through the rod *and* direct your will to the marble at the same time. Have you ever wanted to learn how to juggle?"

Kevin groaned. Jack felt like joining him, but instead

returned to work. By the end of the day, he was once again covered in sweat, but the marble stubbornly refused to budge.

Things were better the next day. By the afternoon, all of them were able to move their respective marbles a few inches before losing it. Reginald expressed pleasure at their progress, but Jack, at least, didn't see what there was to praise. There was never a thought of quitting, though. The morning of the next day ended with them all moving the marbles around with at least a modicum of ease.

They returned from lunch to find the marbles gone and small scraps of paper lying on their desks. Reginald, as usual standing behind the lectern, greeted them as he always did, then produced a paper of his own as well as his focusing rod.

"The next manifestation is Heat. Your goal is to set your piece of paper on fire."

"How does that work?" Kevin asked, voicing Jack's own thoughts.

"It's almost like using Force, but different," Reginald replied, causing Jack to snort softly.

That cleared things right up, thanks, kid, Jack didn't say.

Reginald must have heard the snort, because he looked at Jack askance for a moment before continuing. "Instead of focusing your will at the paper, try to envision the essence of warmth flowing into it." Reginald paused, then added, a bit lamely, "It takes a bit of practice."

That was an understatement. Jack found the process of somehow conjuring the feeling of increasing temperature and forcing it onto the paper to be much more difficult than applying Force had been. He had no trouble imagining how it felt to get hotter. The rest...it just didn't seem to work for him. Kevin, on the other hand, had his paper ablaze by the end of the day.

Sleep was a long time coming that night, as Jack's frustration kept him tossing and turning. He determined to do better the next morning.

Caroline managed to get her paper lit just before lunch the next day. However, the best Jack could do was to cause a corner of the page to smolder. He went to lunch even more frustrated and full of doubts. The short break seemed to work wonders, though, because towards the end of class that afternoon, he finally managed to create a small flame.

The next morning, a small metal bowl filled with tinder was waiting on each of their desks. As he sat down, Jack smirked slightly. It couldn't be that much more difficult to set this alight than the paper, after all. However, he never got the chance to try. Reginald arrived and ordered them to down their doses of elixir. By the time Jack recovered from the initial reaction to the brew, the tinder was burning in his bowl already. Blinking in confusion, he looked around and saw that Caroline's and Kevin's tinder was burning also.

"Draw the Heat away and put the fires out. That is your task for the morning," Reginald said. He patted a bucket on the lectern, which Jack could see was filled with more tinder.

As though the universe was trying to reassure Jack that he wasn't a complete dunce at the Art, he found putting the fire out to be much simpler than starting it. Maybe it was because of his practice the previous days, but envisioning the heat flowing away from the fire felt a whole lot more natural. When he thought about it, though, it made sense; heat naturally flows from hot areas to cold areas, after all. By late morning, Jack had extinguished half a dozen fires.

Reginald nodded in approval as the last of the fires went out on their desks and sent them off to lunch. They returned after an hour to find the room lit up like noon on a sunny day, quite a bit brighter than glow crystals usually achieved. Curious, Jack stepped through the door and found his gaze immediately drawn to the lectern. Where Reginald usually stood was instead a column of light, glowing so brightly it was impossible to look at without shielding his eyes. Kevin cried out in surprise, near panic in his voice, and they all backed away hurriedly.

Then, just like that, the light went out, revealing Reginald standing behind the lectern and wearing a smile of mischief.

"Let there be Light," he quipped, gesturing for them to take their seats.

Jack discovered an immediate affinity for the process of creating Light. He had little illusionary stars weaving around his desk within an hour. It took Kevin and Caroline the rest of the day. He found it interesting how they each found different things to be easy or hard, but again that made sense when he thought about it.

They broke for the day shortly after that. Jack spent a much more comfortable night than he had in the previous few. Two days of good achievement lifted his earlier ill feelings. He slept like a baby.

The next day contained more than just good progress: it was more fun than Jack had experienced since coming to the Citadel. Reginald greeted them with a blowing wind that emerged seemingly from nowhere and left their teeth chattering; the rooms in the Citadel were not particularly warm to begin with and the wind certainly didn't help matters. But his explanation of how to manipulate the energies to create a small Wind soon had them all blowing little gusts. By the end of the day, Jack and his peers had enough control that they were able to blow papers off desks and goose each other.

The following day, Saturday, they moved on to Water, and frustration returned. Everyone was stumped: how do you envision wetness, and then focus that feeling in such a way as to condense moisture from the air? Despite his explanation of the process, Reginald was of little help.

Finally, Caroline managed to create a small drizzle,

earning praise from Reginald and annoyed looks from both Jack and Kevin. Her explanation of how she managed it made Reginald blink in surprise: it was simple, concise, and made more sense than anything he had said. With her help, Jack and Kevin soon made their own small showers, though they were tiny compared to what she had achieved.

Sunday was free, as usual. Jack spent most of the day in the Library with Simeon, helping with his reading lessons and generally enjoying the lad's company. It was a good day. Jack managed to not think about his problems, the mission, or really anything much of import at all. As he lay down that night, it crossed his mind that he was becoming comfortable in this place, a thought he found disturbing. Sleep was a long time coming.

Monday morning, Reginald came in a few minutes late carrying a satchel that clinked as he walked. He nodded familiarly to Jack and the others, then dropped the satchel onto the lectern with a soft thud.

"If you are fully admitted as Acolytes, you will be required to work at various tasks here in the Citadel and out with the Legion," he said. "The skills you learned last week are the foundations for some of the tasks you will be assigned."

With that, he reached into the satchel and pulled out a small object. "You've all used glow crystals," he said, "and you have seen Acolytes recharging them. Today, you will learn how to do this yourselves."

He then passed out crystals, three each to Jack and his peers. "The process is fairly simple," Reginald said. "You all know that lightning is produced by air, water, and heat in a storm. In the same way, the energies of Wind, Heat, and Water will recharge the crystal."

Jack blinked. "Not all at the same time," he stated more than asked.

Reginald's cheerful nod caused a sinking feeling in the pit

of Jack's stomach. "Of course all at once. It's really not that hard, once you get the hang of it."

That began three days of intense labor – Jack never would have thought sitting at a desk was intense labor, but each day left him sweaty and exhausted from the effort – and frustration.

It took all of Monday to be able to grasp how to go about starting the process. He had already learned to concentrate on both the focusing rod and the energy he was trying to direct. That had been hard enough. But trying to then divide his thoughts between first one and then two more energy streams was beyond him. Jack took some measure of comfort that Kevin and Caroline had similar problems, at least at first. But as was becoming her trend, Caroline got the hang of it first.

By Tuesday morning, she had managed to create a warm breeze that flowed through the room quite comfortingly. Jack, on the other hand, was still having problems, and it took him until the end of the day to recreate a small replica of her feat.

It turned out that Reginald was right, though. Wednesday, when they worked on adding a third energy, Jack had faster success. Once he began to get the knack of dividing his focus, adding another division, while more difficult, wasn't more difficult by the same magnitude as adding the first.

To his amazement, by the end of the day, Jack found himself holding a glow crystal with his fingertips on each of its five touch points and sending the energies into it as Reginald directed. Slowly, almost imperceptibly at first, a glimmer of light became visible in the center of the crystal. It gradually grew in luminosity and size until it seemed to Jack that he was holding a tiny star in his hand.

"Enough," Reginald said, and Jack let his focus slip.

The crystal stopped glowing. Had it worked?

"Touch the points that select high illumination."

Jack did as Reginald commanded and found himself grinning when the crystal began to glow just like the ones in sconces on the walls.

"Well done," Reginald said.

Thursday and on into Friday, they worked with Force again, no doubt because Acolytes were expected to help move heavy objects around. Or at least that's how it seemed to Jack, because the sole focus of their exercises during those two days was moving gradually larger and larger things.

Jack noticed an interesting trend. He hadn't noticed the effort it took to move that little marble around. But by Friday morning, when Reginald had them hefting first large books and then their desks, Jack began to feel the effort in his muscles, almost as though he had been physically lifting the objects himself.

"You are lifting them yourself," Reginald said, in reply to Jack's observation. "Energy is not free. It can't just be created. We make use of the Universe's energy, but to compensate for what we use, some of our own is expended." He grinned. "You all will likely be sore tomorrow."

Margaret checked in with them again on Friday afternoon and watched for a time while Reginald continued to put them through their paces. As they performed each technique they'd learned over the last two weeks, Jack felt a sense of accomplishment and no small amount of pride. They'd learned a lot! Whether she was impressed or not was unclear as Margaret left. But shortly before the end of the day, she returned and spoke briefly with Reginald. He nodded his head, an expression of eager pride on his face, and she departed again. Turning to the students, Reginald cleared his throat.

"Well done," he said. "The Dean is pleased with your progress and is recommending to the Master that you be fully inducted into the Order as Acolytes. You will meet with him tomorrow morning, at the usual starting time."

Kevin and Caroline wore beaming smiles as they departed for the day, their eyes alight with pride of accomplishment. To his surprise, Jack realized that he wore the same.

17

ACOLYTE

J ack woke up and groaned. He ached all over, like he'd been working out all day the day before. Or like he had a really bad case of the flu. More like the flu. He sat up reluctantly and cradled his head in his hands for a long moment. Then, sniffing, he stood and dressed.

Looking through the narrow window in his cell wall, it looked like early morning twilight was just setting in. Good, he hadn't overslept. Then he blinked in surprise. It was snowing! At least an inch of snow had already accumulated and it was still coming down; highly unusual for this part of the country, from what he could recall.

He finished his morning routine and got down to the classroom, thankful that he wouldn't have to trudge through the snow to get there, considering his cold weather gear had been confiscated with the rest of his clothing.

He made it with plenty of time to spare. In fact, he was the first to arrive. So he settled down at his desk to wait.

It didn't take long. Caroline and Kevin arrived within moments of each other, followed a few minutes later by Reginald. The Acolyte nodded in greeting with a familiar smile on his lips.

"Good. We're all here. Follow me, please."

He led them up to the second level, then down the corridor and up the spiral staircase to Horbach's audience chamber. It was a month since Jack last came in here, but it felt like longer. It had been a busy few weeks. The chairs were missing this time. Reginald had them line up before the lectern, then joined them, standing at the head of their line like a platoon leader awaiting inspection.

Just as before, even down to the book, the same book as before Jack noted, again held clutched to his chest, Horbach appeared seemingly out of nowhere. And Jack thought that was just a trick to impress the rubes. He half-smiled at the thought. Then Horbach set the book down on the lectern and began to speak and Jack wiped the smile from his face.

"Students," Horbach intoned, "the Dean has briefed me on your progress. You have come to an important juncture. You have proven yourselves able to withstand the most simple Truths of the Order." Jack could hear the capital T in the way Horbach said truths. "You have mastered basic skills so that you can perform useful work. And so we are ready to welcome you into the first circle of enlightenment. You are not now the same people you were when you came here. And so you will be known among us by new names."

Horbach drew a deep breath, his gaze, unblinking, skimming over them for a few moments. With that, he left the podium and approached the line. Stopping in front of Reginald, he returned the Acolyte's respectful, almost reverent, bow with a shallow inclination of his head. Then he moved a pace to his right to stand in front of Caroline. He studied her intently for a long minute, his breaths coming in long, slow inhalations as though he was breathing in her essence. Finally, he spoke again.

"Your beauty is only matched by your loneliness, your sense of loss. You will be called Selene, after the moon Goddess."

Kevin next received Horbach's appraisal.

"You will be called Josephus, after the ancient chronicler of history."

Finally, Jack fell under his scrutiny. Horbach's eyes, unblinking, locked onto his and seemed to burn into him. Jack had to repress a sudden impulse to step back and fall to his knees. It took tremendous effort to meet that gaze and to return it in kind. Horbach smiled faintly and gave the slightest of nods, then spoke.

"You have a warrior's spirit. Unyielding and true. Your name will be Lysander, after the general of Sparta, who defeated the Athenians in all their might."

Turning away from them, Horbach walked back up the steps of the dais to the lectern. There he paused briefly, then turned to face them. He raised his left hand, palm facing them, and slowly drew the index finger of his right hand across the palm. As the finger passed, the flesh of his palm opened, and a slow trickle of blood began to run.

Jack heard his fellow inductees gasp and realized he had done the same.

The blood from Horbach's palm dripped off his hand and fell, but it never reached the floor. Instead, it floated in the air and, dividing into three streams, flew across the intervening distance to the three of them. Again Jack felt the urge to move away, but he felt a...force...preventing him. Revulsion filled him, followed by a macabre fascination, as the blood stream struck his belt and seemed to fuse with its material. Slowly the white belt turned pinkish, then over the span of what seemed minutes, though it really probably only took a few seconds, it became a red crimson, the same color of Reginald's. At that moment, Horbach moved his index finger back across his palm, in the opposite direction as before. The gash in his flesh closed in time with his finger's movement, stopping the flow of blood.

Glancing down the row of inductees, Jack saw the same shock on their faces that he supposed was visible on his. Caroline, Selene rather, almost looked sick. Then Horbach spoke again, drawing Jack's attention back to himself.

"The Order is a family, my friends. I think of all members of the Order as my children. Though you do not share my genes, you can share my blood." He smiled and Jack felt a shiver go down his spine. "You are bound to us, to *me*, now."

It stopped snowing that afternoon, after depositing another inch. Jack was free the rest of the day.

In the early evening, Jack encountered Ortiz again. He was walking across the courtyard toward the Legion's recruit barracks. Ortiz, seeing Jack, veered over to meet him. They clasped hands quickly, then Jack followed him toward the barracks.

"How's it been going, Simmons?" Ortiz inquired.

"Not too badly. The Master made us full Acolytes this morning."

Ortiz eyed him sidelong as they stepped inside. Jack had never been into the recruit barracks before. The first floor consisted of an entryway, where a Legionnaire Recruit stood watch behind a desk, and a long corridor with a dozen or so pairs of doors on either side and a stairwell at the far end. As with everywhere else in the Citadel, glow crystals provided illumination at regular intervals.

The Legionnaire on duty frowned at Ortiz as he and Jack walked past.

"You know the rules on visitors, Ortiz," he said in a whiney tone.

Ortiz grimaced, but Jack stepped in quickly, speaking in a stern tone.

"The last I checked, Recruit, Acolytes of the Order do not require permission to move about from the likes of you."

The Recruit swallowed, paling visibly.

"My apologies. I..." he swallowed again. "I didn't see you. Sorry."

They left him behind and entered the corridor. Ortiz's room was the third one down on the left. Stepping inside, Jack was surprised. The room could almost be a transplanted into a cheap motel from back before the Troubles. A small bed, nightstand, dresser, and a hanging locker. Lighting from several glow crystals. A small privacy screen beyond which, Jack assumed, lay the chamber pot. It was the lap of luxury compared to his little Acolyte's cell.

"Wow, they roll out the red carpet for recruits, huh?"

Ortiz sniffed with derision.

"If they didn't, candy-asses like Holbert out there wouldn't last a week."

"I take it you're not impressed."

"Oh, the Legion is a first class unit, no doubt about that. They're a little lax in their basic training, though. Coddle people too much."

Jack chuckled. He seriously doubted the recruits were actually coddled, though Ortiz seemed to have a...different...perspective on those sorts of things, he'd noticed.

"Where have you been? I haven't seen you in a couple weeks," Jack asked.

"They had us out in the field: practicing maneuvers, learning tactics, that sort of thing. Just another week or so before we get shipped out to our units."

"That could be awkward."

"Don't worry. I made a bit of an impression with the unarmed combat instructor."

Jack raised an eyebrow at him.

"What?"

"An impression?"

"He's almost healed. Anyway, they've asked me to remain here to train other recruits."

"Convenient."

Ortiz looked at him askance.

"You're not going native on me, are you?"

Jack blinked in surprise.

"What? No. No way."

"Ok. But you seem to falling into the mold well. Maybe too well. Watch yourself."

"Thanks for the concern, but I'll be fine."

Ortiz held his gaze for a long moment, then shrugged.

"Fair enough. Do you have enough to take back? We can probably still make the conference if we leave in the next week or so."

Jack frowned. He felt somewhat torn. On the one hand, he certainly had learned enough to scare the bejesus out of Grymanski and his boys, he had no doubt. But... Maybe he *was* starting to go native. Jack found he really wanted to keep learning. Each new discovery, each new trick, promised more exciting things to come. Besides, if he left before he knew how to really apply what he'd learned, what good would it do? Sure, he could describe what the Enlightened were capable of, but if he couldn't counter it? It would be a waste of time.

Finally, Jack shook his head.

"I need more time."

With a sigh, Ortiz nodded.

"Ok, but time's starting to run out. Step things up, if you can."

The next day was free as well. So, as usual, Jack went to the Library in the morning. Also as usual, he found Simeon bent over a picture book along with one of his new friends. This time, it was Kelly. Twelve years old, she was gangly and awkward in that pre-pubescent girl kind of way. But it was obvious she was going to grow up to be a stunner. Jack wasn't surprised at all that Simeon seemed to get more lessons from her than the others.

Settling down on the bench across the reading table from them, Jack returned Simeon's welcoming smile with one of his own.

"How's the reading going?"

Kelly spoke before Simeon. "Really good, Mr. Simmons. He just read this whole page himself."

"Wow, that's pretty impressive."

And it was, considering that just a month ago, Simeon couldn't tell one letter from another. Jack reached out and ruffled the boy's hair, earning himself a look of reproach. Simeon opened his mouth to speak, but stopped, his eyes moving from Jack's face to peer past his shoulder.

"Lysander."

Jack recognized Reginald's voice. Out of habit, Jack stood at once and turned around. He found himself making a quick bow before he remembered that he was an Acolyte too now. His lapse wasn't lost on Reginald. His eyes flashed with amusement as he spoke.

"I wanted to congratulate you personally. You've done very well to this point."

Reginald offered his hand and Jack took it. The younger man's grip was surprisingly limp. Jack would have figured, as assertive as he was in the role of instructor, that he would show more confidence in his handshake.

"Thanks."

"I mean it. I really appreciate the hard work you and your classmates put in."

Reginald paused, glancing toward the two kids at the other side of the table, almost as though he was unsure whether to continue with them around. Kelly picked up on his hesitation and stood, ushering Simeon to another table a short distance away. Reginald looked surprised, then grateful, as he watched them go. When they were out of earshot, he looked back at Jack and continued.

"Your class' indoctrination was my final test. Margaret informed me this morning that tonight I am to be raised to Enlightened."

Jack wasn't sure how he felt about that, truth be told. Every Enlightened he'd met to date had a rather strange air about them, aloof and, in some cases, slightly contemptuous. Maybe it was just an acknowledgment of their superior rank and not wanting to lower themselves to the level of the help. But whatever it was, Reginald's friendly and overall cheerful demeanor didn't seem to fit in that mold. Still, who was he to deflate the guy?

"That's great, Reginald."

He nodded with enthusiasm.

"I've been dreaming of this for years. I owe you and your fellows a debt. If you hadn't done so well..."

Jack waved a hand, dismissing the thought.

"You're advancing on your own merit, not ours. Congratulations."

Reginald shrugged.

"I'd better go prepare for the ceremony. They're coming for me soon."

As he turned to walk away, Jack inquired, "What does the ceremony entail?"

Reginald looked back over his shoulder and smirked.

"Keep working hard and maybe you'll find out some day."

As he watched the soon-to-be Enlightened walk away, Jack pursed his lips in thought. This wasn't the first time he'd heard of the mysterious rite that turned an Acolyte into an Enlightened. He felt an overwhelming surge of curiosity. What went on in that ceremony?

Simeon's voice interrupted him in his thinking.

"Mr. Simmons, did you get promoted?"

Jack turned back toward the boy, smiling broadly.

"I did, just yesterday."

Simeon beamed with pleasure and offered him congratulations. Kelly joined in, also suitably pleased with his accomplishment. From the corner of his eye, Jack noted Reginald stepping through the Library's exit. Maybe if he could find out what this ceremony was about, he would finally have something tangible to bring back to Forest Hills. Time to take a risk. Tonight.

❧ 18 ❧

THE PRICE OF
ENLIGHTENMENT

They came for Reginald at ten o'clock. Four of the Enlightened, walking two by two, escorted him from his quarters with hardly a word. From his hiding place, Jack watched the small procession pass, then quietly followed.

Luckily for him, the Citadel corridors were dark at night. The glow crystals were turned to their dim setting or extinguished altogether; no sense draining their charge when most were asleep. All the same, his white Acolyte robes would stand out, so he was careful to stay back from the quintet.

He paused at each corner, looking around it until they turned the next, then hurried to not miss them at the next one. He almost lost them on three occasions: only the echoes of their footsteps clued him in to which way they'd turned when he moved too slowly to see them.

In reality, he needn't have bothered with stealth. From what he could tell, they never looked back, or even side-to-side. But discretion was the better part of valor, or so they said, so he kept to his cautious approach.

He followed them out of the Acolytes' quarters, upstairs

past the laboratories, and then down a long hall that looked similar to the hallway to Horbach's audience chamber. Except there were no doors save one, at the very end. By the time Jack reached the door, they'd already passed through. He opened it a crack and beheld a narrow set of winding stairs, leading downward.

What was it with the Order and winding staircases?, he wondered for a moment. Then, with a deep breath, he slipped through the door and started down.

The stairwell was lit at regular intervals by a dim glow crystal. The stairs themselves were carved stone, just wide enough that two people could walk shoulder-to-shoulder. Unless one of the people was particularly broad. The walls were devoid of decoration save for a small handrail that was carved into the outside wall of the spiral.

The stairs descended for at least a hundred feet, though it was hard to tell without a reference. Regardless, when he stepped out onto the landing at the bottom, Jack knew he was well below the Citadel proper, deep within the earth of the Citadel's hill.

The landing was a small, round chamber that had clearly been carved out of bedrock. The walls, though smooth, were unadorned. The floor was plain stone as well, except at the center of the room, where tile inlays formed the image of a brightly shining star. A single, straight staircase led out of the room, opposite the spiral stairs Jack had just descended.

Jack moved slowly down the new stairs. They descended about fifteen feet, leading to a good-sized balcony overlooking a large chamber. Three columns, connected by a waist-high railing, prevented someone from falling off the balcony to the floor below. On the far side of the balcony from the stairs he'd just taken, Jack saw yet another staircase, leading down to the chamber proper.

Jack darted back inside the entrance stairs as soon as he

looked out into the chamber. It was full of Enlightened: probably two hundred of them. After a moment passed and no one shouted the alarm, Jack crept back out onto the balcony and crouched down behind one of the columns. Peeking around the column, he beheld something unforgettable.

The chamber was probably fifty yards long and twenty wide. The balcony where Jack crouched was about twenty feet above the chamber floor. Stone benches lined the floor, facing a raised dais which took up the entire width of the chamber at the far end.

The benches were only partly filled by the Enlightened present. Jack hoped the chamber had been built with extra capacity, as opposed to the alternative. A single broad walkway led down the center of the chamber, between the rows of benches, toward the dais. Reginald, with his escort, was walking down the path toward the dais.

Waiting on the dais next to a smoking brazier, clutching his book to his chest as he had when Jack first saw him, was Horbach. It was impossible to mistake him for someone else, even at that distance. The Master wore his usual red robes and had a look of almost exultant expectation on his face as Reginald approached.

The young Acolyte and his escort reached the bottom of the stairs leading up to the dais and stopped. A sound like that of a large gong rang throughout the chamber.

"My brothers, tonight we welcome a new soul into Enlightenment," intoned Horbach. He didn't look like he was shouting; indeed, he could have been whispering for the amount of effort he showed. But his words carried easily throughout the chamber. A trick of the Art, no doubt. Then again, as he looked around the chamber more, Jack supposed it could have just been very good acoustics.

Horbach continued, "Reginald, come forward." He gestured for the young man to come stand beside him.

Reginald complied without hesitation, leaving his Enlightened escort at the base of the dais.

Horbach didn't look at him, but kept his attention on the escort. He spoke again.

"Who will vouch for this man's worthiness: his courage, his knowledge, his judgment, his loyalty, and his skill?"

"I will," said one of Reginald's escorts, followed in turn by each of them.

Horbach nodded his head slowly, then turned his gaze onto Reginald.

"Reginald, you have proven yourself to the satisfaction of these Enlightened individuals. The final test is upon you. Do you feel ready to move onward?"

Reginald inclined his head, replying "I am ready, Master."

A second gong-tone echoed through the chamber as soon as he spoke. Horbach looked at him gravely for a long moment, then made a quick gesture with his left hand.

"So be it."

Jack hadn't noticed the doorways on either end of the dais until Horbach gestured and two Enlightened walked through one of them, dragging a man between them.

The man was lean, with toned muscles indicating a familiarity with physical exertion. His clothing was ragged and his hair and beard were both long, disheveled. He didn't struggle as they dragged him to the center of the dais and pressed him up against the wall. There the Enlightened shackled his wrists and ankles, so that he stood spread-eagle, facing the crowd. He looked as though he'd been beaten recently; he had several visible bruises and a black eye.

"From time immemorable, sacrifice has always marked the path to enlightenment and righteousness," Horbach said.

Seemingly from nowhere, a ceramic goblet and a serrated knife appeared in Horbach's hands. Turning to Reginald, he held out both objects and the young initiate took them.

Reginald approached the prisoner and looked at him for a moment. Then, with a quick flash of the knife, he cut the prisoner's right wrist. The man cried out in pain and blood began to flow freely out of the cut, spurting in time with the man's heartbeat.

Reginald held the goblet beneath the blood stream long enough to fill it, then turned toward the crowd. He raised the goblet in front of his face and spoke in an awed tone.

"The Blood, that we may be pure."

As his words echoed through the chamber, a gong sounded again. Reginald brought the goblet to his lips. Jack felt his eyes widening in amazed horror as Reginald swallowed several times. Then the young man raised the goblet high and upended it, spilling the contents over his head. The blood ran down the cowls of his robes then down his shoulders and abdomen, leaving streaks of red on the white material.

When the goblet was empty, Reginald handed it to Horbach, then turned back toward the unfortunate prisoner. Looking pale already from blood loss, the man nevertheless appeared terrified as Reginald approached. He managed a hoarse, but strong cry.

"No. No, please. *Please!*"

His cry turned to a long, drawn out scream of horrified agony as Reginald bent over and being sawing at his left thigh with the knife. More blood ran and the man jerked and squirmed, but he was tightly confined and could hardly move against the shackles. His screams continued as Reginald turned away from him to face the crowd. In his hand, he held a fist-sized, quivering hunk of flesh from the man's thigh, which he held up for all to see.

"The flesh, that we may know strength."

Jack's stomach heaved and he tasted bile. It was all he could do not to be sick as the gong rang again and Reginald bit into the flesh. The initiate chewed quickly, then swallowed. He continued until he'd eaten the entire piece.

This had to be a dream. A nightmare. There was no way what Jack was seeing could be real.

Reginald turned back to the man, whose screams had reduced to weak, but still heart-wrenching, whimpers. He was almost bled out. Reginald leapt toward him, plunging the knife into the man's chest to the hilt.

The prisoner let out a long, gurgling cry that gradually died as he did. His head lolled forward limply.

Reginald sawed further with the knife, until he'd made a gaping hole in the man's chest. Then, reaching into the hole, Reginald sawed a bit more. When he returned to face the crowd, he held the man's heart in his upheld hand.

"The heart, that compassion and mercy may guide us."

The gong seemed bitterly ironic to Jack as Reginald set the heart onto the brazier. As the muscle sizzled and blackened, then began to burn, Reginald bent forward and inhaled the wafting smoke in long, even breaths. When he backed away, his face and head were black with ash.

Horbach stepped next to Reginald. The initiate turned to face him, his head lowered in supplication.

"You came to us yearning for knowledge and became an Acolyte of the Order," Horbach intoned. As he spoke, the blood and ash on Reginald's robes began to swirl. "You have proven true and have now discovered your true self." The swirling filth covered his entire garment now, which seemed to writhe while it hung on Reginald's frame. "You are Reginald, Enlightened of the Order. We bid you welcome."

As Horbach's final word left his mouth, the gong sounded once again and the fabric of Reginald's robe seemed to stiffen, almost as though it was about to fly off his body. Then the swirling ceased and the garment stilled. Where once it was the white of an Acolyte's robe, now it was black as midnight.

Horbach placed his hand on the new Enlightened's shoulder and turned him to face the crowd. They erupted in applause, shouting his name in one voice. Horbach smiled, almost a grin of triumph as he surveyed the masses before him.

Then Horbach's eyes flickered to the balcony and his smile turned to a near smirk. For a moment, it seemed that his eyes met, and lingered upon, Jack's.

Jack fell onto his backside, his horror at what he'd seen turning to mortal terror as the certainty of being discovered washed over him. Frantically, he pushed backwards with his heels and the palms of his hands and managed to slide back into the stairwell. There, he got to his feet and fled up the stairs as quickly as if hell itself were chasing him.

He suspected it actually was.

Jack pounded on the door to Ortiz's quarters. It was well past midnight, but when the security man opened the door, he was alert and apparently at the top of his game, if not fully clothed.

Not waiting for a greeting, Jack pushed his way inside. His heart pounding, he ran both hands through his hair and fidgeted in the middle of the room. The reality of what he'd witnessed was impossible to accept on one level, but at the same time, he could not deny it. He felt sick, exhilarated, terrified, determined. All at the same time.

Ortiz closed the door quickly and turned to regard Jack. Concern etched his face as he clasped Jack's shoulder.

"What's wrong, Simmons?"

Jack blinked in surprise at Ortiz's concern. Drawing a deep breath, he got a hold of himself as best he could, then spoke.

"I can't do this anymore. We need to get out of here. Now."

"Why? What's happened?"

"You won't believe it," Jack replied, then went on to describe what he'd witnessed in the initiation ceremony. Ortiz's brow furrowed, his expression becoming even more concerned, and troubled, as Jack reached the end of his tale. He was silent for a long moment before responding.

"If we don't get details on how Horbach's men work their magic, our time here has been wasted. Can you recreate their tricks yet?"

Jack shook his head, a sinking feeling in the pit of his stomach. He saw where Ortiz was going.

"Then you have to continue. You know what's at stake."

Jack nodded, reluctantly. Suddenly, a heavy thumping echoed through Ortiz's room. Someone was knocking on the door. The two men shared a guarded look. Ortiz quickly tossed Jack a knife, which he tucked into a fold in his robe. Then, after a heartbeat to collect himself, Ortiz pulled the door open.

Reginald stood in the doorway, dressed in his new black robes. He had a slightly haunted look in his eyes, but aside from that, his expression was serene. His gazed moved from Ortiz to Jack and back quickly.

"Legionnaire Ortiz," he said, his tone dismissive until he refocused on Jack. "Lysander. The Master would have a word with you. Now."

Reginald's tone made it clear he would brook no argument. But Jack knew it would be foolish to refuse, regardless. He inclined his head in a gesture of respect.

"Of course. Good evening, Juan."

Stepping past the security man to follow Reginald, Jack heard Ortiz say "Semper Fi" in a barely audible whisper.

The door closed behind Jack and Ortiz immediately began packing. That summons was bad news. Very bad news. Jack was right: it was time to leave. Good thing he'd managed to retrieve Jack's clothing from the rubbish heap. Assuming Jack made it back, he'd probably need them.

Ortiz just hoped they weren't already trapped beyond hope of escape.

❧ 19 ❧

BITTERNESS AND BETRAYAL

J ack followed Reginald into the bowels of the Citadel, his heart in his throat. Horbach had seen him at the ceremony. Jack had hoped he was mistaken, but why else would he be summoned this way? He unconsciously fingered the hilt of Ortiz's knife. It would probably be useless against the likes of Horbach and Reginald, but Jack still felt better having it.

Reginald led him past the library to a stairwell Jack had never taken before. It led up in a spiral for what seemed an eternity, finally ending at a thick mahogany door that was carved with a re-creation of the man's finger touching a star from the mural in Horbach's audience chamber.

Reginald opened the door and led Jack into a goodly-sized room. Circular, it was sparsely furnished: a large desk along the far wall, two chairs to Jack's left, a fireplace to his right, and a pair of bookshelves flanking the desk. A fire burned in the fireplace, but there were no logs. Behind the desk was a large oval window, allowing a view of the Citadel's dome dozens of feet below. The room must have been atop the Citadel's tower.

Horbach was seated behind the desk, writing in the book he always carried with him. When Jack and Reginald walked in, he looked up. For a moment, the fire reflected off the lenses of his spectacles, making it look as though his eyes were aflame themselves. Then he rose, smiling in welcome.

"Greetings, Lysander," Horbach said, his tone congenial, if not exactly warm. "You've been getting ahead of yourself, haven't you?"

Jack didn't reply. What was there to say?

Horbach chuckled softly and walked around the desk to stand in front of Jack.

"It is understandable, I suppose. I recall well the curiosity of a young student. Wanting to know more. Always more." His eyes went distant for a moment, as though viewing a long lost memory. Then they regained their sharpness, focusing in on Jack's face with a burning intensity. "But some things are not meant for a beginner's eyes, Lysander. You were not ready. Not prepared to comprehend the mysteries of the rite you intruded upon. So I ask you once: why?"

"As you say, Master, I wanted to learn."

"Do not take me for a fool, Lysander. Your progress has been more than acceptable, but others in the past have shown much greater talent and motivation than you, yet they did not dare do what you have done."

Horbach leaned forward, his red eyes seeming to stare through him into his very soul. "Who sent you?"

Jack swallowed. "Master, I don't understand what you mean."

Horbach sniffed, but said nothing. Instead, he looked aside to Reginald, who spoke up promptly.

"I found him conferring with the man who arrived here in his company, Legionnaire Recruit Ortiz, in the Legionnaire's quarters."

"I see." Horbach looked back at Jack. "So, a team effort.

You would steal my secrets, no? You would undermine the new era of mankind. An era of peace and plenty for all. And you come with...a team of two?" He sounded amused at the prospect. "Or are there others as well, Lysander?"

The gig was up. They knew he was a plant. Jack decided to lay it all out.

"Peace? Is that what you call the slaughter at Farrah's Crossing?"

Horbach blinked, his head cocking to the side like a bird for a moment. His lips moved, sounding out the town's name silently, then an expression of recognition appeared on his face and he nodded.

"I recall the incident you refer to. The township in question was offered generous terms to enter into the Order's service and receive my protection, but they refused. They went so far as to assault my emissaries." Horbach shook his head slowly. "Such a thing cannot be allowed. Peace and enlightenment can only be had through harmony and obedience, Lysander. Outright hostility and rebellion is contrary to mankind's best interest and so must be put down."

"...and the people who rebelled eaten."

Horbach pursed his lips. "My son, as I told you when you first arrived, the ancients knew many truths that we forgot, or ignored, in the old world. Among those truths was the passage of a warrior's strength, through his flesh, to the one who vanquished him." He looked back at Reginald. "Tell me true, Reginald. When you tasted his flesh and felt his soul become a part of yours, did you not truly come to understand the man who was sacrificed this night? Did you not feel his strength flow into your veins and raise you to a new height of power and awareness?"

Reginald hesitated for a heartbeat and Jack could hear him swallow before answering. "I did, Master." Whatever his hesitation, Reginald's tone was strong and resolute. Either he truly bought the party line or he was a very good actor.

Horbach's eyes returned to Jack's. He was silent for a time, studying Jack intently. Whatever he saw, it displeased him, as he pursed his lips and shook his head. His expression became one of sadness and disappointment.

"I see that you do not understand, Lysander. And will not allow yourself to. A waste." Sighing, he took a half step back away from Jack. "Reginald will take you below now. I promise you, Lysander, before you expire, you will tell me everything I wish to know about those who sent you. It will be far less unpleasant for you if you decide to speak sooner, rather than later."

He nodded to Reginald and turned away. Jack heard Reginald begin to move and knew if he allowed himself to be taken, there would be no escape.

Pulling the knife from the folds of his robe, he bounded forward and grabbed Horbach by the throat. He plunged the knife hilt-deep into Horbach's back, the blade slipping easily between two ribs. Horbach cried out, an exclamation of surprise and pain that turned quickly into a series of gurgling coughs as he fell.

Jack pulled the knife free and turned on Reginald.

The other man was frozen in surprise, his hand still half-extended where he had intended to grab Jack's arm. Reginald's eyes widened, darting from the bloody blade to Jack's face, and his other hand grasped at the focusing rod tucked behind his belt.

"Lysander..." he began, but Jack allowed him no time to say anything more.

Charging in on the young wizard quickly, Jack thrust his knife upwards through the flesh where Reginald's chin met his throat. Reginald's expression remained one of surprise, even shock, as his eyes filmed over, taking on the vacant stare of death.

Jack allowed the corpse to fall to the floor, his blade pulling easily free as Reginald slid off it. Too bad. He'd halfway liked the kid.

As he turned back toward the desk, Jack crumpled over in pain. He felt as though his guts had been run through with a red hot poker. Groaning loudly, it was all he could do not to fall to his knees. As it was, he found himself bent double.

From the corner of his eye, he saw Horbach, down on both knees with one hand on the floor, a stream of blood flowing out of the knife wound. The wizard's free hand was pointing at Jack, opening and closing in a talon-like grasping gesture.

"Die, fool!" Horbach managed to say, blood spraying from his lips as he coughed out the words.

The pain in Jack's belly increased and he heard himself crying out again. His world became a torrent of agony. Somewhere in the back of his mind, he knew he had only seconds before he succumbed.

If someone asked him how he found the strength to do it, he would never be able to give a good answer, but somehow, Jack stumbled forward toward Horbach and, with all the strength remaining in him, kicked upward with his right foot. Jack's boot caught Horbach in the jaw. The wizard's head snapped up and backward, striking the lip of the desk with a loud *thump*. Horbach fell limply to the floor.

The pain ceased instantly, as though someone had thrown a switch. In a way, Jack supposed someone had. He wasted no time, but quickly snatched up Reginald's focusing rod and a flask of elixir that also hung from his belt. From atop the desk, he took a glow crystal and Horbach's book. Then he fled, bolting down the stairs as fast as his feet could carry him.

Jack's flight carried him past the library entrance before he realized it. Blanching as he became illuminated by the light from the glow crystals within the reading room, he turned away, changing course quickly to avoid being noticed.

And ran headlong into Simeon.

The boy fell down onto his backside. What was he doing awake at this hour?

Simeon looked up at him from the floor, his eyes wide in concern. "Mr. Simmons, there's blood on your robes."

Jack took a step back, but the boy rose and followed. "Are you hurt?"

Jack shook his head. "No. Simeon, I need to..."

The boy's eyes widened, his expression changing to one of shock and fright as he beheld the knife, still clenched in Jack's fist, and the other items he carried.

"That's... That's the Master's book, Mr. Simmons," he said. He looked pleadingly at Jack, his head shaking in denial. "You killed the Master!" His voice raised in volume and he backed away quickly.

Jack moved toward the boy. "Simeon, you don't understand."

"*Traitor!*" Simeon screamed at him. Jack could see tears begin to stream from his eyes as the boy turned and ran toward the library and the Master's tower.

Jack hesitated. He knew the safest answer was to chase Simeon down and shut him up. Even if it meant silencing him permanently. But the image of a flat belly on Susan and Simeon sitting in the back seat of his plane sprang to his mind unbidden. And though he knew it was a false vision, he knew also that he couldn't bring himself to cause the boy harm.

So he fled.

He only had to pound once on Ortiz's door before the security man opened it. Ortiz, fully clothed and looking ready for action, took in Jack's appearance at a glance and, apparently summing the whole episode up in his mind, disappeared inside for the briefest of moments. When he returned, Ortiz tossed a pack and a bundle of clothing into Jack's arms and set off at a sprint for the stables.

Jack recognized the pack and clothing as his own. When and how had Ortiz obtained them? But this was no time for such questions. He quickly stuffed his spoils of war into the pack and shrugged it on, then raced to follow Ortiz, juggling his clothes the whole way.

His burdens slowed Jack down, and by the time he reached the stables, Ortiz had already taken out the stable hands and was busy saddling two horses. He had picked two powerful looking geldings, probably a better choice than the steeds they'd arrived on. It only took a few moments for Jack to strip off his Acolyte robes and put his normal clothes back on. He hastily filled Ortiz in on what had happened as he dressed. Then alarm bells began ringing within the Citadel proper.

"Simeon," Jack said, saying the name like a curse.

Ortiz scowled at him and shook his head, but said nothing, instead mounting his horse and spurring it into motion. Jack did the same. The pair raced out of the stables toward the gate house.

Guards, servants, students, and all manner of other people began spilling out of the various quarters and into the courtyard in response to the alarm bells. All looked around for the source of the emergency. "Is there a fire? What's happened?" Jack heard from numerous mouths. In the confusion, no one challenged the two of them until they reached the gatehouse.

There, one of the guards on duty stepped out, gesturing for them to stop.

Ortiz ran him down.

The security man turned right at the base of the hill, leaving the road and weaving his way through the sea of tents surrounding town.

"Where are you going?" Jack said loudly, to be heard over the horse's hooves. That earned him an annoyed look from Ortiz.

"Weapons Storage," he said in a clipped, business-like tone.

Weapons Storage was a large tent about one-third of a mile further on. Two Legionnaires were on duty when Jack and Ortiz rode up. They perked up noticeably as the pair approached. Reining in, Ortiz dismounted smoothly and raised a hand of greeting to the guards. They relaxed visibly when they beheld his clothing: the uniform of a fellow Legionnaire.

That gave Ortiz all the opening he needed. Moving like an uncoiling snake, he struck the first guard in the throat with fingers curled over at the second knuckle, like a leopard's paw. An audible *crunch* announced the crushing of the unfortunate fellow's voice box and trachea. He fell thrashing to the ground, clutching at his throat and making choking noises.

The second guard shouted in alarm and swung at Ortiz, but the security man was too quick. A high block deflected the guard's strike, then Ortiz, moving in a blur, spun around behind the guard and grabbed him around the head with one arm and around the throat with the other. Quick opposite movement of his arms snapped the guard's neck, who dropped limply to the ground.

"Wait here," Ortiz commanded, then he ducked inside the tent.

Impressed, Jack did as he was told. Unfortunately, Ortiz's

exploits did not go unnoticed. People had begun to spill out of the tents in response to the alarm bells. These were more soldiers than not and it didn't take long for some to notice the bodies and raise an alarm.

A group of four men ran toward the tent. Unarmed except for his knife, Jack prepared to meet their attack, not expecting to survive.

But then Ortiz reappeared. The security man had his revolver strapped to his thigh, a bolt-action rifle slung over one shoulder, a satchel and his M-14 over the other, and a grenade in each hand. He pulled the pin from one grenade with his teeth and tossed it at the charging men.

The men dove out of the way, but the detonation at least wounded a few of them, as Jack heard screams of pain from them. By then, Ortiz had tossed the bolt-action to Jack and mounted his horse. He paused just long enough to toss the second grenade into the weapons tent before spurring his horse to a gallop. Jack wasted no time in following.

The weapons tent exploded in a large conflagration behind them, the grenade apparently having set off other ordnance in storage. The blast drew the eyes of everyone around. Jack and Ortiz covered most of the distance to the edge of the camp before anyone else even tried to stop them. But those attempts were disorganized and the pair evaded capture easily.

As they reached the top of the snow-covered rise to the east of the Citadel, Jack's spirits had begun to rise appreciably. They'd made it! Hot damn!

Then he lost all the wind from his sails completely.

A bright flash followed by a loud concussion from the Citadel drew their gaze. The top of the Citadel's spire was gone, blown apart. Bits and pieces of the stonework flew through the air, landing all over the Citadel complex. An orange-red column of fire erupted skyward from the spire's smoking remains. The flames struck the cloud cover overhead and spread out in an ever-expanding circle, as though the clouds were solid. Louder than the amplifiers of a dozen heavy metal concerts, Horbach's voice echoed throughout the valley, screaming one word with towering fury.

"*LYSANDER*!!!!!"

Stunned, the two men sat still on their mounts for a moment.

Then Ortiz turned a baleful eye at Jack. "You mean you didn't kill him?"

Jack could only shake his head. He had no idea how, but Horbach lived. And he would want revenge.

20

ON THE LAM

They rode through the night, expecting to hear the sounds of pursuit hot on their heels. But by daybreak, they still hadn't seen or heard any sign.

Despite their fatigue, neither Jack nor Ortiz was comfortable with stopping. Memories of Horbach's booming voice and the speed with which the entire Citadel garrison turned out spurred them on. Besides, in the snow, their trail was plain to see. So they continued on, picking their way carefully to avoid unseen holes that could break a horse's, or a person's, ankle. Progress was slow, but it beat being caught by the Legion.

Regardless of the urgency of their flight, neither man was super human. As morning turned into afternoon, Jack found himself nodding off in his saddle. He tried a number of tricks to stay awake, from shaking his head vigorously to bouncing in his saddle to smacking himself on the cheek. He even tried scooping some snow from a low branch and stuffing it down the back of his shirt.

But it only worked for so long.

In early evening, when his horse staggered beneath him,

rousing him from slumber with barely enough time to yank on the reins and prevent the horse from walking into a deep gully, Jack decided he'd had enough.

Pulling his horse to a halt, he turned to tell Ortiz it was time to stop and saw the security man slouched over his saddle, snoring softly. That did it. Jack reached over and grabbed Ortiz's reins. The change in motion woke Ortiz with a start.

"What are you doing, Simmons?"

"We're both falling asleep in the saddle. Time to stop."

Ortiz scowled and looked almost like he was going to protest, but in the end he nodded agreement.

It took several minutes, but they found a deep thicket where they were able to set up a couple blankets as shelter. They then cleared as much snow as possible. Jack didn't get much useful rest that night between the uncomfortable conditions and having to swap watches with Ortiz. But it was better than nothing.

Dawn came much too soon. When Ortiz nudged him awake, Jack would have thought it was still night from the twinkling stars overhead. Only the first inklings of light on the eastern horizon disproved that initial assumption. He wanted nothing more than to lie back down, no matter how unsatisfactory the bed.

This was no time to luxuriate, though. Off to the west, Jack heard the howling of several dogs. He gulped, earning a nod from Ortiz.

"They're on our trail. Maybe a half hour back, I'd say."

Jack hadn't hunted with dogs very often. Just once or twice when Lawrence Herschman joined him and Tobias last year. But from what he recalled, Ortiz's estimate was pretty accurate.

They wasted no time in conversation or in tidying up. Camp was easy to strike: they just yanked the blankets off the thicket branches and mounted up. In less than five minutes, they were on their way.

The growing light enabled them to make better time, but from the sound of things the dogs, at least, were gaining on them. They spurred their mounts to greater speed, but the horses were just as exhausted as the men. The most they could manage was a slow canter. The howling continued to draw closer until a short while later, as they reached the crest of a low hill, Jack, while looking back over his shoulder, saw a group of dogs, followed by mounted riders, break into a clearing no more than a half mile back.

Dropping from his horse, he dragged the animal down below the ridge and shouted for Ortiz to do the same. The security man followed suit quickly. He breathed a curse as he joined Jack on his belly atop the ridge.

"Looks like three dogs and six men," Ortiz muttered as he examined the followers through his binoculars. "If you've got any of that magic brewing, now would be a good time."

Jack raised his hands helplessly. "I have just the one flask. Without the ingredients to make more..."

Ortiz cut him off. "We might as well not have brought any out with us. I know." He shook his head, then added, "Fuck."

Ortiz slid down to his horse and pulled his M-14 from beneath his saddle blanket, then crawled back up to the crest of the hill. "This is going to draw attention, you know" he said as he removed the covers from either end of his rifle scope.

Jack just shrugged. What did Ortiz expect him to do about that? He unslung his own rifle and flipped off the safety. Without a scope, he would have to wait until the men got a bit closer, but he tracked them over his sights all the same.

Bang!

Jack hadn't heard Ortiz's rifle before. That sucker was loud! One of the men crumbled over in his saddle and fell from his horse. His compatriots reined in and Ortiz took another one down. When their second teammate fell, the remaining men scattered, spurring their horses to a gallop as they made for the cover of the woods on either side. A third man fell to Ortiz's sniping, then Jack lost sight of the others as they disappeared into the trees.

"Let's move," Ortiz ordered, sliding down to his horse.

Jack followed suit, his expression betraying his confusion. Why not wait until they showed themselves and take the rest of them out? As they mounted and spurred their horses into motion, Ortiz looked at him and, seeing his expression, spoke again.

"They won't come on as quickly now that they know there's a threat ahead."

That made sense. Still, as they rode away, Jack was painfully aware of the trail they were leaving in the snow. A blind man who'd never set foot outside the city could track them with ease.

"We need to find a stream, a lake. Something we can use to break our trail" Jack said.

"No kidding."

An hour and a half later, they found the water body they needed. It wasn't much: just a swiftly flowing, but shallow, stream. But it was enough. The flowing water kept snow from accumulating along the rocks on either side of the stream itself, leaving them a small area where they were able to ride without leaving a wide trail.

Ortiz turned left, to the north, as soon as they reached the stream. They rode for a mile or so before crossing over to the other bank. Hopefully the water would mask their scent. Another two miles further on, they left the stream near a recently felled tree. The snow was already disturbed there: it seemed the tree had collapsed sometime after the blizzard. Jack hoped their trail would be harder to detect at that location.

After a half hour of cross-country travel, they came to a break in the trees. Strangely symmetrical, the break was only about forty feet across and extended off to the left and right for a good distance before curving out of sight. Jack blinked. That was odd. It took him a minute to realize that he was looking at a road. Old, snow-covered, long-unused, but a road nonetheless.

Grinning, Jack turned his horse to the left and spurred her northwards. "This will help us make time," he quipped.

It took him a minute to notice Ortiz wasn't following. Turning in his saddle, Jack looked back quizzically. "What's the problem?"

"Easy to find us on a road, Simmons."

Jack rolled his eyes. "Juan, we'll be easy to find regardless in all this snow. We need to make time, right? Let's go!"

The security man frowned, remaining still for several moments as he peered first one way down the road, then the other, and finally behind them into the woods. Finally, apparently satisfied or at least not wanting to press the issue, he nodded and joined Jack on the road.

For whatever reason, whether because their pursuers were sufficiently intimidated or because their efforts at concealing where they left the stream were successful, Jack and Ortiz neither heard nor saw anything the rest of the day to indicate they were being tracked. As the shadows grew long in the afternoon, Jack began to imagine they were home free. Ortiz wasn't convinced, however, and forbade a fire in their campsite.

Dinner was almost nonexistent: half a biscuit and a few strips of dried bacon each. The speed of their flight from the citadel left little time to procure provisions. Jack hoped, when they were further in the clear, to be able to take more game, but for now at least they had no time to stop and hunt, so they stuck to strict rationing. It was necessary, but his stomach didn't much care for the rationality of the plan and showed its displeasure with loud rumblings the rest of the night.

Jack was tired enough that he didn't care, though. Ortiz drew the first watch, so Jack gratefully slid into his blankets for some shuteye.

When Ortiz woke him to turn the watch over, it was snowing again. At first, seeing that, Jack's heart sank. It was hard enough traveling in the few inches that were already on the ground. Getting even a couple more would slow them down tremendously! Then that initial chagrin quickly faded, turning to a warm feeling of hope. The fresh snow would also obscure their back trail.

"A bit of luck for us, eh?"

Ortiz nodded. "Hopefully." Then he bedded down. He was snoring in under a minute.

The snow continued until evening the next day. Tempting though it was to remain in place to wait out the weather, neither man voiced the thought. Best to make as much time as possible while the snow fell to minimize the traces of their passing.

It was a miserable day. Jack's cold weather gear, obtained weeks earlier in Forest Hills, was serviceable, but hardly top of the line. By mid-day the wind picked up, naturally blowing directly into their faces. The blowing snow bit at his cheeks and his outer garments seemed to barely impede the wind at all. By mid-afternoon, Jack's teeth were chattering and his feet were numb in the stirrups. He tried to remind himself that the blowing snow would further obscure their trail, but that was little comfort.

He insisted on a fire that evening and Ortiz did not object. Their campsite was the closest thing to ideal he could think of: a sheltered hollow of rock in the side of a hill that was easy to enclose with a makeshift lean-to. The fire was nothing special. It was difficult to find much in the way of quality firewood. But it was better than nothing and it added a bit of warmth to their evening. It seemed forever since Jack had felt warm. It was a welcome change.

Jack was able, for the first time in three days, to relax somewhat, and the full impact of what had happened sunk in. Pulling Horbach's book out of his pack, he looked at the leather cover, darkened in several spots from the blood that had been spilled in getting it. The look in Simeon's eyes as he cursed Jack for a traitor came to mind, fresh and clear, and he felt a pang of guilt and loss. Ortiz was right all those weeks ago: Simeon wasn't his son. But still it hurt to betray his trust, even unintentionally. Jack hoped whatever was in this book was worth it.

The fire was too small to provide adequate reading light, so Jack fished the glow crystal from his pouch. It had only a fraction of its full charge left, maybe another 3 hours depending on what setting he used. Perhaps he should have saved it for a dire need, but right then Jack needed to see what it was he'd paid such a high price for.

The book was penned in a hand that was almost as neat as

a typewriter. Small but plainly legible letters told the tale of Horbach's initial foray into his higher dimension theory at the university, his departure and arrival at the future site of the Citadel, and descriptions of his colleagues. Several pages of techno-babble detailed his experimental setup. Someone more schooled in that sort of thing than him might be able to make something of it later, Jack hoped.

Skipping to the entries after Horbach's experiment, Jack noticed a change in Horbach's writing and voice almost immediately. The handwriting, so crisp and neat before, became more ragged, as though he was writing in a rush. The words themselves became more stream-of-consciousness as opposed to the reasoned and methodical discussion from earlier in the book. Descriptions of Horbach's exploration of his new abilities, his despair over his peers' rejections when he tried to tell them of his success, and his confusion over his inability to replicate his results all came out in a flood. And then...

Oh my God.

Jack re-read the page. It couldn't be.

His breath caught in his throat as the full implications of Horbach's writing struck home. "Juan!" he managed to get out, his voice sounding strangled to his own ears.

Ortiz, busying himself with cleaning his rifle, looked up at Jack quizzically and grunted.

"Listen to this!" Jack said, then began reading the passage aloud.

"'July 17th. Panicked phone call from Petersen. Latest data from the SOHO satellite confirmed my fears. He asked over and over how I knew, but like before he didn't believe my answer. I'd prayed I was wrong, that I hadn't actually affected anything while I was Raised Above. But now I know that I really did touch the sun. The largest Coronal Mass Ejection ever measured, by several orders of magnitude, is in progress.

Petersen said he was going to call the National Science Foundation so they could warn people, but three days isn't enough time to prepare for what is coming. By my hand will our civilization end. God forgive me.'"

Ortiz shrugged his shoulders. "I don't get it."

"I took a couple of Astronomy classes as electives in school. In one of them, we discussed Coronal Mass Ejections. Charged particles ejected from the sun interact with the earth's atmosphere and magnetic field all the time. That's what causes the northern lights. In a Coronal Mass Ejection, the amount of particles hitting us increases by a huge amount and can induce uncontrolled currents in conductors on the planet's surface. There was a big one in 1847 that caused fires all across the country, shorted out telegraph lines, things like that. But there wasn't an electric grid back then, so no one was really affected too badly. My Astronomy professor told me that if a big one ever hit, it could knock out the electric grid in a large area. If a really huge one hit..."

Jack left the rest unsaid, but he could tell that Ortiz got the message. His eyes widened and his brows rose high on his forehead.

"Are you saying that..."

Jack nodded. "According to this, Horbach caused the Troubles."

Not for the first time, and probably not for the last, Jack wished fervently that he had killed the son of a bitch.

21

HUNTED

That night, Jack dreamed the dream again. But this time, when he followed the ghostly glow in the sky up to the sun, instead of the day star, he saw Horbach's face staring back at him.

"You cannot escape me, Lysander."

Horbach's voice echoed in his mind, shattering the dream and making Jack wake with a loud shout of denial.

Jack blinked the sleep out of his eyes and looked around the camp site. The area outside the lean-to was well illuminated by the moon, just past full in a nearly cloudless sky. But within, it was more difficult to see. However, it was obvious he was alone.

But not for long. Jack had barely finished sitting up when Ortiz burst into the campsite, rifle at the ready. The security man quickly swept the small area over his rifle's sights. Seeing only Jack, he lowered the rifle. Jack could hear the soft click from Ortiz switching his safety back on, but it was the other man's expression of ultimate disgust that kept the majority of Jack's attention.

"What the *fuck*??!!" Ortiz whispered in a tone that was as good as a shout.

The memory of Horbach's face in his dream still had Jack shook up. He could only manage a whisper.

"He's in my dreams, Juan."

Ortiz's expression didn't change. If anything, it became more severe. "What are you talking..." He stopped midsentence and squatted down, looking at Jack more closely. "Simmons, you're trembling like you just fell in a frozen lake."

Jack hadn't even realized he was shaking until Ortiz pointed it out. Crossing his arms over his chest, he tried to force the shaking to stop. He wasn't chilled, not any more than he had been all day. It was almost as if he'd been working out hard all day and his muscles were now trembling in protest. He tried speaking again and was able to find his full voice.

"Horbach, Juan. He's in my dreams. He knows where we are."

Ortiz sighed and shook his head. "Impossible."

Jack opened his mouth to rebut, but Ortiz cut him off.

"It's been a tough couple of days, Simmons. And you barely got out of Horbach's office with your head still attached. You're just stressed out."

Jack shook his head in denial. "Damnit, I'm not some pansy, Juan. I can handle stress. I'm telling you..." He stopped and took a deep breath. The trembling was finally beginning to subside. "Look, I know it doesn't make sense. But I'm sure it's real."

Ortiz squatted there in silence for a while, then shrugged. "Nothing we can do about it if it is. It's just about time to turn over anyway. Take the watch and nudge me in two hours. We'll get started early tomorrow. I want to get to the river before full light."

It was still a couple of hours before dawn when Jack woke Ortiz and they set off again. Sure enough, an hour later, they came to the bank of the Red River. There was never any discussion which way to go. West only took them back where they came, so they turned east.

Of course, east was relative, as the river wound back and forth through the land like a serpent. They probably made two miles going north, then south, for every mile east that day. Jack fervently wished for a bridge, so they could strike out directly for home, but none appeared until late in the afternoon, when the sun was only half its own length above the horizon.

The bridge was small and built low over the river. It looked like it was just two lanes. As with the bridge they crossed a month earlier, there were some car hulks on its span. But there was no movement and no sign that anyone had passed over it in some time. It looked inviting.

"If I were to set an ambush, it would be here," Ortiz murmured as he fished his binoculars from a saddle bag. He looked through them at the bridge for a long time, frowning in thought the whole while. Finally, he offered the glasses to Jack. "I don't see anything, but that doesn't mean it's not there. What do you think?"

Jack didn't answer immediately. Through the binoculars, the bridge and its surrounds looked clear. Part of him wanted to make a break for it. All the same... "You cannot escape me, Lysander." The memory of Horbach's words was just in his mind, but it was almost like he could truly hear them carried on the wind. Horbach was a smart guy and Jack knew the Enlightened could communicate over large distances with ease. Ortiz was right. This was ripe for a setup.

"I don't like it. Maybe we should move on. Try the next bridge."

It looked like Ortiz seriously considered it. But no. He shook his head.

"How far is the next one?" He muttered a curse under his breath. "No, I think we wait until midnight and take a shot here."

With that, they turned around and backtracked until the bridge was out of sight, then left the riverbank and took shelter in the woods. They traded off a couple hours of sleep each. Then, at the appointed time, Ortiz led them back toward the bridge.

It was slow going, between the darkness and the narrow area between the trees and the riverbank. There was always the danger of falling in, a potentially very dangerous setback that time of year.

It took an hour, near as Jack could figure, to reach the bridge itself. There they found themselves stymied. The guardrail that ran along the bridge itself continued to the south along the road for another two hundred yards or so. Nearly waist-high on a person, it would be difficult, if not impossible, for the horses to step over it without a running start, and there was no room for that.

"Crap," Jack whispered.

"Damn right. Wait here."

Before Jack could protest, Ortiz slid off his horse's back and set off down the road, hugging the tree line. He vanished from sight quickly.

For several minutes, Jack sat on his horse, alone in the darkness. His breath frosted in the cold night air, but he barely felt the chill as keyed up as he was. His heart felt like it was going to pound through his chest.

A night bird, or maybe a bat, flew overhead and alighted in a nearby tree and Jack started, nearly spurring his horse into a gallop before he could stop himself. Son of a bitch. He needed to calm down.

He took a long, slow breath to relax, but froze midway into it. Did something just move over there?

His rifle was up, the butt nestled into his shoulder, in a heartbeat. He flicked the safety off and carefully searched the area, squinting over the sights to find the movement again. What was it?

"Fire that thing and you'll kill us both."

The whispered voice came from his right side. Even though he recognized it as belonging to Ortiz, the sudden speech made him jump in his saddle. His horse whinnied and stamped, but Jack was quickly able to calm him down. He wished he could calm himself as easily.

"Fuck, Ortiz!"

"There's a roadblock like the one we found at the other bridge, down where the guard rail ends. Two men on duty. And a guard house like before too."

Jack's heart sank.

"Great. Now what?"

Ortiz didn't answer for a long moment. When he did speak, it wasn't very reassuring.

"I can take out one of them easily enough, but no way I'd get both without one of them raising an alarm. They're right next to each other. Do you know how to kill quickly and silently?"

Reginald's eyes, glazing over in death, came into his mind again. Jack swallowed. How much noise had he made when he died? Jack couldn't recall, but it wasn't much. All the same, he didn't feel very comfortable with that kind of work.

"Not sure. Maybe."

Ortiz pursed his lips in thought for a moment, then shook his head.

"If we botch it, we're done. I'll show you sometime later, when our asses don't depend on getting it right."

Jack wasn't sure why, but he felt a bit insulted. He thought better of griping about it though. Meantime, Ortiz began fishing in his saddle bags, pulling items out and setting them on the ground.

"What are you doing?"

"Only way across is to ditch the horses and go on foot."

"Are you serious? It'll take forever to walk back to Forest Hills."

"Then we better not waste any time."

Jack frowned. This was a bad idea. But as he looked down the road toward the guard house, then back to the river, running for miles in either direction, he was forced to agree it was the only available option, short of hoping against hope for another bridge somewhere close downstream. Fat chance of that.

Breathing a curse, Jack dismounted and also began emptying his saddlebags. Good thing they both had backpacks. Even still, there was a lot of stuff they wouldn't be able to bring with them. Jack concentrated on survival gear, the magic items, and ammo. Ortiz had managed to get about a hundred rounds from the weapons tent. A decent amount, but it could go fast.

In just a few minutes, they both were ready to go. As quietly as they could, they removed the bridles and saddles from their horses. A soft pat on their rumps sent the horses walking off upstream, then Jack and Ortiz took a few minutes to dump the items they weren't taking with them into the river.

That done, they crept back to the road. Squatting next to the guard rail, Jack looked anxiously south toward the guard house. No sign that the sentries were alerted to their presence yet.

Ortiz whispered into his ear, "Keep low and hug the guard rail. Follow me."

With that, the security man slipped over the rail and began moving quickly onto the bridge span. Jack followed suit without a word.

The river was about a quarter mile across at that point, with a small island about a third of the way, which the bridge crossed over. It was relatively slow going until the island. There, Ortiz straightened and began trotting forward at a more normal pace. Or as normal as was possible in five inches of snow.

As they passed the halfway point, Jack began to feel good. No sign of pursuit from the south. Theirs were the only footprints in the snow. The gambit appeared to be working. Then, with about a third of the bridge to go, Ortiz stopped, holding his right fist up alongside his head.

Jack stopped as well. He'd seen enough Army movies back before the Troubles to recognize that signal.

"What's up?"

Ortiz looked back at him for a brief moment, then turned his eyes back to the north.

"No more cover between here and the riverbank."

"So? No one else has been through here but us."

"Unless they crossed before the snowstorms."

Wasn't he just a ray of sunshine?

"You don't want to go back, do you? Fuck that!"

Ortiz shook his head.

"Then let's go."

Ortiz hesitated for another moment, then began moving again. As he went, he lowered into a crouch and kept close to the guard rail. Jack mimicked him.

They were almost across when disaster struck.

One moment, they were moving at a steady pace under cover of darkness. The next, the darkness was shattered by a globe of light that rose from the bridge span at their feet. The globe streaked up into the sky, growing larger and brighter as it ascended until, by the time it leveled off a couple hundred feet up, it had increased in luminosity until the entire bridge and riverbank was illuminated as plainly as if it were noon. At the same time, a loud siren, almost like a car alarm, issued from the globe.

They both froze. Ahead, Jack could see a number of figures moving down the road toward them. It was an ambush, after all.

"*Move!*"

Barely had the words left Ortiz's lips before he was running as fast as he could through the snow toward the end of the bridge. He began firing his M-14 as he ran. Jack hesitated for a few seconds, frozen by the shock of being discovered. Then a bullet whizzed by his head and he roused himself from his stupor.

Jack raced after Ortiz and began to fire as well. He was limited by the five round capacity of his rifle, though, and he was soon empty. The rest of his ammo was in his pack, and besides, loading a bolt action wasn't something to be done while running, so Jack focused on just running.

Ortiz continued firing: a twenty round magazine sure came in handy. One of the figures ahead on the road went down, blood spraying from a wound in his chest. But there were three more that Jack could see. He looked back over his shoulder and his heart sank even further. Half a dozen men, one in black robes, were rushing across the bridge from the south.

They were screwed.

Only a hundred feet to the end of the bridge. Jack wondered for a moment about the feasibility of jumping over the side and swimming for it.

Another of the men ahead went down. Two left. Then

Ortiz ceased firing and slid on his back to the other side of the bridge. Jack raced over to his side and dropped to his knees next to him, concerned that the security man was hit. Then he saw that Ortiz was changing out the magazine in his rifle.

"Don't just stand there. Fire!"

"No ammo."

Oritz shot him a disgusted look out of the corner of his eye. Then, magazine change out complete, Ortiz got up onto one knee and, sighting in quickly, squeezed off two more rounds. Jack blinked as another of the men ahead of them fell. Just one more. The man suddenly found the east side of the road to be his best friend as he took cover in a ditch there.

"Are you fucking..."

The bridge rocked underfoot, tossing both men to the ground and leaving the rest of Jack's thought unspoken. What the hell was that? Jack looked back and saw a crater in the bridge about twenty feet away from them. The men to the south were closer. The Enlightened among them was pointing something toward Jack and Ortiz.

No more mystery what caused the crater.

"Juan, we gotta go!"

"No shit."

They rose and sprinted the rest of the way to the end of the bridge, then vaulted over the guard rail on the west side of the road. They landed four feet later and Ortiz immediately turned back to the south. About twenty-five feet back, the bridge was high enough to duck underneath. They did so, despite the ankle deep, frigid water.

Jack was thankful for good boots as they were at least marginally waterproof. But still, it was bloody cold. He moved toward the east side of the bridge, intending to continue moving, but Ortiz stopped him.

"Wait until they're past."

That made sense. But Jack's feet were already starting to go numb. Trying not to think about it, he shouldered off his pack and dug out his ammo. Quickly reloading his rifle, he stuffed a bunch of extra rounds into his pockets and put the pack back on.

Ortiz slung his rifle and drew his revolver from its holster. Passing it into his left hand, he dug into his thigh pocket and withdrew a grenade. How many had he gotten from that weapons tent? He tossed the grenade to Jack, then pulled another out and winked.

Just then, Jack heard the sound of multiple people running overhead and voices shouting back and forth.

"Where did they go?"

"They jumped off and went that way!"

"Then get after them, fool!"

Pulling the grenade pin with his teeth, Ortiz gestured for Jack to follow him, then ducked out from under the bridge on the eastern side.

Jack pulled his pin as well and followed, being careful to squeeze the grenade handle tightly. They ended up crouched on the outside of the guard rail. Their pursuers had reached the point where Jack and Ortiz had gone over the opposite rail. Three of the soldiers were peering over the side. The Enlightened was stalking back and forth impatiently. The other soldiers were trotting to join the man from the ditch, who was making his way toward them.

Ortiz grinned at Jack and tossed his grenade. The Enlightened saw it coming and screamed, his eyes bugging out. Then it went off.

When the smoke cleared, Jack could see that the blast blew the Enlightened's legs clean off. There was nothing to be seen of the three soldiers nearest him, but blood was splattered all over the guard rail.

Even had the explosion not alerted them, the Enlightened's shrill screams of agony would have been enough to bring the remaining three soldiers running. Eyes locked on their leader, they didn't notice Ortiz and Jack until the security man stood and leveled his revolver at them.

They didn't have time to raise their rifles before he gunned them down.

Ortiz gave a satisfied nod and slid over the guard rail. A fourth shot from his pistol put an end to the Enlightened's screams.

"Better put that pin back in," he said.

Jack rose slowly and climbed over the guardrail, feeling dazed. He couldn't believe what had just happened. To go from being certain they were done for to victory so quickly... His hands were shaking, partly from adrenalin, partly from fright, partly from relief. It took a few tries to re-insert the pin in the grenade.

Finally, he found the words to express his feelings.

"Holy shit."

22

ROADWORK

J ack found the missing three Legionnaires easily, on the ground below the guardrail they'd been peering over when the grenade went off. Their bodies were riddled with shrapnel and barely recognizable as human beings, as torn up as they were. To Jack's horror, one of them was still alive when he found them. The unfortunate fellow groaned and squirmed pitifully. Jack took a deep breath. Then, drawing his knife, he climbed over the guardrail and dropped to the ground. By the time he got down there, however, the Legionnaire had passed.

He rejoined Ortiz on the road and the two of them took inventory of the situation.

The light from the globe in the sky had dimmed considerably, to the equivalent of sunset or early twilight. Enough to see by, but it was becoming hard to make out fine details. Though they both felt the need to move on quickly, they took a moment to search their attackers for anything of use.

The Enlightened had carried three elixir flasks and a focusing rod. All but one of the flasks were shattered and the focusing rod was broken in two. But that doubled the amount of elixir Jack had, so he thankfully scooped up the intact flask. If it came down to it, he could use one of them. Not that it would do much good.

Ortiz fared better. The Legionnaires carried an assortment of weapons and ammo, but he found enough of the latter to nearly double their ammo supply.

It got even better as they set off down the road from the bridge. Perhaps a hundred yards beyond the last of the corpses, a small break in the trees, obviously manmade from the number of broken branches and the footprints in the snow, caught their attention. Despite the necessity of putting distance between themselves and the battle site, they took the time to check it out. About fifty feet back was a small camp: a pair of two-man tents, erected in a neat row in front of a fire pit, and, opposite the tents, a picket line where four horses were tied.

Jack couldn't believe their luck, though it made sense that the northern squad would have set up to wait. There was no telling when the fugitives would arrive, after all.

It took only a few minutes for Jack to take down one of the tents and Ortiz to scavenge as much food as he could stuff into a pair of saddle bags and their backpacks. Then they set two of the horses loose, mounted the other two, and set off down the road.

They pushed hard for the rest of the night and on through the next day.

Not long after they set off, the road reached a T-intersection, going east and west. The choice to turn east made itself. After a brief discussion, they agreed on a plan to follow local roads east and north until they hit Interstate 30 at a town called Hope. 30 would take them to Little Rock. From there they could get on Interstate 40 the rest of the way to Forest Hills, just south of Nashville. The Interstates would probably allow faster travel and avoid passing straight through towns, and whoever might inhabit them.

As they rode on, Jack began to see a number of flaws with the plan.

"You know, Juan, I don't think we thought this thing through all the way. If we take the Interstate, it'll be really easy to find our trail. Maybe we should stick to the smaller roads. Or turn north and cut cross-country for a while, then turn east."

Ortiz shook his head.

"It'll slow us down. As it is, we may make it back before the Conference is over."

"Screw the conference. They can call another one."

"Simmons, the conference is the reason for this mission. There won't be another chance to get everyone on the same page. And we'll need everyone if we're to avoid being crushed under the Order's boot."

"I didn't choose this mission, remember?"

Ortiz opened his mouth to reply, but apparently thought better of it. They rode in silence for a quarter hour or so before he spoke again.

"I necessarily don't disagree, Simmons. It'll be a couple days before we get to the Interstate. We can re-assess when we get there."

Jack supposed that was fair.

They stopped in the early afternoon in yet another burned out town. As far as they could tell, it was abandoned, and as they were both exhausted, they decided to hole up for the night in a mostly intact house a couple of blocks off the main road. Exhausted as he was, Jack volunteered for the first watch. As usual, Ortiz was asleep almost as soon as his head hit the pillow. He actually had a pillow, for a change. So did

Jack. They'd found a pair in a closet upstairs and could hardly believe their luck.

During his three hours, Jack took advantage of the natural light to study Horbach's book. He was certain the Legion would find their trail: that beacon over the bridge would have been visible for miles. Once the bridge's outpost failed to check in, contingents would be deployed to investigate and take revenge. He figured they had a day's head start, tops, and he hoped to find something in the book to even the odds a bit.

It was hard, though. There was no table of contents or index, just Horbach's stream of consciousness. When the hourglass emptied for the third time, he'd accomplished nothing except to make himself frustrated. Ortiz took the watch, and for a little while Jack considered staying up to read some more. But the sun was beginning to set and he really was exhausted. The kind of exhausted where he felt light-headed and the world seemed fuzzy.

So, instead, he went to sleep.

A bit before noon on the second day from their borrowed house, Jack and Ortiz passed a neglected airport and then, a few minutes later, saw a sign announcing the town limits of Hope. That Hope was still populated became obvious when they rounded a small bend in the road and saw a roadblock in their path about a quarter mile ahead, just before the inter-section with the Interstate.

They reined in and Ortiz pulled out his binoculars. His lips pursed as he examined the scene ahead.

"Four men. Two rifles. Two bows." Jack could hear more than a hint of dispersion in his voice as he mentioned the later.

"Got a problem with archery, Juan?"

"Nope. Not if the archer knows what he's doing. In my experience, though, most men with bows end up doing more damage to their forearms from the bowstring than to anything downrange."

Ortiz nudged his horse forward at a walk. Jack chuckled and followed.

The men at the roadblock perked up as Jack and Ortiz approached. The bowmen nocked arrows, and those with rifles checked that they had rounds in their chambers. When Jack and Ortiz were about twenty yards out, the men sighted in. One of the riflemen spoke up.

"Hold it right there. We don't want no visitors here. Just turn around and go back the way you came."

Jack and Ortiz exchanged looks. Ortiz rolled his eyes in consternation, then returned his gaze to the speaker and answered.

"We're not interested in visiting. Just want to get on the Interstate."

"Not gonna happen, wetback. Piss off."

Jack had never seen Ortiz look so offended and couldn't say he blamed him. Ortiz's accent marked him as hispanic, but it was hardly noticeable, at least to Jack's ears. Still, with all that was going on in the world, to focus on something as stupid as *that*?

Ortiz surprised him. He muttered under his breath, "I'm Puerto Rican, not Mexican. Bendejo." But his tone when he responded was cordial, almost friendly.

"You want your privacy. I get it. How much to ride as far as the on-ramp? We won't stop. Won't talk to anyone."

One of the bowmen said something to the leader. He shook his head and waved the bowman to silence.

"I'm not going to say it again. Cabron. Go the fuck away."

Even to Jack's untrained ears, the man's pronunciation of

cabron left much to be desired. This was going nowhere. Jack leaned over in his saddle and said, "Let's just move on, Juan. There will be another on ramp a few miles up the road."

Ortiz ground his teeth, but nodded.

"Let's go," he growled. With a forceful tug on the reins, he turned his horse around. Jack took just enough time to give guards at the roadblock the bird before following.

According to their maps, the next exit was in Hope also. Anticipating a similar welcome there, Jack and Ortiz spent the rest of the day navigating smaller county roads and a couple of larger state highways. Shortly before sunset, they came to another on ramp, this one un-guarded. Looking at the map, it was less than ten miles from the one they'd been turned away from, but that was straight-line distance.

As they set up camp, Ortiz grumped about the lost time and the fact that they'd probably covered twenty miles to make those ten toward their destination. Jack tried to be philosophical about it, but he felt an itching between his shoulder blades. Every step they didn't take away from the Citadel brought the Legion that much closer to catching them.

The local road crossed over the Interstate at the on ramp. They camped under the overpass, behind the hulk of an old minivan. As they had each night since the house, they went without a fire, despite the winter chill. The weather was clear, but while that brought the comfort of no snow, it also led to a lower temperature. It was an uncomfortable night.

In the morning, over a cold breakfast, they consulted the map again.

"About a hundred miles to Little Rock," Jack noted. "You guys have any dealings with them?"

Ortiz shook his head.

"Farrah's Crossing was as far west as we've traded so far. But we've interacted with travelers who told us Little Rock is still populated and orderly. Management intended the caravan that discovered the slaughter at Farrah's Crossing to stop at Little Rock and establish relations. You know how that went."

"Doesn't sound so bad. Then it's just Memphis and Jackson, then on to Forest Hills."

Ortiz swallowed the last bite of his meal and began packing up.

"There's no 'just' in passing through Memphis, Simmons."

Jack bit off a hunk of bread and chewed slowly.

"That's twice now you've said bad things about Memphis. What gives?"

"We don't go there without at least a full Company of security guards. There's constant..."

His abrupt stop drew Jack's gaze. Ortiz was looking to the south. His eyes suddenly widened and he dropped into a crouch behind the van.

"Cover!"

Jack cursed and, keeping low, moved over to Ortiz's side. He immediately saw the problem: a dozen men on horses, riding toward them on the Interstate. They were several hundred yards away, but two of them were obviously wearing black robes. Jack cursed again. A dozen Legionnaires would be hard enough to deal with even without those two. But wait. Something was off about the group.

"Is it just me, or are those guys not Legionnaires?"

Ortiz nodded, scowling darkly.

"It's not just you. Three to one those are the same people who turned us away yesterday."

Jack wasn't willing to take that bet.

They crept back to their gear and retrieved their

weapons. As Ortiz removed the covers from his rifle scope, he pursed his lips in thought.

"How far can you shoot accurately, Simmons?"

Jack checked his rifle over and shrugged.

"Without a scope, probably a hundred yards."

"Good enough."

Returning to the van, Jack knelt behind the front bumper and raised his rifle. The approaching group was about two hundred yards out. He could pick out the two Enlightened easily. It was difficult to not start shooting immediately.

"Hold your fire until you're sure," Ortiz said, from his position at the rear bumper. "One shot, one kill. Wizards first."

"Right."

"Ok, I've got left."

That wasn't what Jack meant, but he went with it. Sighting in on his Enlightened, he wished for a moment that he had Vera. He'd seen Tobias take a deer at two hundred fifty yards once using Vera's scope. Jack forced that thought down. What was it the man said, you fought with the army you had, not the army you wanted?

One hundred fifty yards. Plus or minus.

The approaching force was spread out across the road. Three men rode ahead, about twenty yards in front of the rest, and two brought up the rear. Flankers watched the terrain on either side. Jack was no military genius, but they looked like a bunch expecting a fight. Time to give it to them.

His Enlightened was saying something to his colleague. Whatever it was, the wizard clearly thought it important, as he was gesturing vigorously. Jack almost regretted cutting off the conversation as he squeezed the trigger.

Ortiz's shot rang out a heartbeat after Jack's. Jack was gratified to see both Enlightened fall out of their saddles, but he didn't stop to pat himself on the back. Ejecting his brass and chambering another round, he shifted fire to one of the riders in the vanguard. A moment's shocked hesitation on their part gave Jack an easy shot. Ortiz as well, as one of the flankers also fell. The force broke, wheeling their horses around and kicking them into a gallop. Very quickly, the only horses remaining were those whose riders were on the ground.

Jack stood up.

"That was easy."

A derisive snort was Ortiz's initial reply.

"They were sloppy. Let's go."

He set about gathering the gear and packing his saddle bags. Jack hesitated.

"Those Enlightened probably had more elixir. I should get it."

"No time, Simmons. They know right where we are now and they won't be so stupid next time."

Jack knew Ortiz was right, but he still hated to leave the elixir. He hoped they wouldn't come to regret the decision later.

❧ 23 ❧

BLOCKED

Over the next week, there appeared to be little need for regret. They reached Little Rock in the early evening of the third day after the battle. There was one other inhabited town on the way, but they did not stop there and no one from the town gave them any problems. At Little Rock, the plan was to take the city's beltway around to Interstate 40 and strike out east. Neither Jack nor Ortiz had any desire to stop and see the sights, and as it happened there was no need to.

They camped at the intersection with the beltway and by mid-morning were heading east. Four full days of travel found them nearing Memphis.

Jack frowned at what he saw through Ortiz's binoculars. The Memphis skyline was illuminated by multiple bonfires. Several of the taller buildings had collapsed, at least partially. Those that still stood had most of their windows broken and fires lit on several floors. He'd seen a lot of ruins over the years, but never a place that was so intentionally defaced.

"I see what you meant," he said as he handed the binoculars back.

They sat on their horses about a mile and a half west of the Mississippi, where Interstates 40 and 55 split, leading to two separate bridges across the river. It was about an hour after full dark, though from what Jack could see, it was pretty well lit in the city.

"There are three different factions in the city. They're almost always fighting to expand their little pieces of territory." Ortiz looped the binoculars over his saddle horn. "The shortest way is to head straight across on 40, but depending on what's going on in town, it may not be the fastest."

"No way of knowing before we get there, though, is there?"

Ortiz shook his head.

"We can still go around. Head north to where we crossed before."

Ortiz took a long time in answering. Finally, he shook his head again.

"Trying to get through the city will slow down our pursuers."

Jack knew he was going to say that. Damnit.

"Then we might as well take the short route. Let's go."

Jack nudged his horse forward, but before he could move far, Ortiz grabbed his reins and pulled the horse to a stop.

"It's actually better to go through during the day. We should camp on this side of the river for the night."

Jack glared at the security man, but the grave expression on Ortiz's face diffused his anger at being manhandled. After a moment, Jack nodded and turned his horse around, toward an off-ramp a couple hundred yards behind them.

They holed up in an abandoned house for the night and

set out at first light. As they crossed the bridge into downtown Memphis, it occurred to Jack that he hadn't dreamt of the crash the night before. It was strange, but thinking about it, he couldn't remember the last time he had. The closest he could recall was the night before the firefight on the Red River bridge. Jack shook his head in chagrin. To have lived with a thing so long and then to not even realize it was gone...it felt strange.

A mile or so past the bridge, on the other side of the river, the Interstate turned due north for a couple miles before veering back to the east. The way was mostly clear, a few car hulks not withstanding, until that second turn. The glare from the sun, still low on the horizon, made it difficult to see the barrier across the highway at first. But as they drew near, Jack could see it consisted of a number of cars, pushed end to end, with wooden planks fastened together to fill the gaps. The whole thing, while ramshackle in appearance, was probably plenty sturdy.

Ortiz breathed a soft curse.

"I was afraid of this," he murmured as they approached the barrier. "Keep your hands away from your weapon and don't make any sudden moves."

Jack nodded. He felt his mouth going dry, but he swallowed anyway.

When they came within about fifty feet of the barrier, a voice shouted out.

"Where the hell you think you're going?"

Ortiz raised his hands, palms empty and facing the barrier.

"We're bound for Forest Hills, on official business. Let us pass."

A long moment passed. Jack could hear muttering back and forth between at least two people behind the barrier. Then, finally, part of the barrier swung open. A swarthy man of medium height stepped toward them. He had long black hair and a trimmed beard. He carried a shotgun cradled in the nook of his right arm. Jack could see a few knives in leather sheathes on his belt.

The man walked halfway toward them, chewing slowly as he studied them. Then he spat through a gap between his front teeth, a brownish blob of saliva that unceremoniously splattered onto the pavement. Nodding to Ortiz, he spoke in a slow drawl.

"I know you. You come through 'ere before, with them caravans."

Ortiz nodded.

"I have. And I'm on official Company business now. It would not go well with you if we are delayed here."

The man barked a quick laugh, his eyes moving from Ortiz to Jack and back quickly.

"What, the two of you 'r gonna do for me and mine?"

More laughter erupted from behind the barrier, echoing the man's in an unsettling harmony. As the laughter died, the man spat again, then wiped his mouth with the back of his free hand before continuing.

"Tell you what. If you kin pay the toll, you kin pass."

Jack and Ortiz shared glances.

"How much?," inquired Ortiz.

The man grinned, a nasty, mirthless smile that revealed several more gaps in his teeth, the relics of many a fistfight, unless Jack missed his guess.

"Well now that depends, don't it? How much you got?"

Jack rolled his eyes. So that's how it was going to be. He had no money that would be of any use to this thug: just a few of the Order's coins. His few material possessions were vital enough that he had no intention of giving them away. It looked as though they would have to go around after all.

But Ortiz surprised him. Slowly reaching into his saddle

bag, the security man pulled a small leather pouch out and held it up where it could be easily seen, both by the man and his compatriots behind the barrier. Ortiz shook the pouch and it jingled softly.

"There's two hundred Forest Hills Caravan Scripts here. Let us pass, give us escort through your territory, and it's yours."

The man's eyes bulged and he licked his lips, an expression of naked greed forming on his face.

"Two hundred?" He glanced back at the barrier, then, licking his lips again, he nodded. "A'right. You got a deal."

The man held out his hand expectantly. Ortiz chuckled and shook his head.

"Oh no. Twenty-five now. The rest when we leave your territory."

The man's expression soured, but he nodded again. Ortiz withdrew the agreed upon amount from the pouch and tossed the coins to him. The man fumbled the catch and several of the scripts fell onto the pavement. With an oath, the man squatted down to snatch them up. Jack smirked in amusement, but carefully smoothed his face as the man stood back up.

"A'right. Let's go."

With that, he turned and walked back to the barrier. Ortiz clucked and nudged his horse gently with his heels, and followed at a slow walk. Jack followed suit.

Five more men waited on the other side of the barrier, along with a like number of horses. All of the men were bearded and wore their hair in the same style as the first man. Probably part of the gang's colors. They carried an assortment of arms: a couple of pistols, a rifle, a bow, a crossbow. When the first man explained the deal, a couple of them grumbled for a moment, but eventually concurred. Two members of the group, the first man and the man with the crossbow, climbed up onto a pair of horses, then gestured for Jack and Ortiz to follow, and rode off.

Jack and Ortiz followed a few yards behind them. Despite their agreement, Jack noticed that Ortiz scanned the area continuously, as though expecting an attack. Probably not a bad idea.

"Unless things have shifted a lot in the last few months, this group controls this part of town, as far as Summer Avenue, right before the interchange with 240. There's a bit of a no-man's-land between the gangs' territories, so hopefully we won't immediately run into the others."

Ortiz's words were pitched for Jack's ears alone. All the same, he watched their guides warily as he spoke.

A second barrier blocked their way at the other side of the gang's territory. It, too, was manned by half a dozen armed men. They recognized the guides and raised hands in greeting. Then they saw Jack and Ortiz and brought weapons to bear. The first man spoke quickly, gesturing for them to relax. When they heard the details of the arrangement, they lowered their weapons. One of them, apparently the leader, barked orders, and the rest moved briskly to unlock the barrier's gate and swing it open.

Jack and Ortiz's guide turned toward them and held out his hand.

"Ok, yer 'ere. Pay up."

Ortiz tossed him the pouch and they spurred their horses forward. Jack nodded to their guide in farewell as he rode past, and received a grunt in return. That had gone rather well.

The interchange was a few hundred yards past the barrier. They followed the ramp to 40 East, and a few minutes later, they crossed a small river and rode away, downtown Memphis at their backs.

"That wasn't so bad, Juan. And you were worried."

Ortiz nodded. "Cheap too."

"If you think two hundred scripts is cheap, maybe I should work for the Company full time, too."

Ortiz chuckled. "I paid them in expired scripts."

Jack's mouth fell open and he looked at Ortiz in disbelief. The security man raised his eyebrows and grinned, his expression one of amused mischief. Jack didn't know he had it in him.

"Well, Juan, I'm impressed."

Ortiz shrugged.

"We're not out of the woods yet, though. There's more gang territory ahead. Keep an eye out."

Jack opened his mouth to reply. But just then, a shot rang out.

A veritable fountain of blood sprayed as a bullet passed through the neck of Ortiz's horse. The stricken beast reared once, then fell over. Ortiz looked just as shocked as Jack felt, and though he tried to get off the horse before it fell, he wasn't fast enough. The horse took him down with it, pinning his leg beneath its body as it thrashed out its last final moments. The impact was loud: the thud of the horse hitting the ground, the crunch of breaking bones, Ortiz's cry of pain as his leg was crushed.

It seemed Memphis wasn't done with them yet.

❧ 24 ❧

HANDICAPPED

In shock, Jack didn't move for a second. Then the bullet from a second shot whizzed past and roused him from his reverie. Muttering an oath, he jumped from his saddle and unslung his rifle. His first thought was that the gang had double-crossed them, but looking back the way they came, he saw the barrier was still shut. Then he looked south. His heart sank as he beheld a dozen men moving toward them from what looked like an old college campus, just off the Interstate.

Jack knelt behind the corpse of Ortiz's horse and raised his rifle. Sighting in quickly, he returned fire. One of the approaching men dropped; Jack hoped because he'd been hit as opposed to his taking cover. Quickly ejecting his brass and chambering another round, he fired again. This time, the guy he fired at definitely ducked, but kept on coming.

"Get out of here, Simmons."

Ortiz practically spat the words out through gritted teeth. His face was a rictus of agony.

Jack shook his head.

"Not going to happen."

He fired again, then had to duck himself as a couple of the approaching men aimed at him. Bullets streaked overhead, advertising their proximity with their telltale high-pitched whistles. Ortiz grabbed his shoulder and squeezed. The security man looked at him with a grim expression.

"I mean it, Jack. Leave me and go! You have to make it back with what you know."

Ortiz's M-14 had fallen near him. Dropping his bolt action, Jack forced Ortiz's hand from his shoulder and grabbed the weapon. Resting the barrel on the dead horse's torso, Jack, lying prone now, sighted in on the approaching men. It had been a while since he last used a scope, so his first couple of shots were wild, but shortly he was laying down fire at a steady rate. He saw another man go down, blood spraying from a wound in his torso.

Jack spoke between shots.

"You've got people depending on you to make it home, remember?" He shot a third man, who went down grasping at his thigh. "No way I'm going back to tell your wife I left you to die here."

There were still nine men out there, now less than fifty yards away. Three of them, closer than the others, stood up straight and began firing nearly continuously. Bullets struck the horse's torso and whizzed by close overhead, forcing Jack to take cover fully.

"Suppressing fire," Oritz offered. "They'll keep your head down while the others come in. You..." he gritted his teeth and groaned, then, panting, spat the rest of his thought out. "...should have left when...had the chance."

Jack tried to raise himself back up to a prone firing position and almost immediately a bullet struck the horse right next to his head. He ducked down again.

Fuck.

Ortiz was right. They had him pinned. There was no way he could return fire like this. Very soon they would get here and finish him and Ortiz off. Frantic, he looked around for some way to extricate himself. His horse had moved away; the loud noise of the gunfire had no doubt scared her. He wouldn't be able to reach her without moving into the open. No dice there.

Then his eyes alighted on a pile of leather on the ground maybe ten feet away. His saddle bags. In his rush to dismount, he must have kicked them off. One of the flaps had flopped open. Jack's eyes widened as he saw one of his elixir flasks poking out of the opening.

Of course!

Jack belly-crawled to the saddlebag and pulled out the flask and his focusing rod, which was tucked in the bottom of the pouch. Pulling the flask's cork out with his teeth, he quickly downed the elixir and crawled back to Ortiz.

Or tried to.

The ever-present nausea hit him halfway back, followed by the belly-throbbing pain. He doubled over on the ground and clutched himself, groaning loudly, and all thoughts of retaliation fled as the pain consumed his rational mind.

"I got him," someone shouted from nearby.

Jack knew that was bad, but couldn't force himself to do anything about it. He heard footsteps. The pain began to fade, replaced by the tingling and the enhanced vision. His eyes focused on a man with a rifle, about five feet away. He was aiming at Jack, but hadn't fired yet.

The pain was almost gone, but Jack continued to clutch at his belly and groan. The rifleman came closer, then looked to his side.

"Take 'em back to Larry? Might get ransom."

A second voice spoke from off to Jack's left.

"No prisoners."

Jack concentrated and drew the energies in as the rifleman shrugged and stepped next to him. Looking down the barrel at him, the fellow, he couldn't have been more than twenty, said, "Sorry about this, buddy. Nothing personal."

His finger moved to the trigger.

Jack pointed his focusing rod at the young man and pushed with Force. The man's head snapped upward and to the right with a sickening crack and he fell limply to the ground.

Rolling over, Jack saw a second man near Ortiz. He was in the middle of raising his rifle to aim at the security man, but looked away, toward Jack, as his young comrade dropped. The surprised expression on the fellow's face was almost comical as Force struck him and flipped him over the horse's corpse. He didn't get up.

Jack sat up and saw a cluster of four ruffians about ten yards away. Their surprised expressions quickly changed to expressions of blood rage as they saw him. Already with weapons at the ready, they sighted in on him.

He struck with Heat this time. He hadn't had as much practice with it, though, and it didn't quite go as he intended.

The barrels of their rifles quickly went from their normal black to white-hot. One of them had a wooden stock, which caught fire. The others' were plastic and merely melted.

Then the rounds in their magazines cooked off.

Jack flattened himself as the three chambered rounds fired at him. Fortunately, they all missed above and to the right. No doubt the men's aim was thrown off by the sudden Heat. When Jack looked back again, the four fellows were down, writhing and screaming from the shrapnel wounds and extensive burns all over their bodies.

The remaining three, the trio who had initially supplied

the suppressing fire, now wore expressions of fright. Jack couldn't say he blamed them. Seeing five of your buddies taken out inexplicably, and in such a short period of time, especially when you were convinced you'd won, had to be disconcerting.

Jack pointed the focusing rod at them. They turned and fled.

Jack lost sight of the three men and got slowly to his feet. Above and beyond the tingling in his skin from the elixir, he began to tremble. That was close.

This was no time to be standing around, though. He had no doubt the ruffians would come back with reinforcements as soon as they could.

He had to get Ortiz out from under the horse.

Jack squatted down next to the Ortiz and tried to push the horse's corpse, but it would not move. Crap.

"Ok, Juan. Maybe I can pull you out."

Ortiz's eyes went wide and he shook his head. Before he could protest further, Jack grabbed him by the armpits and pulled. Ortiz let out a long, drawn out scream as his leg shifted under the horse, but he hardly moved. Jack tried pulling again. Ortiz screamed even louder, then all at once stopped. Concerned, Jack stopped pulling and looked at his face. Ortiz had passed out.

This wasn't going to work. With all that effort, and all the pain he'd made Ortiz endure, the security man hadn't budged at all. Jack cursed and stepped back from the horse. Wiping his hands on his thighs, he tried to think of another way. If he had a lever...

"Dumbass," he said to himself.

Bending over, he picked up the focusing rod again and

pointed it at the horse's corpse. Drawing the energies, he concentrated on Force and pushed. He'd never tried to move something this big before. As he focused his will, it was almost as though he could physically feel the resistance of the horse's weight. He felt sweat beading on his forehead and he stumbled back a half-step.

The horse hadn't moved at all from what he could see.

Jack took a deep breath and tried again, this time focusing his will, and the Force, at the area between the horse and the ground. He felt the weight on his shoulders as he tried to raise the corpse. Without realizing it, he found himself slumping over. Sweat ran freely. He began panting with exertion, but then, ever so slowly, the horse rolled slightly upward. Maybe that was enough. Jack kept pushing, but reached down and grabbed Ortiz with his free hand and pulled. The security man slid out with only moderate effort.

Jack slumped to the ground, exhausted, and released the energies. He breathed heavily for a number of minutes, but eventually he felt his heart rate return to normal. That was harder than he thought it would be.

Ortiz was in bad shape. His leg was twisted just above the knee such that his foot pointed straight out to the side. Jack was no MD, but he suspected a femur break. From what little he knew of first aid, they could get ugly real quick if they weren't set. Not that he had the equipment, time, or knowledge of how to go about setting it.

First things first.

Jack grabbed him by the armpits again and dragged him over to the horse. It took what felt like herculean effort, but Jack managed to pick the security man up and lay him face down across the saddle. Then he took a few minutes to recover as much of Ortiz's gear as he could fit within his own saddlebags and he led the horse down the Interstate at a walk.

Fortunately, Ortiz slept for a few hours. Long enough for Jack to lead the horse a few miles up the road to an old, overgrown Country Club. Jack expected to see their assailants returning with reinforcements at any minute, but they never did. Thank the Lord for small blessings. Or something like that.

He stopped in a copse of trees that once lined a fairway. Now, of course, it was just a copse beside a meadow. For whatever reason, there was much less snowfall here than down in Texas near the Citadel. Jack thought for a moment, as he cleared an area to use as a campsite, that it was odd, considering how much further north they were. But he wasn't going to complain. In the rush to flee the ambush site, he'd neglected to grab their tent from behind Ortiz's saddle, so they were reduced to sleeping under the stars for the duration of their journey. The less snow on the ground, the better. In short order, he had the campsite ready and spread blankets out on the ground for Ortiz. Then he undertook the difficult task of lowering the security man from the horse without disturbing his leg too much.

He managed, though, and was in the middle of breaking some fallen branches to use as firewood when Ortiz woke up.

"Oh shit," he managed, as he lifted his head and saw the state of his leg.

"Yeah, that's a bad break. We're going to have to try to set it or you may be completely screwed."

Ortiz nodded and slumped back onto the ground.

"Wish...we had some morphine."

Jack sighed. "Me too."

He fished into the saddle bag and found Ortiz's spare belt. Tossing it to Ortiz, he said, "You'll probably want to bite down on that."

There was a young tree growing just behind Ortiz's head.

The trunk was small enough that he could get his hand around it; he took a firm grasp with both. Jack crouched down at Ortiz's feet and took hold of his right boot.

"On three."

Ortiz nodded.

"One. Two."

Jack pulled on the boot at two, leaning all his weight backwards onto his heels to get more pull. Ortiz let out a muffled, guttural cry. Jack could see him grinding the belt between his teeth. The leg wasn't moving. He pulled harder, gave a jerk, and the leg moved a tiny bit. Ortiz's cries became louder. If Jack could...just...get the leg to twist...

He lost his grip and fell backwards onto his back. He heard Ortiz spit the belt out. He was sobbing, his breath coming in gasping heaves.

"Fuck...that...hurt. What happened to three, asshole?"

Jack sat up shrugged his shoulders.

"Doing it that way always seemed to work in the Lethal Weapon movies."

Ortiz gave him a baleful look for a moment, then sighed.

"We're not doing that again."

Jack looked at the leg and shook his head. "No, I don't think we will." He grinned: the foot and knee wasn't completely straight, but it was facing mostly forward now. The bone was set at least a bit better than it had been.

After he got the fire lit, Jack worked on making a brace for the leg from a couple of more stout branches and a spare blanket. Then he spent the rest of the afternoon and a good chunk of the evening after dark putting together a litter. It took a while because thicker pieces of wood were hard to find, but he finally managed to make one that he thought would do the job.

Ortiz looked doubtful, though.

"You want me to get in that thing?"

Jack nodded.

"And the horse will pull it. It's that or you hop all the way back to Forest Hills. You sure can't ride."

Ortiz rolled his eyes.

"It's going to be a long trip home."

❦ 25 ❦

CRAWLING

The good thing about Ortiz's injury was it made taking the watch in shifts untenable. Not only was he immobile, but the pain of his injury left him almost incapable of noticing anything except what was right in front of his face. Besides that, he needed rest. Badly. So Jack made a command decision to accept the risk of getting a full night's sleep.

In retrospect, Jack didn't fault himself for that decision one bit. Because Ortiz's prediction proved true. And then some.

It took a long time to get the litter hooked up to his horse. He ended up looping a piece of rope around his saddle horn, then down the front of the saddle, then between the stirrups and the horse's flanks, and tied it to the ends of the litter just behind the horse's rump. He was careful to leave space between the horse and the litter so Ortiz wouldn't get hit by horse pellets, but it was a jury-rigged setup at best. He hoped it would work out.

Getting Ortiz into the litter was not too difficult, but

they managed to jar Ortiz's leg twice, evoking cries of pain from the security man.

It was very slow going. Jack's horse had not been trained to pull, but to carry riders, and she balked at first. Eventually Jack convinced her to get moving, but they couldn't move at more than a brisk walk without subjecting Ortiz to many jarring bumps. Every one evoked cries of pain from him.

Very quickly, Jack learned to ride on the shoulder, as opposed to the center, of the road: counter-intuitively, it was a smoother surface than the pitted, cracked, and otherwise heavily eroded pavement on the Interstate. Maybe if they'd been traveling in the summer, it wouldn't have made a difference, but with snow, however shallow, covering the road, Jack couldn't steer around those defects until it was too late. They only made a few miles the first day. But Jack made some changes to the litter and its towing apparatus that evening, and each evening thereafter, and gradually the miles began to pass faster.

There were other difficulties, of course. Ortiz couldn't maneuver around to the latrine on his own, for one thing. Back when he was getting ready to be a father, before the crash, Jack had serious reservations about changing diapers on a baby. To have to help a grown man with those same functions was even more distasteful. The more so because it was Ortiz: proud, strong, capable Ortiz. Jack could tell he was humiliated from the whole experience, though he never said anything, and that just made Jack all the more uncomfortable.

If that were the worst trouble, though, Jack wouldn't have minded. As much. But Ortiz's condition deteriorated by the day. He came down with a fever late in the afternoon of the second day of travel. Jack cut his pants leg, in order to better see the injured limb, and was alarmed to see it bruised pretty much all over and pinkish. The bruising actually improved somewhat in the following days, but the pinkish coloration turned redder and Ortiz's waking periods gradually grew less and less frequent.

In the evening of the third day, as he was putting out the fire after dinner, the western sky lit up. One moment, his eyes were beginning to adjust to the darkness of night with just a waning crescent moon to augment the stars. The next, first one, then two more, brilliant flashes of light appeared on the horizon, from the direction of Memphis. A minute or two later, four more flashes appeared, then nothing except for a dim afterglow. They were a bit over sixty miles from Memphis, by Jack's best reckoning. He expected to make Jackson around noon the next day. The fact that the flashes were visible, but there was no accompanying sound, meant whatever made the flashes was very distant. He had a sinking suspicion about what was causing them.

He looked at Ortiz for verification, but the security man was already asleep and Jack didn't want to wake him. With just his own intuition to guide him, Jack felt sure he was viewing the results of the Legion and the Enlightened encountering the gangs of Memphis. He did not sleep well that night at all.

The next morning, Jack pressed his horse to a faster pace. As a result, they made Jackson earlier in the day than Jack expected, though he cost Ortiz several more painful bumps and jarrings. Jack was surprised at the greeting that awaited him at Jackson. A hefty barricade stretched across the offramp from the interstate, manned by a large number of armed men. And was that a howitzer off to the side?

Jack's arrival caused a bit of a stir. As he approached, every man behind the barricade took station and leveled weapons at him. He reined the horse in a good thirty feet from the barrier and raised his hands, empty for all to see.

"Not looking for trouble. We just need some supplies, and if there's a doctor in town, my friend could use some help."

A man near the center of the barricade replied after a brief consultation with the fellow next to him.

"What's wrong with your friend?"

"Horse fell on him and broke his leg."

A few of the men at the barricade winced in sympathy, but they didn't lower their rifles. The leader spoke again.

"Don't know how much help we can give, but Doc'll take a look at him."

He gestured toward a man to Jack's left. The fellow manipulated some mechanism and, a moment later, part of the barricade opened. Jack heeled his horse forward and walked through.

The guards' leader met him on the far side. Jack recognized him immediately as the owner of the Inn they stayed in when they came through before. He saw no recognition on the innkeeper's face, though, until the litter came through the opening. The innkeeper's eyes widened.

"That's Ortiz! What the hell?" He looked back at Jack, and demanded, "Who are you?"

It's always good to know you've made an impression on people. It took several minutes of explaining, and reminding, before the innkeeper remembered that they'd met. Jack was somewhat comforted by the fact he forgot Ortiz had come through with him, those months ago. Maybe the guy was just batty. Regardless, after the drawn out re-introductions were done, he led Jack to the Doc's house.

The Doc ended up being a wiry older man who walked with the help of a cane. Harrison was his name. He set about examining Ortiz, and in particular Ortiz's leg, in a brisk, business-like manner. The examination was quick. Jack was impressed Doc managed to complete it without waking Ortiz up.

Rubbing his eyes, Doc turned to Jack and gave his assessment.

"There's not much I can do, son. It's broken in several places, set poorly, and infected."

Tell me something I don't know, Jack thought. Aloud, he said, "Do you have any antibiotics or anything?"

Doc chuckled ruefully, shaking his head.

"Ain't been none of that here since just after the Troubles. Caravan won't sell what they have 'cept to MDs."

Jack blinked.

"I thought you were a Doctor."

Doc shook his head and waved a hand, as though dismissing Jack's claim.

"Been called Doc ever since the service. Navy Medical Corpsman. Served with the Marines and on submarines."

Well that was great. At least the promise of supplies panned out. The land around town was fertile and they'd had a good harvest. So they had plenty of foodstuffs to sell. Jack had found more caravan scripts in Ortiz's saddle bags, valid scripts this time, when he packed them out from the ambush site. So he was able to purchase food to get them to Forest Hills without too much difficulty.

Jackson's mayor appeared as Jack was finishing his purchases. He was suitably concerned about Ortiz's condition, but was clearly more interested in their mission. Jack obliged him, to an extent. He left off the details of the Art, but was very clear about the potential threat that was following him and Ortiz. The mayor's face became grim when Jack finished. Thanking Jack for the information, he hurried away, calling for messengers to summon people for a conference.

Shortly after noon, Jack rode back out the barricade gate and turned east toward Forest Hills.

According to the map, it was about a hundred twenty miles from Jackson to Forest Hills: about six days at the pace they were making. The first two passed without incident. But when night fell on the third day, there was a glow on the western horizon. It was dim, but noticeable.

"That can't be good."

Ortiz was awake. Jack stared at the glow for a long time before answering.

"There were lights the other night while you were asleep, too. I think the Legion hit Memphis and now Jackson."

Ortiz coughed: hacking, dry coughs that left him gasping. He'd started coughing like this earlier in the day. It had Jack worried. Finally, Ortiz managed to speak again.

"That makes sense. How far to go?"

"Sixty miles, give or take."

Ortiz coughed again, not as bad as last time, though.

"Forty five."

"Huh?"

Ortiz propped himself up onto his elbows and spoke. "The plan we developed had a defensive perimeter set up fifteen miles from Forest Hills. If we can get there, we've got backup."

When the hell was Ortiz planning to let him in on that little nugget? Oh well, better late than never.

"Ok, a bit over two days. Then we'll hook up with your boys, get you to some real Docs."

Slumping back onto his bedroll, Ortiz smiled faintly.

"Looking forward to it."

His eyelids drifted shut. Jack set about getting his own sleeping arrangements ready. With one blanket going into Ortiz's leg brace and another going into the litter, Jack just had his cold weather gear and a thin, patched blanket. But it was better than nothing. He was just settling under his blanket when Ortiz grabbed his upper arm in a surprisingly firm grip, considering the security man's condition.

Jack looked at him and found him fully awake, his eyes fierce in the faint glow from the last embers of their fire.

"Don't trust Grymanski, Simmons."

What was this, revelation night? He sure didn't need *that* advice, thank you very much.

"Never have, Juan. Never will."

"No, I mean it. Do not trust him, with anyone. Or any thing."

Ortiz's eyes flickered from Jack toward his saddle bag, where Jack kept the flask of elixir, his focusing rod and glow crystal, and Horbach's journal. Then he spoke again.

"Only reason you're here, Simmons, is to..." he coughed again. "To give Grymanski leverage on your pal Miller. Give him a reason to do what Grymanski wants him to." Ortiz drew a deep breath. "Sending you out put Miller into his hands nicely. And if you didn't make it back, so much the better."

Jack felt a chill in his bones.

"What, you're supposed to do me in?"

Ortiz shook his head.

"I don't do that kind of work, and he knows it. But if you happened to get taken out by a bandit, or the Order, he wouldn't shed a tear. He's wanted you out of the picture ever since Graeber and he figured you for easy meat." Ortiz paused for a moment, then added, "He docked me a month's pay over that Graeber incident, you know. Wanted you whacked right then, whatever your mayor said."

"So why..."

"Because I'd have done what you did to Graeber, or more, if I were in your shoes." He coughed again.

"But. That makes no sense. You and he are in lockstep."

Ortiz rolled his eyes.

"Never contradict the boss in public, Simmons. Disagree all you want in private, but in public, his policy is your policy."

"Well...thanks. I guess."

Ortiz issued a half-laugh that sounded more a snort.

"Whatever. Just remember, don't trust him an inch."

Ortiz drifted off to sleep again and Jack sat awake for a while. He'd always figured Grymanski for a weasel, and recent events seem to have born that assessment out. Maybe Ortiz was right. If he went waltzing into Forest Hills with all this loot, Grymanski would likely try to take it. If he did try, there would be precious little Jack could do to stop it, with the quantity of men-at-arms the Company controlled.

There was a small hillock not far from their campsite with a number of snow-covered boulders and smaller rocks scattered about the summit. That would do nicely. There was a collapsible shovel in Ortiz's pack; Jack had actually thought to grab that when they fled Memphis. Happy at his foresight, Jack grabbed the shovel, then dug out Horbach's journal and trudged to the top of the hillock, where he began to dig.

❧ 26 ❧

THE BATTLE OF FOREST HILLS

The morning of the sixth day since they left Jackson dawned clear and brisk, with only a very few clouds in the sky to the west. They'd camped under an overpass again, and from the nearby mile marker, Jack figured they had less than ten miles to go before they reached Ortiz's theoretical perimeter.

As nice as the morning was, Jack couldn't shake the feeling that the Legion would come marching into view any second. So he wasted no time, but quickly got their equipment squared away, helped Ortiz onto the litter, and got moving.

They set a pretty good pace initially, despite fresh snow. The morning after Ortiz's warning, Jack had awakened to find himself dusted with snow and fresh flakes falling from the sky. Over the course of the day, a little more than two inches fell, slowing them down appreciably. Jack had been comforted that it probably slowed the Legion even more, if they were lurking on his and Ortiz's backtrail, and that it would obscure their tracks. But the slower pace still rankled.

Now, feeling that much closer to freedom and safety with each step, it seemed to Jack they positively flew down the Interstate. The sun slowly rose in the sky ahead of them. When it was about halfway to its zenith, Jack began to relax. From the mile markers, they'd covered five miles. They were just about home free.

He shouldn't have been surprised when, at that precise moment, it all went to hell.

"Simmons," exclaimed Ortiz, from the litter.

At first, Jack was surprised he was awake, but that was it.

"Yeah, Juan."

"I'm going to need my rifle."

"What are you..."

He turned around in the saddle as he spoke, but the words caught in his throat. Topping a rise about a mile behind them was a party of about thirty or forty riders. It was too far to tell who they were, but Jack knew.

The Legion. They were caught.

Jack's spirits, high just a moment before, sank like a stone. The worst part was that it happened so close to their safe haven.

Ortiz's M-14 was tucked under Jack's saddle blanket. It took some doing to pull it out without stopping. But he managed after a minute or two and tossed it back to Ortiz in the litter. Spare magazines were in the saddle bags, which he tossed back as well.

Then he spurred the horse to greater speed. Or tried to. Between the litter and snow above her fetlocks, the horse could barely manage a fast walk. The Legion was not so encumbered. Jack had no doubt they were catching up quickly.

Jack looked back once, a few minutes later, and blanched. They'd already given up half their lead. Now he could see that four or five of the riders wore black robes. The others wore red.

"Juan," he shouted, and was surprised to not hear a tremble in his voice.

"I'm on it," came the reply, steady and cool as normal. "Just ride."

Jack kicked the horse's flanks harder and she responded by surging forward into a canter. But it didn't last long. Within a few minutes, she'd fallen back to a walk again. Her burden was just too great.

"Zig-zag," Ortiz shouted.

At first, Jack didn't understand what he meant, but then a bullet whizzed past his head and it clicked. He turned the horse first right, then left, then right again. It slowed their forward progress, but at least they weren't riding in a straight line and making themselves an easy target.

"You going to shoot or what," Jack shouted. If they were getting shot at, they might as well return fire.

He wasn't pleased by the reply.

"Shut up and ride."

Jack looked back over his shoulder again. The Legionnaires were at best a tenth of mile back. What was Ortiz waiting for?

Almost as though he was reading Jack's mind, the security man picked that moment to open fire. The shots came steadily: one every five or six seconds. Still looking back, Jack saw Legionnaires topple from their saddles almost in time with Ortiz's shots. What was it he said, back north of Hope? One shot, one kill? It looked like he was living up to his words, or trying to.

Jack turned the horse again and kicked her flanks. If he could keep the horse going at a good pace, maybe Ortiz could pick off enough to make the rest of the pursuers fall back.

Suddenly, a massive concussion lifted him out of the saddle.

Jack landed in a snowdrift. He lay there for several moments, his ears ringing and his equilibrium totally lost. The world spun around him; he could barely tell up from down. After what seemed forever, he managed to sit up. What the hell happened?

His heart sank as he looked around. His horse was on the ground. He was sure she was dead. The litter was broken. Ortiz lay sprawled in the middle of the road. A fair-sized crater told Jack all he needed to know: the Enlightened.

Jack tried to stand and stumbled back down to his knees again. Apparently he hadn't fully gotten his bearings back. He managed to get to Ortiz by a mixture of crawling and stumbling. The security man was breathing, but his pulse was thready. Jack was dismayed to see his leg brace was broken and he was bleeding from a deep gash in his belly.

There was no time to worry about Ortiz's wounds, though. His rifle lay a small distance away, as did the saddle bag with the magazines. The Legionnaires were only about a hundred yards away and Ortiz had only felled a few of them. At least Jack could take a few more before the end. The scope on the M-14 was broken, the front lens shattered.

He raised the rifle anyway, sighting in as best he could. He fired and was taken aback at the result.

An explosion at the head of the Legion's column sent three of the riders tumbling as their horses fell. Suddenly, Jack heard gunshots from all around him. Eyes wide, he looked to the right and his heart leapt. A squad of men in full battle rattle, red FH emblazoned on their breasts, charged through the snow on foot, firing quick bursts at the approaching riders. A similar scene played out to Jack's left. He and Ortiz must have travelled farther than he thought.

The Legion adjusted quickly. They pulled up short and dismounted, quickly taking cover wherever available, then returning fire. Several went down in the transition from pursuit to firefight, but as Ortiz had noted back at the Citadel, the Legion was well drilled and professional.

But so were the Forest Hills troops. Advancing steadily and methodically with supporting fire, they didn't give the Legion time to regroup, instead pressing the attack. Jack took advantage of the Legion being distracted to grab Ortiz and pull him back behind the horse's corpse. Crouching there under cover, he watched the battle play out, fascinated. It looked like the Forest Hills men were about to completely overrun the Legion.

Then the Enlightened came into play. Flames burst from the ground at the advancing men's feet, turning part of the charge into a throng of screaming, thrashing bodies. A long-abandoned car lifted from the Interstate and flew into a group of Forest Hills men, crushing them beneath its weight. Another group stumbled and fell to their knees, then all the way to their bellies, as though being forced down by a large weight. Then they screamed, long drawn out cries of agony that were abruptly cut off.

The Forest Hills advance stalled, the remaining troops ducking for cover. One man, near the rear of the advancing men, turned and made a frantic "Come on" gesture in Jack's direction. Sure that he didn't mean the gesture for him, Jack looked over his shoulder and his spirits rose. Another group of Forest Hills soldiers, at least a platoon, if not a full company, was advancing in a second wave.

In moments, they reached Jack's position. Most pressed

on, barely giving him a second glance. But a few remained: a squad of mortar men, who set up behind a car near him, and two men on horseback. Each wore full battle rattle, but one of them, a stocky fellow in his early forties, had gold letters for his insignia, just as Ortiz had all those months ago. Despite the firefight just a football field ahead and the bullets flying around, they sat straight in their saddles, the gold-lettered man in particular surveying the battle as though looking at a puzzle that he would crack. Jack was impressed.

Ahead, the Forest Hills reinforcements were forcing the Legion into a slow retreat. The mortar support in particular seemed effective, as it equalized the punch the Enlightened provided. More and more, the Forest Hills troops appeared to gain the advantage. Then, all at once, the Legion broke. Mounting their horses, they turned and rode away to the west at the best canters their horses could manage in the snow. The Forest Hills troops did not pursue them very far, instead allowing them to make their escape.

"Why let them go?" Jack wondered aloud.

The gold lettered man answered in a clipped tone, "Because if you don't leave a man room to retreat, he'll fight to the death. And maybe take you with him." He looked down at Jack and added, "Good thing for you we shifted our deployed position forward a few miles, stranger. Two weeks ago, we would have neither seen you, nor been in position to help."

"I appreciate it," Jack said, standing up straight for what felt the first time in years. "We need to get to Forest Hills as soon as possible."

The commander frowned at him, then looked from Jack to Ortiz. His eyes widened. "That's Ortiz!" he exclaimed, then looked back at Jack. "Are you Simmons?"

Jack nodded.

"I'm Bob Webster. We've been on the lookout for you two

for weeks." Turning to his lieutenant, Webster said, "Get Isaac up here with the cart and a litter, then send word to base that the scouts have returned and we're inbound. Tell the Doctors to get ready for an assist."

The Lieutenant nodded and, turning his horse around, rode east with all the speed he could muster.

27

HOMECOMING

I t only took a few minutes for the Lieutenant to return
with the cart. More a sleigh than a cart, really, since the
wheels had been removed and replaced with runners.
Webster's men moved quickly, getting Ortiz onto a litter and
loading him into the back of the cart. Jack hopped into the
front of the cart with the driver and they set out with
Webster and three others riding escort.

Word of Jack and Ortiz's return spread quickly. They
arrived at the Country Club building an hour or so before
sunset and found a small crowd gathered, waiting for them.
Guards, servants, important-looking people Jack couldn't
identify, kids, women, and a few men in lab coats waited
amongst the columns in front of the building.

Jack wasted no time checking out the welcoming committee. As soon as the horses stopped, he dismounted and
rushed to help another soldier carefully slide Ortiz's litter off
the back of the cart.

"Juan!"

The pretty woman Jack remembered from their departure

rushed forward, a stricken expression on her face, as she saw Ortiz's condition. She bent over the litter and embraced him, sobbing. She remained there for a long few moments, speaking softly to him, until Webster came over and put a gentle had on her shoulder.

"Mrs. Ortiz, please. We need to get him inside so the doctors can help him."

She looked up at Webster and nodded slowly. Then she kissed Ortiz on the forehead and straightened. They moved into the building quickly and she followed, wiping her eyes with a handkerchief.

The doctors led them upstairs to a small room at the corner of the building, the same room they'd used to treat Tobias, Jack recalled. Within was a narrow bed in the middle of the room. Along one wall was a series of basins, pitchers sitting at the ready next to each, atop a long wooden table. What looked like surgical instruments were laid out on a similar table on the opposite wall. A number of compressed gas cylinders stood in a corner near the door, attached to breathing masks through clear plastic tubes. Large windows along the wall opposite the door admitted light from outside and there were a number of mirrors mounted from swivels in the ceiling. Small oil lamps were mounted to each mirror, to add additional light.

Jack and the soldier carefully set the litter down on the bed and backed away. No sooner had they finished than one of the doctors ushered them out and, without a word, shut the door in their faces.

Outside the room, Mrs. Ortiz stood alone, looking forlorn and terrified. Jack walked over to her and extended a hand.

"Mrs. Ortiz, I'm Jack..."

She pulled back from his outstretched hand, cutting him off in an angry tone.

"I know who you are, Mr. Simmons. It's because of you he went off. And look what happened." Her voice broke, and she wiped her eyes with her handkerchief again. Turning away from him, she waved him away. "Leave me alone."

Jack hesitated for a moment, then, with a sigh, he turned and walked away. He passed a trio of women in the hallway. They were hurrying toward the medical room; her friends, probably. As they passed, they eyed Jack with accusing, contemptuous gazes. Oh yes, definitely her friends.

Jack got back to the Country Club's foyer, then he was stopped abruptly by another body crashing into him. Arms grasped him in a fierce embrace and a face buried itself into his shoulder. The person was half sobbing, her body, he could tell it was a woman without trying, heaving from deep inhalations.

"I thought you were dead," she cried.

He knew that voice, but before he could reply, a hand clasped his shoulder, drawing his eye. Tobias stood at his side, grinning.

"Good to see you, boy," the old man said.

Jack blinked in surprise, then grinned sheepishly. Why should he be surprised? He knew Tobias would be here. Still, the suddenness of the greeting took him aback. Awkwardly, he patted Serena, he finally put the voice to a person, on her back. It was far from adequate, but it was all he could manage for the moment.

"It's good to be seen," he said. "Didn't think I'd make it back a few times there."

Serena released him and took a step back. Wiping her eyes, she smiled, looking somewhat abashed.

"What are you doing here?" Jack asked, earning himself a long-suffering look from her.

"The conference, you big dummy. Someone has to keep Beatrice and Geoff from giving away the farm just to spite each other."

"And she's done a great job of it," Tobias interjected. "I think Grymanski and his boys expected us small town folks to be pushovers. Didn't count on the likes of her."

That was good to hear. Much as he had hated to think about it, or rather, much as he'd felt ridden with guilt every time he thought about it, a good part of what made Serena so appealing was her stand-up attitude. Jack had never seen her back down where her rights were concerned. Even when Graeber attacked her, she did her best to fight back despite the odds being so heavily weighted in his favor. If Jack hadn't... But that was long past. No need to revisit it.

"Well, it's good to see you." Jack gave Tobias a gentle punch in the shoulder, adding, "Both of you," for the old man's benefit.

Serena looked surprised, then pleased. Her lips turned upwards into a warm smile. For that matter, Tobias gave Jack a weird look also. What was that for? Whatever. He returned Serena's smile in kind.

"Where's everyone else?"

"They were finishing up some business when word came you'd returned. Come on, they'll be anxious to see you also."

With that, she and Tobias led him out of the Country Club building and to the road he'd first seen through the slats of the labor pens. He found himself grinding his teeth as they walked past those pens, the memory of his and Tobias' earlier treatment coming back in a rush.

Their destination was a large house a short way down the road to the left. Built in two levels, with a wrap-around porch on the first level and a detached garage in back, it was the sort of thing that a doctor or big-time attorney would have owned, back before the Troubles. Inside, the ground floor was dominated by an open great room, complete with leather furniture near a big fireplace in the wall and a fancy-looking dining room set over near the doorway to what Jack presumed was the kitchen. Geoff and Beatrice were seated at the dining table, along with Dwight Goodwin and, Jack was surprised to see, Logan Pierce.

"Hot damn, Logan, what are you doing here?" Jack exclaimed as he walked into the room.

They gave each other a quick back-slapping hug of greeting and Logan quipped, "Just picking up your slack, brother."

Jack looked at Logan quizzically. With a chuckle, he elaborated.

"After you up and disappeared, I got the good deal. They tapped me to come here in your place."

"At no small expense and inconvenience to my business operations, I might add," said Geoff, giving Logan a sidelong look that contained a hint of reproach. He was just as cheerful as ever, Jack saw.

Rolling her eyes, Beatrice snorted. "Logan's done a great job for us on this trip. You have more than enough hands to run things back home for a while without him. Besides, the town's covering all the expenses of this trip, so stop your grumping."

Geoff's eyes flashed with annoyance and he half-opened his mouth to respond. But he stopped, apparently thinking better of it; a remarkable show of restraint from what Jack recalled of his temperament. Instead turning his attention fully to Jack, the ranch owner said, "Glad you're not dead," and shook Jack's hand in a quick, almost dismissive manner.

Beatrice was more friendly in her greeting, giving him a warm embrace. "I can't tell you how glad we all were when we got here and learned you still lived." Her eyes flickered toward Tobias, and she added, "Both of you." Looking back at Jack, she smiled broadly. "Welcome back, Jack."

Jack didn't know Dwight very well, but they had always been amicable. He completed the round of greetings by shaking Jack's hand with a firm, confident grip and nodding silently, his gaze conveying a great deal more respect than the last time they had interacted.

Jack's neighbors wasted no time in plying him for details of his expedition. Even Geoff was eager to hear of it, though Jack could tell he was trying hard to appear nonchalant. Jack hesitated. There was a lot to tell, and he wasn't entirely sure where to start. But if he couldn't figure out how to tell the story to them, how could he tell the other delegations in the conference?

So he obliged them, telling the tale as simply as he could. They were suitably impressed and more than a little amazed when he described the Order and Horbach's discoveries. He thought he saw tears welling up in more than one pair of eyes when he described Simeon's experience on the road, and again when he described how Jack and the boy parted ways. And of course the drama of the last few days on the road evoked exclamations from all of them.

Jack had just finished the telling and was feeling pretty good about how it went when a loud knock on the front door drew everyone's attention.

Logan opened the door, revealing Grymanski, along with two other men in suits. He barely acknowledged Logan's presence; his gaze instead swept over the people present before coming to rest on Jack.

"Ah, Mr. Simmons. I thought I'd find you here. May we have a word with you?"

They spoke on the porch, just outside the front door. Grymanski didn't want to have the conversation in front of Jack's friends. Jack wasn't about to invite Grymanski into a bedroom or to kick everyone else out of the great room, so outside it was. Besides, it was turning into a nice evening, as winter evenings went; it was considerably warmer than it had been just yesterday, though it was still far from t-shirt weather, and the stars were especially bright. Grymanski wasted no time in getting to the point.

"Were you successful?"

Jack looked over the two strangers momentarily before nodding.

"I found them. You're in a lot more trouble than you thought. Who are these guys?"

Grymanski tsk'd softly.

"Mr. Edwards and Mr. Chu are two of my partners. Our fourth, Mr. Goldberg, is in another meeting."

Jack inclined his head slightly in greeting. They did not return the gesture.

Grymanski cleared his throat.

"Mr. Simmons, tomorrow is the last scheduled day of the conference. We have made little headway toward establishing the alliance so far. What did you learn?"

"I learned enough to make it clear you're going to need that alliance if you want to hold them off."

Grymanski opened his mouth, but Jack silenced him with a raised hand as he continued.

"But I'm not going to tell you alone. I'll tell everyone tomorrow, at the conference meeting."

"Mr. Simmons, we need to plan what you're going to say. There are ways to..."

"Tomorrow. At the meeting."

Grymanski's jaw worked; he didn't look happy with Jack's proposal at all. Nor did his partners, though they kept their silence. Jack didn't give them a chance to protest further.

"Good evening, gentlemen," he stated flatly, then stepped back inside and shut the door.

The guys and Beatrice were gone, though Jack could hear their voices coming down the hallway from another room. Serena sat on the couch alone, watching the fire consume a large log in the fireplace. She looked toward him as the door closed.

"That was fast."

"Got nothing to say to him. He can get my report in the morning, with everyone else."

"Is that a wise way to play it?"

Jack settled down into a stuffed chair and, with a shrug, replied, "Maybe not, but I'm sick of dealing with that prick."

Serena watched him silently. Her gaze almost made him uncomfortable in its directness, except that it also carried a warm affection. Finally, she spoke again, a gentle smile on her lips.

"You've changed."

Jack blinked. Had he changed? He didn't feel any different. But then, he found it difficult to recall how he had been, back before the raid on Tobias' house. So much had happened since then. He'd seen so much. His dreams had changed...

His dreams had changed.

Starting, Jack looked back at Serena and was, as always, entranced by her beauty. But unlike before, he felt no guilt at noticing it. He shook his head in amazement.

"I guess I have."

He reached out and took her hand.

"I'm sorry for how I treated you. I don't have any good excuse."

Serena looked down at his hand, her eyes widening for a moment. Then she squeezed it gently.

"I always understood, Jack."

Then she laughed and added, "It took you long enough, though."

28

DIPLOMACY

The old dining area on the first floor of the Country Club building was opulent. Wide and long, with intricate crown moldings along the ceiling and a number of expensive-looking paintings on the walls, once upon a time it was probably a popular place to rent out for wedding receptions and the like. For all Jack knew, the people of Forest Hills might still use it for that purpose now.

But today, at least, the room filled a different role. Roughly twenty round tables, with room for eight people, but only set for four or five, were positioned in a semi-circle around a lectern near the wall opposite the entrance doors.

Jack followed Serena and Tobias into the room and toward a table near the end, on the speaker's right. Several other embassies were already present and seated, as were the other members of the Glennville contingent. Beatrice nodded and gave him a warm smile of greeting as he sat down at the table. Logan grinned and bumped fists with him. Dwight and Geoff nodded in greeting, the former giving him an encouraging grin. Serena sat next to him on his right, Tobias on his left.

Jack certainly had never thought to be part of a gathering like this. Looking around the room, he saw place tags for many settlements he had heard of and some he had not. Glennville, Jackson, Atlanta, Morgantown, Harper's Ferry, Birmingham, Fayatteville, Richmond. The list went on. These tables were about to be filled with important people who were here to represent their citizens. What the hell was *he* doing here?

A new contingent of three men entered the room and walked toward the tables. Their clothing drew Jack's gaze immediately. They wore camouflage fatigues, but the camo was in blues, greys, and blacks. Though faded and dirty, they had rank insignia on their collars, sewn on nametags over their right breast pocket, and another sewn on tag that read "US NAVY" over their left. Above the Navy tags, each wore insignia that Jack supposed must have some military significance.

"Who are they?" he asked.

Serena leaned over and spoke softly into his ear.

"The embassy from Mayport. It was a Navy base before the Troubles, you know. They claim to be the crew off a submarine that escaped damage during the Troubles. Apparently they were submerged when everyone else lost power and didn't know what was going on except they'd lost communications. After a few days, they headed home to Norfolk, but found the channel blocked by wrecked shipping. Mayport was the easiest port to get into, so they went there instead and managed to dock."

She raised an eyebrow at him. "They say their electricians were able to repair some of the wiring in the base, and they're supplying electrical power to a number of buildings with their reactor."

Jack blinked. Wouldn't *that* be nice. Of course, if he could get Horbach's notes figured out, they wouldn't need tricks like that for much longer. He hoped.

Over the next several minutes, the rest of the embassies arrived and took their places. Finally, Grymanski and his three partners entered. They took seats in the table at the far end of the semicircle from Glennville. All except Grymanski, who walked up to the lectern and called the meeting to order.

"Good afternoon, ladies. Gentlemen. As you know, we recently dispatched a team of two volunteers to discover the facts concerning this 'Master,' of whom we've spoken the last few days. I am pleased to inform you that they returned yesterday afternoon. The leader of the expedition was badly injured and is currently resting, but his second is prepared to give you his report. Please welcome Mr. Jack Simmons, from Glennville."

Grymanski turned and went back to his seat. Serena squeezed Jack's hand briefly before he stood and took Grymanski's place at the lectern. Well, here goes nothing, he thought. Taking a deep breath, he told the story of his and Ortiz's journey. It took a long time to tell the whole thing and by the end Jack really needed a drink of water.

Finally, he finished. The response was not exactly what he expected.

"Really. Magic. You expect us to believe that bullshit?" The speaker was a delegate from Morgantown, but Jack saw a number of others nodding in agreement.

Jack spread his hands helplessly.

"I'd offer a demonstration, but as I said, I only have one flask of the potion left. And it cannot be reproduced without someone directing the correct energies into the new batch, so if I use it now..."

The Morgantown rep snorted and leaned back in his chair, crossing his arms over his chest with a look of disdain. Jack looked over at Grymanski. The old man looked alarmed.

He made a 'get on with it' gesture with his hand. What did he expect Jack to do?

Tobias got him off the hook for a moment by standing and directing a withering glare at the Morgantown folks.

"Look here. I've known Jack for ten years. If he says that's the way it is, that's the way it is."

The leader of the Mayport contingent, a fellow with gold oak leafs on his collar, spoke up.

"We're not questioning his honesty, Mr. Miller. But extraordinary claims require evidence. Perhaps he was fooled by a clever trick."

Tobias frowned, but sat back down. Jack couldn't believe what he was hearing. A clever trick? Was he kidding? After all he'd gone through at the Citadel. All the struggles to get back safely. Now, to be essentially accused of being a shill or a liar was too much. Irritation turned to anger and he slammed his hand down onto the lectern loudly.

"Damnit, I'm not making this stuff up! I'm sorry, Major, but this isn't some sleight-of-hand parlor trick. It's real."

"Commander."

"What?"

"I'm in the Navy, not the Army. I'm a Lieutenant Commander, not a Major."

"You're going to argue with me over semantics? When the hell were YOU at sea last? Unless you hadn't noticed, there isn't a USA anymore, let alone a US Navy. For the love of..."

Grymanski stood and cleared his throat. All eyes turned to him.

"This is getting us nowhere. Mr. Simmons, what would you require to provide the demonstration the delegates requested?"

"I need another flask of the elixir. But I haven't found the recipe in Horbach's journal yet and..."

"As I recall, Mr. Simmons, you and Mr. Ortiz were

followed by a not insignificant force of Legionnaires, and our forces engaged them while seeing you to safety."

"Yes."

Where was he going with this?

"Is it possible, Mr. Simmons, that one or more of those who call themselves Enlightened were with the pursuers?"

Jack nodded. Son of a bitch. Why hadn't he thought of that?

Grymanski turned to the other delegates.

"In that case, if you will consent to remain here an extra day, I suggest we adjourn until tomorrow to give our scouts time to search the site of the battle for the items Mr. Simmons needs."

There was a long several moments of murmured discussion among the gathered delegations. Looking around, Jack could tell that some of those discussions were more than a little heated. Crap, had he blown it? Were they all going to just leave in a huff and ruin all his efforts?

Finally, the murmuring died down and, one by one, the delegations expressed concurrence with reconvening the next day. Relief filled Jack as he sat back down. He had one more chance.

A few bits of formality followed, but very soon the delegations stood and, one by one, filed out of the room. One and all, they looked at Jack as they left, some with curiosity, some with amusement, some with contempt. As the final group departed, Grymanski walked over to Jack and fixed him with an icy stare.

"This, Mr. Simmons, is why I asked you to brief me *before* I allowed you to address the delegates. This is a waste of time we do not need."

"I don't work for you any more, Grymanski. You don't allow or forbid me anything."

Grymanski opened his mouth to say something more, but

Jack turned and walked away before the old man could speak. He met Logan, Tobias, and Serena at the door. She took his hand, and Tobias gave him a wink and a clap on the shoulder as they walked out together.

The next day, shortly before noon, Jack answered a knock on the front door and found Webster waiting on the porch. He looked exhausted.

"Mr. Simmons, Mr. Grymanski asked me to bring this to you."

Jack looked at the man's outstretched hand and felt a burst of excitement.

"Thanks," Jack said as he took the pair of flasks Webster held. Carefully unstoppering one of them, Jack sniffed the contents, and his excitement mounted. It was the same slightly sour, metallic odor he had come to recognize during his time at the Citadel. He gave Webster a broad grin.

"Really, thank you. You may have just saved our butts."

Webster merely shrugged. "Just doin' my job. But if you don't mind, I've been up all night. I'm going to hit the rack."

He didn't wait for Jack's response, but turned and quickly walked down the stairs of the porch, then down the street.

Jack watched him depart, his grin fading. This afternoon would be a big deal. It had been almost two weeks since he last tried to use the Art. Hopefully he wouldn't screw it up too badly. Even if that went well, there was the rest of his plan to consider. Tobias and Serena both agreed it was the right way to go, but Jack knew there would be a lot of people in the room who would be incensed.

The delegates assembled again at 3 o'clock. This time there was no pomp and circumstance. Jack simply walked up to the lectern and held up the flask. Then, without a word, he removed the stopper and drank the fluid down.

As always, he had to force himself to swallow the hideous fluid. The nausea and pain hit him full force and it was all he could do not to double over. He had to support himself on the lectern to keep his feet. But soon enough, the initial rejection passed and he felt the tingling sensation begin to spread. Was he imagining things, or did it happen faster this time? Looked like Reginald was right about something else.

The image of the young Enlightened's eyes as Jack's knife struck home ran through his mind, and with it, a flash of guilt. Reginald hadn't been an evil person, near as Jack could tell. But he was on an evil path, that was for sure.

Jack closed his eyes and took a long, deep breath. Then he slowly exhaled. Focus on the here and now. Can't afford to screw this one up.

When he opened his eyes again, his vision was altered, the sure sign that the drug had fully attuned him. He looked around the half circle of delegates and smiled thinly.

"Who would like to volunteer?"

The Morgantown rep snorted. "Who the hell are you, David Copperfield? Get on with it, Simmons, so we can go the hell home." To one of his comrades, he muttered, "Wasted enough time here as it is." The fellow nodded in agreement.

Had his senses not been honed by the drug's effects, Jack probably wouldn't have heard the last remark, but even had he not, the Morgantown man singled himself out. His derisive comment pissed Jack off and sealed his fate.

In retrospect, he probably went a little overboard.

The man was wearing work boots, jeans, and a collared cotton shirt. And a bad tie. Not that any tie was good when paired with jeans. But really. A naked woman dancing on a stripper pole? How does that become tasteful? Jack shook his head and pulled the focusing rod he'd filched from Horbach's office out of his pocket.

He took a moment to clear his mind, then he focused his will. Jack heard a number of delegates gasp as the crystal began to glow.

A moment later the Morgantown man shouted with chagrin as, with a flick of the focusing rod, Jack used Force to pull the tie straight up into the air and force the delegate to his feet.

Jack managed not to grin as he pulled the tie forward with Force, toward the lectern, and the man stumbled to follow it. "Nice tie," Jack said to the man as he came to a halt before the lectern. Then Jack made a twirling motion with the rod and the man turned in time, again being pulled by the tie, until he was facing the other delegates.

Jack paused again, considering. Combining Force and Heat wasn't something he'd tried before. He frowned. It was harder than he thought. But if it worked...

The Morgantown man shouted an oath as the end of his tie caught fire. Again the delegates gasped, as much because the flame was blue-green as because of the sudden ignition. Jack let the flame spread halfway down the tie before releasing the Heat and Force that touched the tie. The man yanked the tie off (it was a clip-on!) and threw it to the ground, then stomped on it to put the fire out.

He turned on Jack, his eyes alight with fury. Fists clenched, he rushed forward. But before he could move a step, Jack raised the rod again and pressed forward with Force at the man's chest. The man stopped as though hitting a wall and fell back onto his rather sizable backside. Several members of the various delegations chuckled. From the corner of his eye, Jack saw Tobias and Logan doing all they could not to let out full-on guffaws.

The chuckles stopped when Jack raised the rod over his head. Every eye watched the glowing crystal. Jack could see wariness painted on most faces. Perfect.

"Would you see more? I only had a month of training at the Citadel. The Enlightened of the Order train for years before they put on the black." Jack glanced over toward the Forest Hills partners. "Mr. Grymanski."

The old man looked surprised to be called upon, but he recovered quickly.

"Yes, Mr. Simmons?"

"What were your casualties in the battle when Ortiz and I returned?"

Grymanski frowned, and for a moment it didn't appear he was going to answer. But his partners nodded an affirmative, so, with a sigh, the old man replied.

"Twenty-five out of sixty men killed or wounded."

"And how many of the enemy killed?"

Grymanski's frown deepened. "A dozen Legionnaires and one Enlightened."

The disproportionate numbers were not lost on the delegates, particularly those from Fayatteville and Mayport. Jack could see worried frowns on virtually all of them. If one Enlightened could do that much harm, what could ten, or fifty, do? Did the settlements have anything that could stop such a force, even with the weapons and expertise of Fort Bragg? Jack didn't think so, and from their expressions, neither did they.

A man from Fayatteville broke the silence.

"What will it take to put together a force of our own magic users?"

Jack felt a weight lift he didn't even realize he'd been carrying. It looked like he'd done it. The first part, at least.

"First, I need time to study in a secure place. Horbach's notes are detailed, but complicated. It will take a while to decipher them. And I'll need people to obtain supplies for the potions and focusing rods. Then, of course, I'll need volunteers who want to learn. In the Citadel, less than ten percent are able to learn at all, so if you want a sizable force, I'll need a *lot* of volunteers."

The room filled with a general murmuring as the various delegates talked with each other. Jack overheard a number of interesting, and stupid, ideas being voiced. Then the Commander from Mayport rose and the murmuring ceased.

"I propose you do your studying in Mayport. We're located furthest from the Citadel. We have electricity, so it'll be easier for you to work. And worst case, we can cut the mooring lines and take you out to sea." He flashed a quick grin. "Can't ask for more secure than that."

Several voices rose in protest, but after several minutes, most came to accept the Commander's idea as the best way to go. Fayatteville held out the longest against the motion, no doubt due to Army-Navy rivalry more than anything else, but eventually it became unanimous.

Once that was settled, a woman from Atlanta took the floor and began discussing the logistics of shipping the supplies Jack needed. It was time to put a stop to this. Jack raised his voice.

"You didn't ask my price."

Stunned silence greeted him. The Atlanta woman, a plump woman in her thirties with curly red-blond hair, stopped her sentence mid-word and looked at him as though seeing an alien.

"I beg your pardon?"

"I said, ma'am, that you didn't ask my price."

She sat back down, clearly unsure how to respond. The Commander was not so reluctant.

"We're talking about ensuring the survival of every settlement east of the Mississippi, Mr. Simmons. What do you mean, your price?"

Jack glanced at Grymanski and was gratified to see him looking a bit worried.

"Commander, I've recently learned the value of quid pro quo. If you want my help in saving yourselves from Horbach and his Order, you'll have to meet my price to get it."

The Commander scowled, but gave a small nod of acquiescence. "Name your price then, Mr. Simmons."

Jack looked at each delegation table in turn. He saw worry in every face. Good.

"Some of your settlements make use of slave labor."

He held up a hand to cut off indignant cries of protest from several delegates.

"Don't bother trying to deny it. The Caravan Company makes a good profit selling them to you, do you not, Mr. Grymanski?"

Grymanski, looking pole-axed, nodded weakly. He trembled as he pulled a handkerchief from his pocket and wiped his brow. Jack smiled again.

"This practice will stop, now and forever. All slaves in your settlements will be immediately freed and either paid a fair wage for their labor or else given money and supplies to see them to a new home of their choosing."

Groans of chagrin emanated from several mouths, but Jack continued.

"Furthermore, the forces of the alliance of settlements will make it their business to hunt down and eliminate any and all raiders and slavers from within the alliance's borders. Do this, and I will help you. Do not, and I'll go someplace where neither Horbach, nor you, can find me, and leave you to deal with him on your own."

The Morgantown rep, still on the floor, growled up at him.

"How 'bout we just beat you down, take the book, and learn it our damn selves?"

His colleagues voiced concurrence. Jack couldn't say he was surprised. He had a fair notion which West Virginia settlement it was that Grymanski mentioned to him before. It was good to be prepared, it seemed. Jack favored the Morgantown man with a mocking grin.

"You could do that, I suppose, but good luck finding the book."

The man looked confused.

"You don't think I was stupid enough to bring it here, do you? It's buried out there somewhere." He made a vague gesture toward the west. "I'm the only one who knows where. But it wouldn't matter anyway. It took me an entire afternoon to even achieve this much with the Art..." he gestured toward the glowing crystal at the end of the focusing rod, then continued, "...and there are just two doses of the potion available between here and the Citadel."

The Morgantown man glowered, but didn't say anything else. Jack looked around at the remaining delegates and saw acceptance on most faces. Tobias, Serena, and Logan wore expressions of open amusement and pride. This was going quite well.

The Commander spoke up again. "It appears you've left us no choice, Mr. Simmons."

Jack chuckled. "There is always a choice, Commander. The question is whether you are willing to pay the price for making it." He looked back at the Forest Hills folks. "Wouldn't you say, Mr. Grymanski?"

The old man looked at Jack with unbelieving eyes that seemed to be bulging out of his head. Yes, quite well indeed.

❦ 29 ❦

THE PRICE WE MUST PAY

J ack stepped into the recovery room and shut the door quietly. Ortiz lay in bed, looking almost like a mummy from all the bandages he wore. The security man's leg was heavily bandaged and braced, raised in a traction device. In all, he looked like hell, but he was alive. He was also asleep.

Jack cleared his throat and Ortiz's eyes sprung open in a heartbeat. Seeing Jack, he managed a half-grin.

"Simmons," he said by way of greeting.

"The nurse said you wanted to talk with me."

Ortiz nodded and gestured to the chair beside his bed. Jack walked over and lowered himself into it, finding it surprisingly comfortable. After he was settled, he looked at Ortiz and waited. A moment later, the security man spoke.

"I never thanked you, Jack."

Jack blinked in surprise and made a dismissive gesture.

"There's nothing to thank me for."

"You could have left me there when I told you to. Hell, you *should* have. But you didn't. You saved my life, and for that, I thank you."

Ortiz held out his hand. Slowly, almost gingerly, Jack took it and they clasped hands for a moment. Ortiz's grip was still strong, whatever his injuries.

"I like to think you'd have done the same," Jack stated, earning a shrug from Ortiz. Jack looked at the traction unit and changed the subject. "What's the verdict?"

Ortiz's eyes followed Jack's to his leg. His expression lost what cheer it had.

"Doc says it had already begun to heal wrong when we got here. He thinks I'll walk again, but..." He spread his hands in an expression of helplessness. Jack saw the pain of loss in Ortiz's eyes and felt for him.

"Damn. I'm sorry, man."

Ortiz shrugged again.

"It is what it is."

They sat in silence for a few minutes. Jack was just beginning to think he should leave when Ortiz finally spoke again.

"I heard what you did in the meeting yesterday. Even though we lost the Morgantown delegation, that was damn good work."

"Yeah, well, you should have seen your boss' face at the end," Jack remarked, letting his amusement, and his pride of accomplishment, show through in his tone.

Ortiz chuckled softly.

"What's your plan now?"

"I think I'm going to take the Navy guys up on their offer. Go to Mayport. Horbach's still going to want to kick my ass. For that matter, he'll probably want a piece of Forest Hills as well now. At least if he tracks me to Mayport, there's no one I care about in the crossfire if he sends his goons there. You? Probably can't keep doing what you were."

Oritz replied, "Grymanski asked me to take over coordinating our defensive forces' positioning."

"And you're going to accept? You warned me not to trust him. How can you?"

Ortiz looked away, toward the window. He took a short moment to answer, his expression contemplative.

"This is my home, Jack. I need to do what I can to serve and protect it. No matter if I trust the men in charge or not."

Jack could understand that and respect it.

"In charge of the defenses. Isn't Webster doing that?"

"He only has command of the western units. I'd be overall in charge."

"So it'll be General Ortiz then, eh?"

Ortiz's jaw dropped. He looked back at Jack, his expression shocked, as though he'd been pole axed.

"Really? You didn't put two and two together there, Juan?"

Ortiz shook his head. "I suppose I hadn't thought about it. General." He suddenly frowned. "I don't think the raise he mentioned is big enough."

For a moment, they looked at each other in complete seriousness. Then first Jack, then Ortiz, burst out laughing. It felt like all the tension of the last several weeks came rushing out of him. From his laughter, Jack could see that it was the same for Ortiz. They kept on guffawing for what felt to Jack like an eternity. But in reality, it was only a minute or so. Wiping his eyes, Jack got himself under control and stood up.

"I never thought I'd say this, but it's been a pleasure."

Ortiz, also wiping his eyes, nodded.

"Take care of yourself, Simmons. We can't afford to lose what you learned at the Citadel."

"Good to know I'll be missed," Jack quipped. "You take care as well, General. I won't be there to pull your chestnuts out of the fire next time."

Ortiz snorted and Jack clasped hands with him again. Then, with a last smile and a nod, he turned and walked out of the room.

They stopped atop the hillock long enough for Jack to dig up Horbach's book. He'd taken pains to wrap it as securely as possible, but all the same, the book showed evidence of moisture damage when he finally pulled it free of the earth. He breathed a curse and thumbed through the book, hoping the moisture hadn't ruined the important parts. He couldn't see anything obviously illegible, but he would have to thoroughly examine it later to be certain. He shuddered to think what would have happened had he left it in the earth for much longer though.

Jack stood and walked back to his companions. Geoff and Dwight had balked at detouring west, wanting to return to their businesses as soon as possible. So Logan had offered to see them safely home, leaving Jack, Tobias, Beatrice, and Serena to retrieve the book and follow along after. It was silly, but Jack had come to expect nothing else from Geoff after having listened to Tobias' bitching about Council meetings over the years.

"Find it alright, boy?" Tobias queried as Jack pulled himself up into his saddle.

"No worries. Let's get going."

They turned their horses east and, after a few minutes, came upon their escort. Ortiz had insisted on sending a platoon to guard them while they were beyond Forest Hills' western perimeter. Beatrice and Tobias were very reluctant to accept. Had the offer come from anyone other than Ortiz, Jack would have been also. After a brief, fiery discussion, they acquiesced, but they'd been on edge the entire two days out here.

Not that Jack was entirely relaxed. He had no illusions about Grymanski's love for him and wouldn't put it past him to pull a fast one without Ortiz's knowledge. But the days passed and they left Forest Hills behind without incident. Maybe Grymanski figured there'd be no profit in making further trouble.

A couple of days past Forest Hills' eastern perimeter, they held a palaver over the campfire after settling down for the night.

"Should be home tomorrow afternoon. You still intend on going to Mayport, Jack?" Beatrice inquired, her tone conveying her disapproval plainly.

Not again. They'd had this argument once already, back before leaving Forest Hills. Serena surprised him by interjecting, though.

"Yes, we are. You're not going to change our minds, Beatrice, so stop trying."

"We?"

Serena gave him a direct, almost predatory, look.

"If you think you're going to slink away and leave me behind again, Jack Simmons, you've got another thing coming."

In fact, he'd been thinking exactly that that. He opened his mouth to say as much, but Tobias beat him to it.

"Not gonna win this, youngster. Do yourself a favor and just say yes."

Frustration welled up. Didn't they get it? He was a marked man. Anyone near him would be in danger. Better to subject the Navy guys to it. At least they were military types. But looking at first Serena's, then Tobias' faces, Jack could tell the older man was right. He was going to lose this one.

With a deep sigh, Jack nodded.

"Guess that means you're coming too, Tobias?"

A loud snort was the older man's initial reply.

"Hell no. Beatrice and me'll have our hands full enough making sure Geoff doesn't fuck this thing up. Won't have no time to gallivant across creation with you, even if I wanted to."

They rode into town a couple hours before dark. Jack was pleased to see the palisade wall complete. The guards at the gate beamed with excitement as they rode into view. One of them sprinted away into town ahead of the travelers. Jack and Tobias exchanged glances and smiles at the reaction.

Mayor Lang and the rest of the council met them about a third of the way between the gate and City Hall. There were handshakes all around and warm smiles of welcome. The pleasantries lasted for quite some time before the council led the weary travelers to the high school. They wouldn't say why, but that became clear as soon as the troupe walked into the gymnasium.

Cheers erupted. It looked like half the town was gathered there, applauding Jack and his friends as though they'd done something truly heroic. Gena's band was set up on the far end of the room. They started playing almost as soon as the applause ended and the crowd closed in on the small group of travelers.

The party lasted well into the night. It was almost as festive as the opening party for the caravan market. Of course, with all that had come to light recently, Jack couldn't help but wonder if the caravan market would ever be as joyful an occasion as it had been before. That was a thought for another time, however. For now, he was home. Safe. And surrounded by friends.

The lone dark spot on the evening occurred twenty minutes or so after the party started. Tobias had left Jack and Serena shortly after they arrived. When he returned, he looked concerned, almost distressed.

"What's wrong, old man?" Jack quipped, in between sips from some of Harlan's best whiskey. It was excellent. But then, it was free for him that night. Even rubbing alcohol would probably be better than average under those conditions.

"Liselle's not here," Tobias replied. Jack was shocked to hear the older man's voice break. Her absence was really hurting him!

"I'm sure she's around," Serena offered.

Logan, standing at Jack's side, cleared his throat and stared at the floor. "No, she's not," he said, his suddenly subdued tone drawing all eyes to himself.

Tobias rounded on him. "What's happened?" he demanded.

Speaking softly, Logan told the tale. "The day after Dwight, Geoff, and me got back, one of the other ranch hands asked me if it was true that Liselle killed her older girls and replaced them with slaves she bought from the caravan. I told him he was full of it, but I could tell he didn't believe me."

"What?" said Serena. "We agreed to confront her in private. How did the word get out?"

"Crenshaw," growled Tobias, his lips compressing into a snarl.

"We don't know that."

"Who else could it be, girl? Dwight ain't that dumb."

"Well, however it happened," Logan continued, "word spread like wildfire. Folks started grumbling about seeing justice done. Grumbling became talking. Then shouting. Next thing we knew, a mob formed and headed out toward the Hempstead House to string her up and free her girls. The Mayor tried to stop them, but..." Logan shook his head.

"No," Tobias breathed. "Did they...?"

Logan shook his head. "She got away. Barely. Word is, she rode out of town as fast as her little carriage could carry her, heading north." Shrugging, he added, "Funny thing was how her girls reacted. Some were relieved. Said they'd never have taken up whoring if they hadn't been forced into it and blessed the leaders of the mob. But more than a few got really mad and said that Liselle was the kindest, most generous person they'd ever known. Strange, huh?"

Jack agreed that it was ironic at least. The difference in reactions was lost on Tobias, though.

"I'll kill him," he growled, turning and beginning to shove his way through the crowd toward where Geoff and the Mayor were talking.

It took both Jack and Logan to restrain him, and a lot of fast talking to convince him that violence was the last thing he wanted to resort to, especially without proof of his suspicions.

Tobias fumed for most of the rest of the evening. Finally, as the party began to die down, he almost came to resemble his normal self again. Jack noted that he watched Geoff depart for his house through narrowed eyes, though.

Before long, the rest of the townsfolk began to follow Geoff's lead, heading off to their beds. With only a few exceptions, they stopped to clap Jack and Tobias on the shoulder and say well done. It gave Jack a warm feeling of accomplishment, greater than he'd felt after the negotiation in Forest Hills. More genuine, for these were people who knew him giving their approval. He found himself beaming.

As the last of the people left and Jack, Tobias, Serena, and Logan turned to depart as well, Beatrice walked up to them.

"Where are you planning to stay now that you're back?"

Jack and Tobias glanced at each other. Tobias' house had burned down during the raid that resulted in their kidnapping, something he had informed Jack of shortly after leaving Forest Hills for home. They'd talked briefly on the road about how to handle living arrangements once they got back, but hadn't decided on anything definitive.

With a shrug, Tobias replied, "I figured we'd bunk down

in the inn tonight, then head home tomorrow and start rebuilding."

Beatrice shook her head, making a soft tsk-ing sound. "I thought as much. Don't even think about paying for a room. You can stay at my place for as long as you need. You won't get much work done rebuilding until spring anyway." She offered Tobias a warm smile. He hesitated for a moment before nodding and returning the smile with a grateful grin of his own.

From where she stood at his side, Serena squeezed Jack's hand. "You can stay with me if you'd like, Jack," she offered.

Jack blinked, finding himself flushing slightly. He opened his mouth to refuse, but the other options available to him raced through his head. He realized they were all fairly lacking. And, he had to admit, not nearly as good looking as the option Serena offered. After only a moment's hesitation, he nodded acquiescence, evoking a pleased smile from her.

They all went their separate ways, Tobias and Beatrice to her farm, Logan to Geoff's ranch, and Jack and Serena to her place. She had a moderate-sized house in the central area of town, near City Hall. Jack had never been inside, but as they paused in the entryway for Serena to light an oil lamp, Jack decided the house fit her. It was neat and tidy, furnished with simple, but obviously high quality, objects. Very much like Serena herself, it was not ostentatious, but elegant. He liked the place instantly.

Serena led him upstairs and paused before a door adjacent to the landing. She looked at him, her expression suddenly uncertain. "This is my room," she said.

Swallowing, Jack took in the sight of her in the dim lamplight. He could tell she wanted to ask him to join her, but that desire was what spawned her uncertainty.

A part of him wanted nothing more than to sweep her up and take her to bed. But the larger part knew it was too soon.

He wasn't ready to go there yet, however tempted he might be. Better to take it slow.

"Is that the guest room?" Jack asked, gesturing toward another door a short way down the hall.

Serena nodded, disappointment mixing with understanding and acceptance on her face.

"Good night," said Jack as he leaned forward to kiss her on the cheek.

❦ 30 ❦

TO STRUGGLE AGAINST
LONG ODDS

"What the hell are you in such a hurry for, youngster?" Tobias asked.

It was a week later. Jack and Tobias had ridden out to Tobias' property to survey the damage. The place was a total loss. It wasn't burned down to the foundation, but it might as well have been. Only the stone fireplace still stood, but it was blackened and warped, leaning over at an uneasy angle. Beatrice was right. They'd need weeks or months to rebuild, and winter was no time to get started on a project like that.

But there would be no "we" in that project, not for Jack. He'd come to a decision and had broken it to Tobias during the ride to the house. He and Serena were leaving for Mayport in the morning.

"No sense wasting time, Tobias," Jack replied.

The older man snorted. "It just snowed again, boy. You'll make horrible time, and if you get caught in another snowstorm in the mountains, you could freeze to death. Better to wait for spring."

Tobias had a point. Jack had to concede that. But over the

last few days, he'd felt a growing pressure to get moving. Behind every building, or every tree, he half expected to see the charge of Legionnaires in red blouses, supported by Enlightened in black. But how to explain that, when he knew weather prohibited a large-scale excursion? And even if it didn't, it would take the Order weeks, maybe months, to find Glennville.

All the same, he couldn't shake the feeling that time was slipping away from him.

"I get what you're saying, Tobias. But I really feel I need to get moving."

"But..."

Jack held up a hand, forestalling the older man's response. "Horbach's after me. We both know that. Do you really think Percy, Emilio, or any of the other guards on the wall could hold off even a small raiding party of Legionnaires and Enlightened?"

Tobias sighed, then shook his head. "No, Jack. I s'pose not."

"I've made my decision, Tobias. Tonight we'll all have dinner. Then tomorrow, I'm off."

Tobias nodded and clapped Jack on the shoulder.

They spent the rest of their inspection in silence. The memories around that place were thick for Jack. He imagined it was even more so for Tobias, though the older man kept a stoic exterior.

Looking around, Jack could see the porch where he'd spent more than a few summer evenings looking at the stars. The corral where he'd first learned to ride a horse. The curing shed, where Tobias had taught him how to dress out and skin game, and how to preserve the meat. The woods, where he'd learned to live outdoors. And where he'd first crashed into Tobias' life.

The tree line where his plane went down was more or less

fully healed. If Jack didn't know where to look, he probably wouldn't notice the difference in the trees and undergrowth any more, at least from a distance.

Unbidden, Jack felt a surge of heartache as his eyes lingered on that spot. Unlike in the past though, the heartache did not come with overwhelming guilt and self-loathing. What happened wasn't his fault; he knew that now. He supposed he'd always miss Susan, always feel the pain of her loss. But standing there, he finally realized that he truly had moved on. It almost felt good.

That evening, Jack and Serena invited Tobias, Beatrice, Logan, and Dwight over for dinner. Jack almost invited Geoff, since he'd also been with them in Forest Hills. But Tobias was still furious with him; they'd almost come to blows twice in the last week, so Jack thought better of it.

Though Jack tried for a festive air, dinner was subdued at first. Everyone knew he and Serena were leaving in the morning and that put a damper on things. But slowly, inevitably, the conversation grew lighter, more reminiscent. Soon they were laughing about old stories and simply enjoying one another's company.

But the evening had to come to an end. Goodbyes were long and, in some cases, tearful. Logan and Tobias, in particular, lingered for a long time as though unwilling for the night to end. But finally weariness won out and they departed after exchanging hugs; manly, companionable hugs with Jack and warm, endearing hugs with Serena.

Serena shut the door behind Tobias and turned back to Jack. Wiping her eyes, she asked, "Are we doing the right thing?"

Jack took her hand and squeezed it gently. "You know the answer to that. It's better for them if I'm gone."

Serena hesitated, then nodded, acknowledging what she

already knew. They took a few minutes to clean up, then went up to bed, Jack still in the guest room.

———

The next morning, Jack and Serena got up with the dawn. Already packed for the trip, they quickly loaded their gear onto their pack horse. Then, mounting up, they set off. They didn't get far, just to the outskirts of town, before they were stopped.

Logan was waiting for them on the road, dressed in winter traveling clothes and packed for a long journey. Seeing him, Jack shook his head vigorously.

"I know what you're going to say, Logan, and the answer's no. It's too dangerous for you to come."

"But not too dangerous for her?" Logan smirked playfully. "Shit, Jack, I thought you knew me better than that. You need all the help you can get. Now, you can say no all you want." He leaned forward in his saddle, resting his hands on the saddle horn and raising his eyebrows meaningfully. "I'll just follow along a half day back."

Jack rolled his eyes. But, of course, Logan was right. It's not as though Jack could physically stop him. Finally, reluctantly, he nodded and got a thankful grin in response.

"What's the plan when we get there?" Logan asked as he fell in alongside.

Jack noticed Serena eyeing him curiously while he answered. They hadn't really talked about it and, truth be told, Jack hadn't thought it through. But they did need a plan, however vague.

"Not sure, exactly. Get there, figure out how to make more of Horbach's elixir. Next, figure out how to make better use of the Art. Then try to teach others so we can balance the scales a bit."

"And do our best not to get found and whacked," Logan added.

"There is that, yes."

"And work hard to not be co-opted by the Navy guys," Serena added.

Jack started. He hadn't even thought about that aspect of things, but she had a good point. How the hell was he going to manage that, along with everything else?

"Sounds like a whole lot more fun than managing Geoff's herd."

"Logan, the odds are stacked so far against us, we might as well admit defeat now."

"Yeah. Like I said: fun."

Logan began to chuckle, and before long Jack found himself joining in. Serena did as well.

Louis Horbach grimaced as he rose from his padded leather chair. Sharp, stabbing pain from his back accompanied even that small movement: the remnants of Lysander's treachery, almost as painful as the loss of the Book of Knowledge.

Julius bowed from the waist, his white Acolyte robes rustling softly. "Master, a report from Enlightened Yolanda," he said, holding out a small cylinder, barely larger than a man's finger and capped at one end.

Horbach returned the Acolyte's bow with a shallow inclination of his head and accepted the message tube. He paused for a moment, studying the younger man's features intently. Julius was far enough along in his training that he was almost ready for the indoctrination, the final training of the mind that readied a man or woman to become Enlightened. Horbach remembered when Julius began, just as he remembered every one of his children's arrival. He was upright and true.

Wasn't he?

Finding himself clenching his empty fist, Horbach forced down the doubt and altered his attention, focusing on the universe more fully. Lines of energy, always at the edge of his vision and ready to dominate his whole perception if he allowed it, flowed from Julius to himself and back again. They were linked in ways that even the Highest of the Enlightened didn't understand.

Horbach smiled. All was well with Julius.

With Lysander, that fateful night in his office, it had been different. Horbach had sensed that their bond was off, wrong somehow. He had seen the signs of a child's loss of faith more times than he could count in the past and had always taken the necessary actions to deal with it. He'd assumed he would also succeed in Lysander's case.

He'd paid the price, once again, for his hubris. And the world had nearly paid the price as well. For a second time. Never again.

"Thank you, Julius," Horbach said as he forced his attention back to normal. The Acolyte bowed again and left the room.

With barely a thought, Horbach directed the energies that would unlock the message tube, then thumbed it open. A small scroll within carried the message, written in a cypher of his own devising. He read it as easily as he read his native language.

"What does it say?"

Horbach broke off reading, annoyed, and looked over at Margaret. She was seated in the room's other chair, a thick tome cradled in her lap. She'd been with him from the beginning of his quest to discover the Higher Truths. He cherished her counsel, her wisdom, her warmth. But since Lysander...

He looked away from her toward the two Legionnaires standing at attention on either side of the door and scowled. He was never alone anymore.

No matter. Yolanda had been ordered to report once she had Lysander in custody and the Book of Knowledge in her possession. Soon all would be well again.

He turned back to the message.

"Yolanda reports..." he began to say. Then his eyes reached the bottom of the page and he found himself at a loss for words. Unbidden, rage flowed through him. The message crumpled in his hand and, with a roar, he cast the paper across the room. A flick of energy set it alight, and it burnt to ashes in a flash.

His roar became a groan as pain stabbed through him. The movement of throwing the paper aggravated the wound again. Before he realized it, he found himself doubled over and coughing.

Then Margaret was at his side, supporting him with a gentle arm around his shoulder.

"He escaped," she said, not even a hint of a question in her tone.

Horbach nodded.

"You should rest, Louis," she said, concern etched on her face. "It can wait until you're fully healed."

It was tempting. But no. His mission required strength. Perseverance. He could not heal the world without pain. If the unrighteous must feel it as they became purified, it was fitting that he should as well, to atone for what his hubris had wrought.

He shook off Margaret's arm and, straightening himself, turned to face her.

"Summon the others in the Council of the Highest, Margaret," he ordered. "The time has come for a council of war."

MESSAGE FROM THE AUTHOR

Thank you for reading my book. I hope you enjoyed reading it as much as I enjoyed writing it.

If you're willing and have a minute, please leave a review where you bought it, and/or on Goodreads. Every review helps an author out, even the bad ones. So whether you loved this book, hated it, or something in between, please take a minute to tell other readers what you thought. All of the online retailers make it very easy to do, and I would really appreciate it.

Feel free to come say hi at my website, on Twitter, or on Facebook. I always enjoy hearing from readers, especially since you all are, collectively, my boss.

Finally, I'd like to invite you to join my newsletter. Don't worry, I promise not to spam you with incessant annoying emails. But if you want to get the first word on what I have going on, new releases, and special deals, come on over and sign up. No pressure, no obligation.

Thanks again. My best to you and yours.

Warm Regards,
  Michael Kingswood

ABOUT THE AUTHOR

Michael Kingswood is 20-year veteran of the US Navy submarine force and a lifelong fan of science fiction and fantasy literature. He holds a bachelors degree in Mechanical Engineering as well as a Master of Engineering Management and a Master of Business Administration. He currently resides in San Diego with his wife and four children.

Find Michael Kingswood online at:

www.michaelkingswood.com

www.facebook.com/michael.kingswood

twitter.com/michaelkingswd

MORE BOOKS BY MICHAEL KINGSWOOD

GLIMMER VALE CHRONICLES

Glimmer Vale

Out-Dweller

Tollard's Peak

Robbed Blind

Wedding Gifts: A Glimmer Vale Chronicles Story

The Falconer's Stairs

Glimmer Vale Chronicles Omnibus Edition #1

THE PERICLES CONSPIRACY

Passing In The Night

The Pericles Conspiracy

DAWN OF ENLIGHTENMENT

Masters Of The Sun

NOVELLAS

What Lurks Between

The Necromancer's Lair

The Champion

Veritas Morte

STORY COLLECTIONS

Tales Of Adventure #1

Tales Of Adventure #2

Short Story 10-Pack

A Jar Of Mixed Treats

SHORT FICTION

Michael has also published a number of shorter works, links to
which can be found on his website.

PATREON

If you enjoy Michael's books and are interested in supporting his quest to be able to write these books full time, please come over the his Patreon page. For as little as $1 per month, you can make a big difference.

Thank you for your support!

Copyright © 2011 by Michael Kingswood

Cover Art Copyright © 2011 Jeroen ten Berge

This story is a work of fiction. Names, characters, places, and incidents are either products of the author's imagination or used fictitiously. Any resemblance to actual events, locales, or persons, living or dead, is entirely coincidental.

All rights reserved.

No part of this book may be reproduced in any form or by any electronic or mechanical means, including information storage and retrieval systems, without written permission from the author, except for the use of brief quotations in a book review.

🏵 Created with Vellum

www.ingramcontent.com/pod-product-compliance
Lightning Source LLC
Chambersburg PA
CBHW020941120726
47905CB00008B/2627